HERMINA B

SWEET PILGRIMAGE

HODDER PAPERBACKS

*The characters in this book are entirely imaginary
and have no relation to any living person*

First published by Robert Hale Ltd., 1943
Hodder Paperback Edition (Reset) 1962
Second Impression 1969

*Printed in Great Britain
for Hodder Paperbacks Limited,
St. Paul's House, Warwick Lane, London, E.C.4,
by Richard Clay (The Chaucer Press), Ltd.,
Bungay, Suffolk*

SBN 340 02145 4

This book is sold subject to the condition that it shall not, by way of trade or otherwise, be lent, re-sold, hired out or otherwise circulated without the publisher's prior consent in any form of binding or cover other than that in which this is published and without a similar condition including this condition being imposed on the subsequent purchaser.

CHAPTER I

JENNET, leaning over the ship's rail, had the strangest feeling of unreality. Of course life could not seem quite real ever, in these days when the world was changing from hour to hour, all the secure things one had grown up with threatening to crash about one.

It had often seemed like a nightmare, but during these last few days it had turned into a dream. A dream in which one drifted along a broad stretch of water, and whatever landscape that could be seen looked vaguely like the pictures on willow-pattern plates, or those Chinese prints which had always fascinated her so much.

Beyond the distant bank now, she could see the outlines of what looked like a temple, the remains of a square tower, steps leading upward, terraces which appeared to be more than half destroyed. It was almost impossible to realize that from a continent threatened by the shadow of war she had come to a land which had known war for years, before the crisis which had just ended had shaken Europe with the knowledge that it, too, was very near the brink.

And yet, this extraordinary peace, and this odd-shaped little ship making its way downstream! It was almost impossible to believe it.

How very far away seemed the big, busy wards of the emergency hospital where she had worked before she left England. The research wing, the students' hostel, the staff quarters. Was it possible that she had been part of it all? It was as though her strange journey had thrust it all back into a different world.

Yet here she was, still herself, Jennet Grey, with the right to put M.D., F.R.C.S., after her name. And she had earned that right! Gruelling hours of study—the horror that she was not going "to pass." The days of despair and self-distrust when she had thought: I ought to have made up my mind to just be a nurse, after all——

But she had made up her mind to be a doctor; she was a doctor. And that was that. All the same, she had certainly never expected to come to China, of all countries in the world, to do her doctoring. That was perhaps why life had taken on an unreal tinge since that day when Sir Bruce Ferguson had sent for her (an invitation to lunch with the redoubtable old man of Harley Street was a royal command, so "sent for" her was the only way to express it), and told her that if she was really interested in the work she had taken up, she would not be fool enough to refuse the appointment of assistant medical officer to the Eldred Chambers Hospital in the province of Mangtong.

"But—Sir Bruce," she had protested, "there's a war on in China——"

"There'll soon be a war on here!" had been the grim retort. "And China is a much bigger country than this is. Anyway, it is the chance of a lifetime for anyone as young and inexperienced as yourself." He had glared at her from under his bushy brows. "Seems perfectly ridiculous for you to be a doctor at all——" But no one knew better than he did that she had been one of his most brilliant students, and at least she was not fool enough to doubt that unless he had thought a good deal of her work he would never have suggested her for this or any other post. . . .

The pagoda, or whatever it was, disappeared into the distance, and with a sigh Jennet turned to meet a pair of bright brown eyes fixed on her.

Bright, inquisitive eyes like a robin's, which in spite of the lined and rather raddled face in which they were set, were curiously young and keen.

Jennet had noticed the owner of those eyes before—watched the old lady coming on board with mounds of luggage and a Chinese amah. That she was someone important was obvious from the attention she received. Jennet put her down at once as one of those redoubtable old women who have a habit of making themselves felt wherever they may be, and while endeavouring to dismiss her as not being likely to have anything to do with her affairs, was still curious to know who she was.

At first she could not make out whether she was English or American, then, hearing her addressed as "Lady Amanda," decided on the former.

But Alice, when spoken to by the White Rabbit, was not more startled than Jennet when, before she even had time to look the other way, Lady Amanda, still staring at her with what in most people would have been a lamentable lack of manners, announced abruptly:

"That lovely complexion of yours will soon be ruined in this climate, if you don't protect it. Better not spoil it before you've caught a husband."

Horrible old cat! Jennet frowned, flushed, and then burst out laughing. She had a particularly charming and infectious laugh, and almost immediately the wrinkles round Lady Amanda's eyes became more apparent, and the corners of her mouth twitched. "Well?" she demanded. "Isn't that important?"

"Not to me," replied Jennet, still smiling. "About the last thing I have come to China to do is to catch a husband, as you——"

"Vulgarly express it! Well, sit down and tell me what you have come out here for," was the retort. "I noticed you when you first came on board, and since I take it you are bound for Mangtong, sooner or later you will have to give me an account of yourself. I'm Lady Amanda Trent. Don't suppose you have ever heard of me. But you will."

Rather to her own surprise, Jennet found herself taking the chair next to this extraordinary old woman quite meekly, and supplying the information: "My name is Grey—Jennet Grey."

"English—but you've hardly come from England?"

"Yes; I came from England," said Jennet.

"Going to relatives?"

Jennet hesitated, but there did not seem to be much sense in trying to be reticent, though she loathed telling strangers her business. She said: "I am going to take up a post at a hospital—you probably know it, the Eldred Chambers——"

"Know it!" snorted Lady Amanda. "I ought to. I'm on the committee and heaven knows what. But I didn't know any new nursing staff was coming out."

"I haven't come to nurse," said Jennet quietly. "I'm Doctor Grey. I have come to take up the post of assistant to Doctor Sinclair."

There was a moment's complete, blank silence. Then: "What the devil——!" exclaimed Lady Amanda. "You!" And then, more calmly: "I knew there was a new assistant on the way, but I understood it was some man with a good hospital record——"

"There was a man coming." Jennet spoke calmly, though she felt a stab of annoyance. "He was prevented from taking up the appointment at the last moment. I was chosen as the most suitable person to take his place. I also have excellent hospital experience."

"But, good heavens, you're an infant, and——" Lady Amanda broke off, for once curbing her too frank tongue; what she had been about to add was, "a darn sight too ornamental for a medical woman." Instead she added quite mildly: "And who, if I may ask, thought you the next most suitable choice?"

"Sir Bruce Ferguson."

"Eh!" The old lady sat up abruptly. "Bruce is no fool—I've known him for years. Knew him when he was a young man and came to Boston to take up a post there—a brilliant young man.

Good Lord! I nearly married him. I was Amanda Chambers then—the Eldred who founded the hospital you are going to was my uncle. He was mad on the medical world—the house was always full of 'em. So you know Bruce."

"I studied under him," Jennet told her, not bothering about what a small place the world was, in her sudden pleasure at meeting a friend of "the chief's." In less than a quarter of an hour, Lady Amanda had all the information she wanted, and while Jennet thought she was only giving the briefest answers to questions put to her, had gathered that this young woman, for all her over-allowance of good looks, no doubt had a more adequate amount of brains.

For herself, unlike many women of her generation (maybe because she was of American birth), Lady Amanda had no prejudice against women doctors. For all that, she was not at all sure that in sending this girl out here, her old friend Bruce Ferguson had not made a mistake from other standpoints.

Then suddenly something seemed to strike her, and she asked abruptly: "And what about Ivor Sinclair? Was there any time to consult him on your appointment?"

"I don't think so," said Jennet. "But I believe Sir Bruce cabled him."

"Land sakes!" Lady Amanda stared blankly, unaware that she had reverted to the idiom of her girlhood. "You don't mean to tell me that Ivor Sinclair doesn't know they are sending a woman out?"

"I couldn't tell you." Jennet flushed. "You—you don't mean that he is one of those hidebound creatures who object to working with a woman? It's a woman's hospital, anyway. I've specialized in everything to do with women, and in tropical diseases. You see, I had some idea at the beginning of becoming a medical missionary in India. Then the war came——" And as Lady Amanda still continued to stare at her with the oddest expression on her face, she urged: "Will he mind my being a woman?"

"Mind!" Lady Amanda seemed to rouse herself from a stupor. "My poor child," she said patiently, "what you have to learn is that your future colleague has not just a prejudice against women—he simply manages to ignore the fact that they exist. But I can't talk to you any more now," she added. "Here's Amah, and I am going to rest. We will have dinner together this evening, and I'll explain a few facts to you."

But Jennet was no longer interested in scenery. She was face to face with a thing which she had somehow never contemplated. All through her training and afterwards she had found nothing but good fellowship from the men she had worked with. There had never been any question of her sex making things difficult—except, of course, that two or three times there *had* been occasions when she had been reminded that she was young and attractive, and men considered there might be sidelines to being a doctor. She had learnt, though, to know that look in a man's eye, and to nip any budding aspirations very swiftly, or turn them down so determinedly that they were not revived. She might have gone into life partnership three or four times over, with doctors who did not in the least object to a woman as a partner in their work, and wanted one particular girl in their lives. But the last thing Jennet meant to do was to marry at the beginning of her career. Of course, if she had fallen in love, she had to admit frankly that she might have thought very differently.

But then, she had never been in love. At least, the only time she had ever come near it had been "the desire of the moth for the star," but it had taught her to know that if ever she wanted something a little nearer than a star, she was as capable as the next girl— perhaps more capable than many—of sacrificing other things that had been dear to her.

The one thing she passionately resented was the idea of her sex being used as an excuse to prejudice anyone against her work.

Ivor Sinclair.

She had looked forward to meeting and working with him, after what Sir Bruce had said. He was brilliantly clever—could have been at the very top of the tree at home, in spite of the fact that he was still in the early thirties, and had thrown up everything to go out to China, when the hospital of which he was the head had been founded ten years ago.

He had not been the head of it at the beginning, but he had been one of the pioneers who had fought prejudice and gracefully made the institution do what it was primarily intended to do—alleviate the suffering and the death roll among the women and children of the province. The man who founded it was a rich American who, coming first for business reasons to this remote province which, even in the war-scarred China of today, remained practically untouched, had stayed because the spell of the country had taken him; married under the most romantic circumstances an English girl who was doing missionary work out there, and remained to die in his adopted land.

Jennet, with the born doctor's burning desire to serve humanity, had looked forward with the thrill of her life to serving in that hospital. And now suddenly everything seemed spoilt in advance.

She wished she had never met Lady Amanda. It is only human to want to cling on to illusions as long as possible! But somehow, even at the beginning, she felt a curious lack of resentment at the old lady's frankly curious interrogations regarding her affairs—and that was not just because she had learnt that Lady Amanda was a friend of Sir Bruce's. If she had felt inclined to be amused at anything, she would have quite enjoyed the fact that the announcement that she was to dine with her ladyship had sounded like an order rather than an invitation. But Jennet's sense of humour was in abeyance; she was remembering that announcement in that slightly hoarse voice: "Your future colleague had not just a prejudice against women—he simply manages to ignore the fact that they exist——"

Heavens! What *sort* of a man——?

While Jennet fumed, Lady Amanda lying in her bunk wrapped in a silk wrapper in which a few moments before, with that frankness which she never failed to extend to herself, she had described herself as looking like a scarlet porpoise, suddenly began to shake like a not quite set jelly, while the tears coursed down her face.

Su-Ching, her amah, who was entirely used to such phenomena and was merely glad when anything happened to amuse her beloved mistress, took not the slightest notice—though anybody else might have been alarmed in case the old lady's paroxysm of silent mirth caused trouble. Presently it quieted, and, wiping her eyes, her lips still twitching, the widow of the late Sir Roger Trent, who had been born Amanda Chambers of Massachusetts, murmured: "I'd give half a million dollars to see Ivor's face when his new assistant walks in on him. That girl! A darned sight too good-looking for a woman doctor, anyway! She will cause trouble outside the hospital, I'll bet. But, oh, the trouble in it! Darling Ivor, I wonder if at last you're going to meet your Waterloo?"

CHAPTER II

DOCTOR IVOR SINCLAIR replaced the last of the test tubes he had been examining with the loving care anything so important demanded, and, straightening, glanced at the watch on his wrist.

Half an hour before the boat was due in. If he left in twenty minutes he would be in plenty of time to greet the new man. Meanwhile, there were things to do. There always were things to do. There was not a moment of the day, and few of the night, which he could not have filled in.

Having washed his hands and removed his white coat, he went

across from the laboratory to his own private quarters. He had been oddly restless all day, and sitting down now, he forced himself to face the reason for that restlessness. He hated the idea of a stranger around the place—not only because that stranger would fill the position which had once been occupied by the man who, from being his student and protégé, had become his colleague and his best friend, but because he never knew what a stranger would be like to work with. The annoying thing was that the man who had been originally chosen, and whom he had known all about—a young, enthusiastic doctor with an excellent record—wasn't coming at all now.

It was a pity Lady Amanda was not clairvoyant, or she might have found more food for mirth in the knowledge that at that particular moment "darling Ivor" was wondering what the substitute Doctor Grey would be like.

He glanced at his watch again, and began to make some hasty notes. And as he sat there at the big desk in the cream-walled room, however true the description which Jennet had been given of him might be, it would have been obvious to almost any observer that no matter how little interest Doctor Ivor Sinclair might take in the opposite sex, they were likely to take plenty of interest in him. The clear-cut face, bent over the paper on which he was writing, was exceptionally good looking; but there were lines on it which are seldom seen on the face of so young a man, and the mouth, which at rare moments had a suggestion of tenderness, was grimly set and almost bitter.

It ought to have been a much younger face and a very much happier one than it was. It was not the suffering its owner had seen—and been so often able to alleviate—which made it neither of those things; the causes lay elsewhere.

As he finished his notes, his "number one boy" came to announce that the car was waiting, and it was "plentee late!" Taking his sun-helmet up, the doctor hurried out. He had given himself less time than he had meant to, and as the drive lay through the crowded quarter of the town he only arrived just as the boat which he had come to meet drifted alongside the jetty. He was hurrying on board when he came face to face with Lady Amanda Trent.

"Hello, Ivor." The familiar, hoarse tones of the old woman's voice arrested him, as she laid a hand on his arm. "Don't look like that—aren't you thrilled to encounter your best girl friend again?"

"Madly." He smiled down at her, a different sort of smile to that which anyone else ever received from him. The most maddening woman in Mangtong she might be, but there was an odd understanding between this shapeless grande dame and the doctor, an understanding amounting to affection which no stranger who had overheard their acid duels of words would ever have believed possible. "So you're back——"

"Yes. Ready to make more trouble for you! I know whom you are looking for," she informed. "We have been getting acquainted on the trip down. Come along and I'll introduce you." She took his arm, turned him about and beckoned. "Doctor Grey—let me make you two known to each other. This is Doctor Sinclair—Doctor Jennet Grey. I shall see you both again soon." And with a nod and swift, sardonic glance distributed between the two, she proceeded on her way, followed by Amah, Chinese chauffeur, and mountains of suitcases, to the grey Rolls-Royce which waited ashore.

For a completely silent moment Doctor Ivor Sinclair faced Doctor Jennet Grey. Long afterwards he remembered that moment—the tall, slender girl who did not seem tall because he towered above her. Dark gold hair framing a cream-coloured skin beneath the brim of her sun helmet, high cheekbones, a mouth which, if a man was interested in such things, might interest him very much; eyes the colour of speedwell flowers in an English hedgerow, set between short, thick lashes which were startlingly dark against the gold of her hair. It hardly seemed likely that one of those details should register with a man on top of whose blank surprise the most furious anger was following; therefore he naturally failed to note the rather square cut of the firmly modelled chin beneath that intriguing mouth.

As for Jennet, her first impressions were no more than great height, and a pair of eyes that reminded her of smouldering amber.

Then Ivor Sinclair spoke. "I think," he said, "there must be some mistake——"

Confound him; he had a lovely speaking voice! Jennet was very glad that she managed to keep her own cool and slightly amused as she replied, "I'm afraid there isn't any mistake, Doctor Sinclair. Didn't you receive the cable saying that I was coming?"

"I received a cable saying that Doctor O'Brien was unable to come, and Doctor Grey was coming as a substitute——"

"But you didn't expect a woman? Too bad. You'll get used to it, though," said Jennet coolly. "I assure you, I shan't kill off the patients. I have a letter for you from Sir Bruce Ferguson, which may explain things better. I'll find it later, if I am allowed to go on shore."

"I beg your pardon!" Sinclair suddenly realized that whatever he might feel this was hardly the time or place to go into this matter. "I'm afraid you took the wind out of my sails," he said with a slight smile. "Come along. My chauffeur will see to your luggage, and I'll drive you back to the hospital at once. I hope your journey has been as comfortable as circumstances allowed." He was walking beside her as he spoke. Jennet noticed that he had not attempted to shake hands, and decided that there was evidently to be war of some sort, even if the Japanese did not bring it.

He was detestable! Well, he wasn't going to get her down. She was here to do her work, she told herself, and she jolly well meant to do it! Of course, the man thought he was a little god! She had met doctors like this before, but they were not usually the clever ones.

"You will find all this very remote," he told her as they drove along. "There is a small European and American colony—but I expect Lady Amanda has told you about it."

"Yes; Lady Amanda explained quite a lot to me." Jennet's tone was non-committal.

But if he noticed anything behind it, he gave no sort of indication that he had. He went on speaking in that musical voice which she couldn't fit in at all with the hardness of his personality; the sort of voice which made Jennet tell herself: There's Celt somewhere in him—you don't get voices like that otherwise.

He said, "Lady Amanda rules the roost all right—that is, outside the walls which enclose the Ling homestead. Behind those another personality asserts itself. The Lings still own most of Mangtong— they must be one of the very last of the old Chinese clans who have not been broken up by this necessary but less picturesque modernism. You'll learn about them later."

"Surely Lady Amanda does not rule everything?" Jennet turned her head, raising her eyebrows slightly.

"Well, she doesn't run the hospital, if that's what you mean," he answered. "But—she's on the committee."

And she can make you uncomfortable sometimes, I hope! thought Jennet with unusual vindictiveness, for in spite of the red in her hair she was a good-tempered young woman. When she did lose her temper it was as devastating as it usually is with controlled people.

She nodded. "I see. Is that the hospital?"

"Yes—at the top of the hill."

She could see it as they climbed. The beautifully designed white building set in its acres of gardens. As they drew nearer she could see also the fronding wisteria which covered the private staff quarters, hanging down in great bunches of pale and deeper mauve. There were roses rioting in the gardens and beds of peonies of every known and unknown colour. Here was beauty that should heal the heart while one helped in the lovely work of healing broken bodies.

Suddenly Jennet could have cried that all her happiness should have been spoilt, because the man beside her was filled with prejudice. She had heard so much about his work. He ought to be *bigger*. What was the use of a brilliant brain, if you had a limited mind to go with it?

Of course it was quite probable that women themselves had helped him to despise them. But she was not a patient—she was a fellow-doctor! And heavens! surely the man was not afraid that she was likely to fall in love with him.

If so, he need not worry. She had never disliked anyone more cordially in her life than she was disliking Ivor Sinclair at that particular moment.

The car turned in at the gates, opened by an old Chinese porter. They turned from the main drive and stopped before the wisteria-covered building she had noticed.

Ivor Sinclair got out and held the door open for her. Then to her amazement she saw that he was holding out his hand, smiling down at her. "Welcome to the hospital," he said. "I hope that while you are here you will enjoy your work."

Feeling the cool, firm clasp of his fingers as they closed on hers, Jennet experienced a sudden glow of warmth. This incredible man meant what he said. He would never have said it otherwise——

She did not realize that though he might welcome her arrival—since she was here!—he would quite as sincerely welcome her departure.

And neither of them thought of considering that this was only the beginning of the story. . . .

* * *

As it was already late in the day when Jennet arrived, it was taken as a matter of course that she should not see anything of the hospital until tomorrow.

She found herself, in fact, being treated as an honoured guest; and even though she was burning to learn all about everything and get down to work, it was rather nice to have these hours to settle in.

She was taken straight to her own quarters—Ivor Sinclair accompanying her to introduce her to the Chinese houseboy and his staff. The staff quarters at Eldred Chambers left nothing to be desired for comfort and well-being of those who ran the hospital. The founder of the place had had his own ideas, and they had been carried out to the letter. The hospital was built after the Chinese style, around courtyards—and although the white buildings were modern in design they seemed to fit in perfectly with the scenery around, and the buildings in the city at the bottom of the hill.

The nurse's home was on its own. Ivor Sinclair had his segregated quarters, the research workers—four of them—shared a house; and Jennet to her delight found herself in possession of a white bungalow over which the mauve wisteria grew in glorious profusion.

Bedroom, sitting-room, bathroom—with the servants' quarters at the back. Her woman servant took possession of her luggage as a right, and by the time she reached her bedroom everything seemed to be unpacked and in its place. Ivor Sinclair had shown her round the whole domain. She had begun to realize by now that in spite of the doctor's almost unforgivable welcome—or lack of it—he certainly had charm.

"I hope you will dine with me tonight," he said. "Then we can talk things over."

"That's very nice of you. I'd like to," Jennet replied.

"You won't see Matron until tomorrow, I'm afraid. She's very busy at present, and I understand it's her 'night off'," he added.

Jennet wondered what Matron was like, knowing only too well that a matron can be a thorn in the side of the medical staff, if she happens to be difficult and doesn't like them; but she had a feeling that no woman would have stayed here long whom Doctor Ivor Sinclair found any difficulty in getting on with. For her own part Jennet had never failed to get on with the nursing staff, and had been most popular in her last job.

Having seen her in, Ivor took his leave in that abrupt way which she had a feeling she would have to get used to. She went to the window when he had gone, and watched him striding across the court. Because she had a great admiration for physical perfection, she appreciated the fact that he was so very well built. Tall, without being too tall, broad shouldered, slim hipped. He walked like a man who had done a lot of fencing—later she learnt that it had been a hobby of his when he was studying in Paris.

She turned, and glanced round the sitting-room, appreciation deepening in her eyes. Oh, she could be happy here if she was allowed to be. The cool, cream walls, the empty bookshelves which seemed to be crying out for that case of books which was coming with her heavy luggage from the boat. Deep chairs in plain linen covers, one beautiful turquoise coloured rug on the polished floor. The desk was near the window—very plain and workmanlike.

She saw at once what could be done with this room. It was almost severely masculine now. Jennet liked it that way, though anything less masculine than she herself looked, in spite of the severe tailoring of her linen suit, would have been difficult to imagine—this girl who was so ready to compete on an equal footing with the sex which had once had everything to itself.

If the servants were surprised that a woman had arrived when they expected a man, there was no sign of it.

Lai-Ling was the sister of the number one boy. She had held any sort of position in the household of Jennet's predecessor. Yet there she was, calmly slipping into the rôle of lady's maid as if there had always been a woman at the head of the house. In fact, Jennet suddenly wondered if she had been mistaken in thinking that the former inmate had been a bachelor. When she came from the bath which had been drawn and prepared for her, she asked if the last doctor had been married.

"No married. He bachelor—poor gentleman," replied the woman gravely. While the maid proceeded to brush her hair, Jennet elicited the information that she had been "serving matron" in several European households, and evidently knew all about "maidery" and took the fact that she would wait on Jennet hand and foot as a matter of course. Jennet, who was used to looking after herself with almost fanatical independence, was not quite sure whether she was going to like this, or whether it would drive her mad.

When it came to dressing, she deliberately chose the very plainest of her dinner frocks—dull surfaced black crepe, cut high at the front and rather lower at the back, with touches of pink embroidery. It was a model from a famous house, and she had bought it at a bargain price, and against the advice of the friend who had been shopping with her, who had insisted it was too mature.

Jennet thought the fact that it was not quite a girl's frock was to its advantage. She had to admit that the effect was really rather nice —severely plain, and she had made Lai brush the thick waves of her hair so that they lay close to her head and didn't seem to curl too much behind. She considered her hair a menace—it would have looked so much more business-like if it had been straight. She kept it as short as she could—to have cropped it closer would only have been to sacrifice neatness, as it would merely have stood up in a short mop.

How disappointed she would have been if she had realized that all her careful preparation failed entirely to get the effect she wanted. That when, having gone across the court to Ivor Sinclair's house she was shown into the room where he was waiting, Ivor, looking across at her from the rug on which he was standing, was startled by the picture she made as she came towards him. So startled that for a moment he remained where he was; then, as he remembered his manners and went to meet her, that swift surge of anger which he had felt when he first knew "the trick" the people at home had played on him, came back in full force, making his greeting a little constrained—at least, if he had analysed it he would have been quite sure that it was anger.

Jennet said, "I hope I am not early."

"Not a bit. Rested after your journey?"

"Well, I don't feel at all tired. But then I'm afraid I've a horrible amount of energy," she laughed.

He drew forward a chair for her, and as Chang, smiling and urbane in a blue linen suit, handed cocktails, Ivor asked: "You feel rather strange, I expect?"

"I do—and I don't. I'm adaptable." She glanced at him over the rim of his glass. "I seem to be explaining myself. But you wouldn't know unless I told you."

"I expect I should find out."

She wondered if she would always hate, or whether she would get quite used to, that abrupt way he had of speaking. Yet his manner could be charming when he liked. However, she was quite determined that he should not ruffle her—they had to work together and therefore they would have to get used to each other.

"Of course—it's your business to find out things—and mine," she replied calmly. "By the way, I have a letter for you." She opened the black sequined evening bag she carried and took it out. "From Sir Bruce. He said I was to give it to you."

Ivor took it and put it in the pocket of his dinner jacket. "Thanks."

Jennet thought: I wish I knew what the old man has said about me. I bet he's tried to put me across. Then taking the bull by the horns: "I'm afraid you had a bad shock when I arrived, Doctor Sinclair—it really was rather steep to spring me on you like that. They might have put 'female of the species' in the cable."

He shrugged his shoulders. "It is a wonder the cable arrived in time in these days. In any case—I ought to be immune to shock."

Just then dinner was announced, and they went in together. She had been noting the surroundings—everything about this place where Ivor Sinclair lived was in perfect taste. He evidently liked nice things.

Ivor was a charming host. He talked to her quite gaily, explaining Mangtong and its population. It was practically a miracle that this island should have remained almost untouched when war was devastating China. Life went on quite normally, and it was the last remaining life of the China that had been. Of course it had changed since the revolution and the wars, but not terribly. The great clan of the Wongs still owned practically the whole province—still lived behind their courtyard walls in the feudal way which had been that of all the great families of China.

"Wait till you meet Madame Ling-Mai," said Ivor. "Lady Amanda and the doyen of the great house are bosom friends. Those two old women run this place between them. Only Madame—thank heaven!—keeps behind her walls."

Jennet told him. "I've always loved reading about China. Lady Amanda told me she had lived in Mangtong for twenty-five years—and, war or no war, nothing would get her out of China."

"No. She says it's in her blood. She was married to a man who adored it too. Good thing he didn't live to see the Japs running about in great portions of it. He wrote a history of it, you know; and he was in the Diplomatic. When he retired they settled here."

"Are there a lot of Europeans?" Jennet asked.

"A fair amount—quite a gay colony. But I'm afraid I'm not social."

"Doctors don't have much time to be." She shrugged her shoulders.

"That depends——" An odd shadow flitted over his face, and once again she had that strange impression that something had made him very unhappy. To her surprise she suddenly discovered that she was smitten with shyness. Talk about the Great Wall of China—this man seemed able to build a stone wall round himself all in a minute. Here she was, longing for him to talk shop to her; but not a word did he utter regarding the hospital.

The course was changed silently and adroitly, and Ivor was talking again. Asking her about her voyage, about London in these difficult days, touching on the situation in Europe, but all the time she had that feeling that he was withdrawn.

Then the meal was over, and they rose to go back into the other room together. Coffee was served, and tiny glasses of liqueur.

Then deliberately thrusting aside her inhibition, Jennet said, "You'll be wanting to go your round soon, won't you?"

"Not for an hour." He hesitated, there was something he had made up his mind to say. In the shaded golden light he glanced across to where she was sitting.

What the devil was Sir Bruce thinking about, to have let them choose her? Ivor asked himself again. Why, even if he had been inclined to accept a woman to work with—this was the last type he would have chosen. And to think of a woman in Simon's place——

A spasm of bitter pain shot through him, and his mouth set grimly. It was no use wasting time. He would have to be drastic, and, by jove! he meant to be.

Jennet turned her head suddenly, and smiled. "May I look at your books?" she asked, rising. "Then I think I must go to bed——"

It was his opportunity to announce: "First I have something to say to you——" But she was already standing in front of the bookshelves. "I suppose you make time to read," she said, "one does, if one really cares about it. I've brought as many as I dared——" She broke off as the door behind them opened, and Chang announced:

"Mister Devenham and Missis Danvers."

Jennet had time to see the dark frown on her host's face, but it was gone immediately, though he was quite unsmiling as he turned to greet the new arrivals. Watching from the background, she thought involuntarily: What an extremely ornamental pair!

They were. The man with his good-looking face burnt to a light bronze which was in strong contrast to his fair hair, and made his grey eyes appear startlingly light. The girl, wrapped in a white silk shawl embroidered in yellow and cream roses. Black haired, with one of those thick matt white skins which never seem to be affected by sun or wind, but keep their magnolia tint unsullied. Eyes like velvet, that dark pansy brown which might be either black or purple; a study in ivory and jet, with a curved scarlet mouth.

This vision came swiftly across the room, exclaiming: "Ivor, we've been dining with the Venners, and I felt I simply must look in as we passed. You don't mind, do you—I'm simply dying to know——" She broke off, suddenly aware of Jennet. "I say, Chang didn't say you had a guest——"

If Jennet could have known it, for the first time since her arrival Ivor was near to enjoying himself. "It's quite all right," he said. "Doctor Grey and I have been getting to know each other. She arrived today. May I introduce Doctor Jennet Grey—Mrs. Danvers."

"Oh! Are *you* the new doctor? But how frightfully interesting." Iris Danvers held out her hand; as she put her own into it and met those amazingly dark eyes Jennet, who among other things was a very excellent psychologist, knew instantly that this exotically lovely creature did not like her at all.

Iris continued in that drawling voice, which somehow had a hard quality behind it, and did not seem to match her appearance: "This is my brother—Philip; isn't it too exciting to think of a woman doctor instead of some boringly stuffy man to take poor Simon's place." The speech was in extremely bad taste, but Jennet did not know enough yet to realize just how execrable the taste was.

But Philip Devenham shook hands, smiling straight into her eyes. "Frightfully—exciting," he said. "I hope Doctor Grey isn't going to be entirely professional all the time."

It was the sort of remark which, coming from most men, would have annoyed Jennet intensely, but somehow she laughed, and without knowing it flushed a little under the open appreciation in Philip Devenham's eyes.

"Oh, doctors sometimes relax," she said lightly.

"A cigarette—if you have any mercy in you, Ivor." Iris had seated herself on a corner of the Chesterfield, and held out her hand imploringly.

"There's a box next to you," he replied curtly. "And in ten minutes I shall turn you out. I'm due in the hospital—— Cigarette, Doctor Grey?"

"No, thanks. I think I must run along now," replied Jennet. "If you will forgive me. I am really tired."

"Right." He did not attempt to keep her, and with a smiling nod to each of the recent arrivals she moved towards the door.

Without any apology to his other guests Ivor followed her, escorting her as far as the courtyard. "You can find your way?" he asked.

"Thanks very much, yes. And thanks for a most pleasant evening." She hesitated. There was bright moonlight outside, and in it she saw that he was very pale. She had the instinctive feeling that he was blazingly angry, but this time his anger was not for her. And suddenly: "Doctor Sinclair—you will give me a chance, won't you?" she asked impulsively. "I mean—you will try and forget that I am a woman, and—judge me by my work and my capacity to—adapt myself?"

For a moment he looked down at her in silence. Then: "I shall certainly judge you by your work," he said. "Please meet me in the entrance hall of the main building at eight tomorrow morning. Good-night."

"Thank you. Good-night." She hesitated again, then, deciding not to offer her hand, turned and walked away. He might have been nicer—he might at least have shaken hands, said something to cheer her. If anyone else had behaved like that, Jennet, who was a good hater and had not learned yet to curb an impulsiveness which made her take violent dislikes to people, would have told herself that she hated Ivor Sinclair. But, surprising as it was, she did not hate him— did not even dislike him; and a few minutes later, when she had firmly dismissed the waiting Lai, she thought as she sat before the dressing-table vigorously brushing her hair: He isn't nearly as hard as he would like people to think. He gives me the impression that he is wearing armour. And yet—he could be hard. Even cruel. What a pity—if he's really as clever as they say—that he isn't broader-minded! (How very pleased Doctor Sinclair would have been if he had known of that conclusion!)

Then she found herself thinking about those other two whom she had only just glimpsed.

Now why should Iris Danvers have taken that instant dislike to her? As for Philip—he was an easy type to sum up. The too good-looking man, who is almost a professional lady-killer, and yet—with a certain charm.

She thought: I don't somehow see myself having much in common with those two. She had yet to learn that the handsome Philip and his sister were not to be so easily dismissed.

Doctor Jennet rose, and crossed over to the bed. She noticed for the first time that with the bag she had laid down on the coverlet when she entered was a small, slim volume.

She picked it up with a start of dismay, remembering that she had drawn it from the bookcase by which she had been standing when Iris Danvers and her brother were announced. She had obviously gone on holding it with her bag. Bother! One only borrowed books from one's friends, and that with reverence, in Jennet's creed. And here she was running off with one of Ivor Sinclair's volumes without "by-your-leave," the first day they had met.

Donne's poems. She had been going to ask him how he liked that strange Elizabethan, when those wretched people arrived. Frowning, she turned the pages, and was suddenly arrested by a verse which stood out because of the faint pencil markings under it:

> "*And sweare*
> *No where*
> *Lives a woman true and faire.*
>
> *If thou findst one, let me know,*
> *Such a pilgrimage were sweet;*
> *Yet do not, I would not go,*
> *Though at next doore we might meet:*
> *Though she were true when you met her*
> *And last till you write your letter,*
>   *Yet she*
>   *Will be*
> *False, ere I come, to two or three.*"

She stared down at the book. Who had marked those lines? Surely—— She turned back to the flyleaf. The name was written firmly enough: Ivor Sinclair—and a bookplate to emphasize the ownership. So that was how he felt? Was that the reason for that bitter mouth—for the fact that he had no use for women? Because once—some girl had hurt him, disillusioned him?

Jennet told herself she wouldn't know. She had not come to China to think about anything but the romance of mending broken bodies.

And if somewhere on High Olympus the Gods laughed, Doctor Jennet Grey did not hear them.

CHAPTER III

IVOR SINCLAIR finished examining his morning's mail, and sat back to stare for a few moments out of the window beside him. It was not often that the picture beyond that window failed to please him, for there was something in the young man which reacted very strongly to beauty of line and colour.

But today he was not thinking of the exquisitely falling wisteria, or the riot of colour that filled the flower-beds in his private courtyard. There was no room for anything in his mind, save the unpleasant fact that this day marked the beginning of the most unprecedented thing he had ever contemplated—the sharing with a woman of the running of his hospital.

For the twentieth time he asked himself what in the name of all that was impossible the trustees had been thinking of. He could not imagine. If they had to send him a woman, it would have been easier for him if they had sent what he called "the usual" type— he could very well have coped with that. But Jennet Grey was not even grown up. What on earth real experience could she have had?

And then a passage from Sir Bruce's letter came very clearly back to him—"The most brilliant of my students. Knocked the boys clean out of it. Don't take any notice of her ornamental looks, she's a worker. And quite soon you will be grateful to me for sending her. Anyway, there is no pick of decent men over here now. They may all be needed."

In spite of that, Ivor had fully made up his mind yesterday evening that he would tell her she could not stay. And it was not Sir Bruce's letter which had stopped him from doing so. He frowned darkly, knowing perfectly well that if Iris had not come in like that, just to have a "look see" what the new man was like, and then enjoying what she must have guessed to be his discomfiture, his parting with Jennet last night would have been a very different one.

Then suddenly he seemed to hear a clear, soft voice asking: "You will give me a chance, won't you? You will try and forget that I am a woman, and judge me by my capacity to do my work and to—adapt myself?"

But hang it all! even if they had sent her out as a matron—though, thank heaven! there was not the remotest chance of his needing a new matron, and the present one—Rose Hilton—was the most capable woman who had ever run a nursing staff in any hospital he had been in.

He had not had time to talk to Matron about this yet—Great Scott! he hadn't said a word to her about the new arrival. She had been dining out last night. She must know by now, but——

The sharp ring of the telephone bell interrupted his thoughts, and with a muttered imprecation he unhooked the instrument which stood on the desk beside him.

"Hello! Is that Dr. Sinclair?"

"Speaking." (Now what?)

"Lady Amanda would like to speak to you, sir."

"All right," said Ivor, resigned but not cordial.

A moment later Lady Amanda's voice came across the wire. "Good-morning, Ivor. I will say that trying to get you is rather like attempting to speak to Royalty!"

"Sorry," he said. "In another minute I shouldn't have been available at all."

"Well," she enquired, "how do you like your new colleague?"

"I shall probably be able to answer that question better when I know more about her."

But Lady Amanda was not to be put off. "You give her a chance, young man," she said crisply. "She will be handicapped enough, if I know anything about it."

"What do you mean?"

"Too good looking to be an unqualified success in our small European colony." There was a touch of grimness in the old lady's voice. "Two's a crowd, if you understand me." And then, without waiting to see if he made any comment: "Anyway, don't start by disliking her."

"Good heavens! Why should I? As long as she does her work well—that's all that concerns me."

"That's good. Couldn't be better."

Half amused, and knowing his antagonist too well to be annoyed, Ivor observed: "You seem to be interested in the young woman."

"I am—extremely interested. Also in the experiment and its repercussions."

"Look here——"

"I know, I know. You want to get away. You can run along—but bring her to tea on Sunday."

"I don't think——"

"I'm not asking you to think. I'm telling you to come!" snapped Lady Amanda. "I'm not having that girl thrown to the wolves—if they think *I* am behind her they'll mind their p's and q's."

"Oh, all right!" said Ivor. "Good——"

"Just one moment. I must say I am glad that you are not starting by loathing her. That would have been just too dangerous."

"Dangerous! What on earth do you mean?"

"Well, I have often noticed that when a man starts by disliking a girl too much, it's very often the prelude to falling in love with her—and think what a complication that would be!" Lady Amanda chuckled, and rang off abruptly.

Of all the old——! thought Ivor furiously. Falling in love! Good Lord! that was very likely! But there again was the snag. Outsiders—especially in a place like this—were not going to accept the fact that a man and a girl could work together on an absolutely impersonal basis.

There was no time to nurse his anger then, but his temper was far from improved by the fact that he was already several minutes late for his appointment. If there was one thing he loathed, it was unpunctuality.

His face was set and unsmiling when a few minutes later he strode into the square entrance hall of the main building.

Jennet was already there, the tall, slender figure of the Matron beside her. They broke off their conversation to turn towards him.

"Good-morning, Doctor Grey," he greeted curtly. "Good-morning, Matron."

Jennet said: "Good-morning, Doctor. I have been getting acquainted with Matron."

"Excellent." His eyes softened as they rested on the pleasant face under the stiff white cap, and as their glances met he raised his brows very slightly.

Rose Hilton knew that look. He always did that when he was particularly exasperated. She knew him so well, and guessed almost exactly how he was feeling, but she was one of those blessed women who prefer to be on the side of their own sex. She already liked

Jennet; and even while her loyalty to Ivor was an unshaken thing, she thought: He really must give her a chance!

"Then there is no need to introduce you," he observed. "Sorry to have kept you. We had better get in."

No time for good manners! I hope he doesn't treat his patients so curtly, thought Jennet, who after last night had somehow hoped for better things.

But she soon discovered that however he treated his equals, he had something quite different in reserve for those helpless people in their beds. It was only necessary to see that quick turning of heads when he entered a ward, the eager welcome on a sufferer's face, to realize that there was not a soul to whom the quick, light sound of his footsteps was not welcome.

He walked her quickly through the first two wards, but when they reached the entrance to the third he said: "These next two will be in your charge, so it will take us rather longer to go round. Have you a good memory?"

"Excellent," Jennet told him calmly. No one would have guessed from her serene manner how sick with nervousness she was. But very quickly her burning interest in the work she loved took hold of her. She thanked heaven that she had swotted up enough of the language to be able to make herself understood, and though he said nothing, he was pleasantly surprised on that score.

It became evident to him very quickly that she was no fool—though he was still sceptical about how she was going to handle a job of this size.

He was oddly aware of her as she stood beside him—hang it, she looked even younger in her white coat! But how quickly she grasped a thing. Ivor Sinclair, whose keenness on efficiency was almost a mania, began—though he was not yet ready to own it—to feel a little less alarmed over the immediate future of the hospital that was his life.

It would have helped Jennet if she could have known that.

Finally, he turned her over to Matron, and went away to do his own work. Glad to be rid of me! Jennet thought, looking after him.

Beside her Rose Hilton said quietly: "You will soon get used to it all, Doctor. And you will find Sister very helpful."

"I am sure I shall." There was something Jennet liked instinctively about this woman. She had the feeling that the convention that exists in hospitals of keeping the medical staff on a businesslike, more or less aloof, basis from the nursing staff must be rather relaxed here. She had sensed already that Ivor Sinclair and Matron were excellent friends, and that without knowing—or perhaps just without admitting it—he depended on the elder woman quite a lot. And to Jennet herself, Rose was a pleasant surprise—how well she knew the difficulties a Matron could cause. Of Sister she was not quite so sure; she would probably need careful handling, not being used to working with a woman.

Jennet said impulsively: "I'm afraid it will be a little while before I feel at home."

"You have come a long way," said Rose. "But—if I may say so—you'll be all right. And though," she smiled, "I'm not supposed to give a personal opinion, I would like to say that I think it's a very good idea of the trustees to have sent you."

Jennet raised her brows. "You haven't any prejudice against women doctors?"

"Good heavens, no! Look at the splendid work they do." Then she added: "You will find the Chief marvellous to work under. He is the most generous-minded person. The only things he is really fierce about are if he thinks anyone is letting the hospital down, or any sort of inefficiency. He lives for this place and his work is in it. But he is terribly helpful."

Jennet said, a little dryly: "I'm sure he is." She thought privately that she would go to Matron if she really wanted putting wise on anything.

As she went back into the ward she was feeling unusually depressed. For the first time her self-confidence failed her—supposing she fell down on this job?

* * *

The Sister in charge of both the big wards which Jennet was taking over was very polite and seemed ready to co-operate, but Jennet was not sure that she altogether liked her. They discussed cases though, and Jennet got most of the information she wanted, gathering one thing on the way—that evidently her predecessor had left quite a lot with Sister and enjoyed a popularity which was going to make it difficult for anyone following him. Another paragon!

She naturally did not ask Sister, but she was determined to ask Matron about him as soon as an opportunity presented itself.

Of one thing she was certain—she was going to find a great deal to interest her here. It certainly was a perfect hospital, the sort of place many doctors dream of but few attain. There was unlimited money behind it, as well as people who knew how to, and were determined to, spend that money to its best advantage.

Walking through the broad, white-tiled corridors, Jennet thought:

If I can't do good work here, I may as well write myself down a failure. No wonder Ivor Sinclair thinks the world of it.

Ivor Sinclair! What an odd mixture he was. So much unconscious charm, and so much that was difficult in him. She thought: He gives me the oddest idea that he has deliberately built a barrier round himself. I wonder why he found it necessary. Then suddenly she was remembering that book of poems which was still up in her room.

> "*And sweare*
> *No where*
> *Lives a woman true and faire.*"

Had some woman really let him down badly? she wondered. But the first impression that he was a woman hater, which Lady Amanda's description of his attitude towards the opposite sex had given her, somehow did not seem the right one. No man who really disliked women could be quite so universally adored by them—as it seemed pretty obvious this one was. Nurses and the female patients, and even Matron, seemed to get that same sort of look on their faces when he was about.

He must be a little spoiled! thought Jennet. He wouldn't be human if he was not. Well, *I'm* not going to spoil him. No eyes raised in worship from *me*! I'm meeting the man on an equal footing—that's what I'm doing.

Nevertheless, if the question had been put to her, she would have been quite ready to admit that already she was much oftener inclined to like than to dislike Doctor Ivor Sinclair.

CHAPTER IV

AT luncheon Jennet met the rest of "the house." There were two research workers, a young Irish doctor, the anæsthetist David Macdonald, and two others. They were all very nice, and they all seemed to take her advent as a matter of course. For which she was suitably grateful. Whatever they had to say among themselves did not concern her.

Afterwards, she was glad to escape to her own room, where she made notes and wrote steadily for an hour before she began to unpack some of her personal belongings.

When she saw her own books on the shelves, her own funny little mascots scattered around, she began to think it looked more like home. She was standing looking around, her back to the long open window, when a man's voice asked:

"May I come in? I'm so tired of waiting for someone to announce me in the conventional way."

Jennet swung round, and found herself looking into the handsome face of Philip Devenham.

"Don't say you have forgotten me already," he begged. "It was only last night we met!"

"Of course I remember meeting you," Jennet replied calmly. "Mr. Devenham, isn't it?"

"That same useless person." Without asking again for permission, he stepped over the window-ledge. "I say, can I make myself useful?"

"No, thanks. I've done everything I am going to do today," she replied. Quite aware that her visitor had charm, and sure that he was aware of it too, she was neither cordial nor otherwise. She had not made up her mind whether she was going to like him or not.

He said: "I say, I hope you don't mind me butting in like this. I had an idea that you would probably be taking a breather about this time. And I had a message for you."

"A message for me?" she repeated.

"Yes; from my sister."

Now that, thought Jennet, I *could* do without. She had not taken long to make up her mind about Mrs. Danvers.

"But that can wait." Philip smiled at her. "May I sit down for a minute?"

"I'm sorry—please do," said Jennet quickly. And as he lowered himself into a chair: "You'll find cigarettes in the box next to you."

"I say, you do seem to have settled in beautifully. You look exactly as if you belonged."

"I suppose I do," said Jennet calmly.

If she had meant it for a snub, he was quite unembarrassed. "Yes I suppose so," he agreed. "But, Lord! what a shock I got last night. If you had seen some of the medical women I have seen—but no doubt you know the type. Cropped hair and——"

"Forgive me saying so, but you're a long way behind the times you know," she told him. "Sorry if I gave you a shock——"

"I like pleasant shocks." Those handsome, rather sleepy eyes met hers. Not trustworthy eyes, she decided. How like his sister he was in spite of the difference in colouring—almost too good-looking for a man.

Philip Devenham was thinking: It's quite impossible that anyone as attractive as this should be as unaware of her sex as she pretends to be. Had Sinclair known that a woman was coming and kept it to himself? That, of course, was what Iris wanted to know—naturally.

Philip had decided with cynical amusement that the arrival of Doctor Jennet Grey was going to cause some fun. And whenever there was the particular brand of "fun" which contained an element of mischief, he liked to be in it.

Hang it, life was dull enough. It needed waking up.

During the next quarter of an hour he pretended to entertain Jennet with information regarding the small European colony at Mangtong. It was impossible not to be entertained by him—he was certainly amusing. A soft-footed houseboy brought in tea—she had not ordered it, but she had to offer her visitor some.

She was laughing gaily at a remark of his when she broke off with a start as something leapt through the window, landing on the back of the chesterfield.

"Hang!" exclaimed Philip. "It's that darned cat of Sinclair's. I say—do you mind taking it away from me?—I can't endure cats."

"All right," said Jennet. "Some people can't—though I can't imagine why. Come here, you beauty——"

"Take care, it scratches like the devil!" said Philip, which she could not help thinking rather good, considering he had asked her to move it.

However, she calmly approached the interloper, a big Siamese, who regarded her from its blue eyes, giving no indication of what it intended to do.

"We're going to be friends," she informed, as she picked it up. Just then a shadow darkened the window, and Ivor said quickly:

"I say, I'm sorry! Ming suddenly got the idea that he ought to call on you—I hope he didn't startle you."

"I like him," replied Jennet. "How do you do, Ming? Since we are now introduced."

"He's behaving himself very well, but I think I'd better take him." Ivor held out his hands. "He has rather a propensity for sharpening his claws on people's furniture."

"I don't mind. Come in and have some tea, won't you?" What an amazing person this was—somehow she would never have thought of him as owning a pet of any sort; certainly he had his human side. She liked men who liked cats.

"Well, if you don't mind the creature." He stepped into the room. At the same moment he saw the other visitor, and his expression changed.

"Hello, Devenham," he said curtly. "I didn't know you were there."

"I think your blinkin' cat did. It seems to pursue me," said Philip sulkily.

Whether his dislike of cats was genuine or not, Jennet was certain of one thing—there was no liking lost between these two. She had noticed Ivor's expression of annoyed surprise when he saw the other man, and suddenly she found herself wishing that the doctor had not arrived to find her already entertaining—though what it was to do with him she really did not know.

He accepted the cup of tea she gave him with a rather curt "Thank you," and then: "I wanted to talk to you about one or two things," he told her.

Really, he could be rude!

"Do you play tennis?" Philip asked Jennet.

"I have played a good deal," she replied. "But I'm hardly up to Wimbledon form."

"Good. And don't forget if you like to ride, I can mount you——"

"Aren't you forgetting," enquired Ivor before Jennet could even reply, "that Doctor Grey has not arrived to become a social asset to the community. She will have quite a lot to do."

"I suppose she'll get time off," replied Philip coolly. "Barton seemed to get plenty——"

Jennet saw Ivor go suddenly white, but whether with anger or pain she could not tell, although she had the swift impression that he had winced.

"Of course," he said. "I have yet to find out which Doctor Grey prefers."

"I should think there's a happy medium." Philip rose. "I must run along now. And"—he smiled at Jennet, who had the annoyed feeling that for some reason she had become a bone of contention between the two men—"I might as well remember to deliver my message. Iris wants you to please come to tea on Sunday afternoon."

"That's very nice of her——" began Jennet, wishing she knew how to say no.

Ivor cut in curtly: "She can't. I have already arranged to take her out to tea."

Really, this was a little bit much! Jennet thought: If I let him go on in this way, he'll be writing out a list of what I'm to do with my spare time. She felt Philip's amused eyes on her, opened her lips to speak, and closed them.

"Oh well, of course if you've made your arrangements there's nothing else to be said," Philip observed in that sort of pleasant voice which is so much ruder than open contradiction. "Iris will be disappointed, but—another time. Thanks awfully for the tea. I'll ring you up." He held out his hand, and, as Jennet put her own into it, gave her a look which was altogether too understanding. "I'll go the way I came, if I may," he said, and stepped once again over the window-ledge.

Jennet turned back to the tea-table, amazed to find that she was angry enough for her hand to be trembling as she moved the teapot.

Then, across the brief silence Ivor spoke. "Sorry I didn't have time to explain," he said, "but Lady Amanda rang up and asked me to take you to see her on Sunday."

She raised her head and looked at him coldly. "Did it occur to you to ask if I wanted to go?"

"No!" he retorted. "Or to her. An invitation from Lady Amanda is a royal command."

"Oh!" She flushed, biting her lip.

Then, as their eyes met, she realized he was laughing at her. She longed to be dignified, but somehow it was quite impossible, and the next moment they were both laughing frankly.

Then: "You like your own way, don't you?" she asked.

"Don't you?"

"Yes—but I am reasonable."

"That's unusual for a woman."

"Must you generalize?"

He smiled again—that particularly charming smile. She carried the memory of him long afterwards, sitting there, one leg dropped loosely over the other, scratching the head of the cat on his lap with that beautifully formed, sensitive doctor's hand. "You know," he said, "you will usually find that when I make a decision it is the right one."

She forgot to think that it sounded a little arrogant. What she did think was: He can be persuasive too. It's rather difficult to combat him.

Then he sat upright, putting Ming down decisively. "There are one or two points I am anxious to hear your opinion on," he said. "Will you tell me exactly what——" The rest concerned technical details regarding the patients she would be in charge of.

Jennet would have been very annoyed if anyone had suggested that listening to that charming voice made it all so much more interesting. . . .

* * *

Ivor Sinclair had had a particularly busy day.

When he found himself free at last to sit back, light a pipe and open a book, it was later than usual.

He read the first page, and, laying it face downwards on his knee, remained studying the lovely Chinese print on the wall opposite. But he was not seeing the print. He was seeing a girl's face, grave, intent; hearing the low, eager voice expounding the sort of things which had always formed the deepest interest of his life.

She was certainly intelligent.

He thought: I'll give her a free hand for a month. If she falls down on it, I can't be blamed for sending her home again. But—she'll have to discriminate and not philander. He frowned darkly.

Now—what the deuce was Devenham hanging round for this afternoon? I wonder if she is sensible enough to size him up? I doubt it, he thought. If the Devenhams will keep away from this place I shall be darned pleased. Anyway, the Amanda will look after Iris.

He picked up his book again. But while he read he seemed to hear Lady Amanda's rather hoarse voice.

"If a man begins by disliking a girl too much—he's very likely to fall in love with her; and that would be a complication——"

She need not worry. It was the sort of complication he had finished with long ago.

But it was curious how the remembrance of Philip Devenham looking so very much at home in Jennet's room annoyed him. . . .

CHAPTER V

JENNET had asked Matron to come in on the Sunday morning and drink a cup of tea with her. Pouring the straw-coloured liquid with its exquisite aroma into the lovely little handleless cups, Jennet glanced across at her companion. She was still thanking whatever gods had been instrumental in making Rose Hilton the head of the nursing staff of this hospital; she knew that if the Matron had been the sort who was inclined to resent her coming, things could have been made difficult. Besides, the short time which had elapsed since their first meeting had sufficed to strengthen the impression that she was going to like Rose.

And though Jennet preferred to consider herself entirely independent of other people's likes and dislikes, it nevertheless gave her a warm sort of feeling when she knew that anyone was on her side! As she instinctively felt Matron was.

"Cigarette?" she asked, holding out her case.

"Thanks—seeing that I'm not on duty." Rose helped herself. "Are you liking the new life, Doctor?"

"I think I'm going to like it," Jennet replied. "That is—the hospital part of it. But—to tell you the truth, it scared me to discover that there is a social side to life out here."

"Why on earth?" Rose raised her eyebrows, laughing frankly. "You can't shut yourself behind the hospital courtyards—you'd wake up one fine day to discover that you were going crackers with boredom—probably wanting to assassinate everyone on the staff. Why, even Doctor Sinclair has a few outside interests."

"To tell the whole truth," Jennet confessed, "from what I've heard and read of European communities out East, I don't think the people will be a bit my type."

"But it takes all sorts—even to make up a Legation set." All the same, Rose thought, they won't be too ready to be nice to her; at least, the women won't. Especially her ladyship! The title was an ironic one, and she was not thinking of Lady Amanda.

Jennet said: "I believe I'm going to be vetted this very afternoon. Doctor Sinclair accepted an invitation to tea for me—with Lady Amanda Trent."

"Good," nodded Rose. "If Lady Amanda sets the seal of approval on you, believe me, all the sting will be taken out of any social obligations. She's a redoubtable old lady; what she says today, all European Mangtong must say tomorrow (whatever they may think!). You'll probably find her difficult and exacting, but she's really nice—if she likes you."

"I've met her," said Jennet; and went on to explain how.

When she had finished, Rose nodded. "You'll be all right," she comforted. "I'm extremely glad she got hold of you first, if I may say so."

"First?"

"Well, there's a rivalry between herself and Mrs. Danvers, who is——"

"I've met Mrs. Danvers too," informed Jennet. "She called on Doctor Sinclair when I was dining with him on the night of my arrival."

She would! thought Matron, and, seeing her expression, Jennet said impulsively: "You don't like her?"

"I suppose I ought not to say it," replied Rose, "but she's a snake. It may be very indiscreet to tell you so, but frankly I have been wanting to ever since I first saw you. I do like my own sex; and, in spite of years of hospital experience, I've come to the conclusion that the best of us are capable of quite as strong *esprit de corps* as men are. Cats are not all of one sex! Therefore I resent the Iris Danvers type. She couldn't be real friends with a woman—not even a really plain one!—if she tried; but she wouldn't try."

Hello! thought Jennet. The lovely Iris must be even worse than I thought.

She said: "She is very beautiful."

"Oh, she's good looking enough!" Rose would have liked to add: And makes as much capital out of it as she can. But she did not want to say too much. It was the first time her tongue had really loosened against her *bête noire*; but something urged her on to put Jennet on her guard. As far as Jennet was concerned, Rose thought: She is quite capable of taking care of herself—up to a point. But she's a woman, and we've a wisdom the opposite sex don't possess as far as our own is concerned. I wish to heaven I could be sure that—someone else is capable of maintaining immunity against that Danvers cat. Though, to be sure, it's an insult to Ming to call her one. . . .

"You are looking fierce!" exclaimed Jennet, laughing.

"I feel fierce," Rose answered. "Silly to let things that don't matter rattle one—as long as they don't matter. But you look out for yourself."

"I will. I've learnt to do it, you know."

"I expect you have," said Matron. "I hope you don't think I'm impertinent."

"Certainly I don't. I'm looking to you to put me wise to things," Jennet told her warmly.

"There is something I want to ask you. I don't know if I am imagining things, but it seems to me as though—there's a certain amount of reticence about my predecessor here. I do so want to know exactly what sort of man I'm following. . . . Oh, I've gathered already that he was very popular," she added a little dryly. "But popularity doesn't always mean——"

"Brains and efficiency," supplied Rose. "How right you are. Only Simon Barton certainly had brains. When he put his mind to his job he was fine. He could have gone a long way if only——"

Jennet looked at her quickly. "You're talking in the past tense—did something go wrong? Don't tell me if you feel you ought not to."

Rose said quietly: "Simon Barton was killed in a motoring smash. Something went wrong—we will never know what, because the car was smashed to bits and ran into a tree. It was late at night, and they didn't find him until the next morning."

"But how awful!" exclaimed Jennet. "He—he was quite young, wasn't he?"

"Twenty-eight. The worst of it is——" Rose glanced from the closed door to the open window. "Do you mind if I shut that for a minute?" she asked.

"I will." Jennet rose and attended to the window. As she turned back she said: "Don't talk about it if you would rather not——"

"I'm glad you asked me. I've been wondering how I could give you a hint," Rose said. "You'll think this very 'hush-hush' and rather mysterious, as of course everyone knows about the accident. But, you see, there is a sort of tacit understanding that it isn't talked about in the hospital, because we all know how terribly Doctor Sinclair feels it. There were not so many years between them, but Simon was like the Chief's younger brother. He'd been his fag at school. The worst of it was, Simon's parents were going to buy a practice for him in England, but there was this job going here, and Doctor Sinclair suggested he should come out. I happen to know that made him feel much worse. Though he'd hate people to guess it, Ivor Sinclair is extraordinarily sensitive. He thought the world of Simon, and the tragedy hit him hard, especially as they had not been seeing eye to eye lately, and there had been—disagreements."

"Over Doctor Barton's work?"

"Partly. The one thing Doctor Sinclair won't stand for is if he thinks anyone on the staff is slacking. And—— He has felt it most terribly," she finished. "And—we simply don't mention it if it can be helped."

"How dreadful," said Jennet. "I had no idea. I am glad I asked you."

But she still had the feeling that there were things which Rose had left unsaid.

When she was dressing to go out that afternoon she found herself thinking about her predecessor, picturing him as young—perhaps younger than his age; high-spirited, the sort who would not in the least mind making himself socially amiable. She wondered if he and Iris had been friends. Was that why Iris had been so eager to find out what his successor was like?

Another scalp!

How uncharitable I am! Jennet thought. But she was much nearer to the truth than she imagined.

It touched her strangely to find how this conspiracy of silence had been formed to stop Ivor from being hurt. And as she sat beside him in the car and glanced at that strong, rather stern profile, she suddenly seemed to be seeing him through new eyes.

That odd feeling she had experienced that he was not happy was right, then. And—he was capable of really human feelings. But surely she had sensed that already? She thought suddenly: I don't believe he would be capable of half-measures. When he loved somebody, it would be with no holding back. But he would be quite as ruthless—perhaps even more ruthless—with someone he cared about than——

Her companion turned his head, and, furious with herself, she realized that she had been caught staring at him. She could have kicked herself the harder because, as she looked away, she knew that she had gone scarlet, but if she had thought about it she would have decided that, of course, it was annoyance which was playing such queer tricks with her heart, making it beat at twice its normal rate.

He did not seem to notice that there was anything wrong, though, and he asked with a note of amusement in his voice:

"I suppose you know you are going to be very thoroughly inspected this afternoon?"

"I rather guess so." She shrugged her shoulders. "Probably I shall behave badly. I'm not awfully good at party manners."

"Nonsense!" he retorted. "Think of them as patients—a bit abnormal! And honour them with your best bedside manner. For the honour of the hospital, you must make a good impression."

She had the curious feeling that he meant it—he really wanted her to make a good impression. Perhaps it was because of Lady Amanda. Nevertheless, she asked a little defensively: "Do these people really matter?"

"Not a bit!" He sounded quite cheerful. "Except, of course, that they can make you feel at home, or a complete stranger—and I suppose that for your own sake it is better for you to be able to feel at home."

She could not very well ask if that meant he had accepted her, and was quite prepared for her to settle down—but she experienced an odd, quick little feeling of warmth. There was something terribly nice about this man. It was a shame if anybody had let him down.

A wide door was opened, and he turned the car into a courtyard gay with flowers. The white house that faced them was tiled in lovely blue; there was a wide verandah on which a few people were sitting, and a servant came quickly to open the door of the car; another, smiling broadly at the doctor, bowed them in. But before he could announce them, Lady Amanda came swiftly to the entrance of a room on the right of the hall.

"Ah! there you are, Ivor," she greeted. "Well, my dear," she took Jennet's hand, "how are you liking China?"

"Very much indeed."

"Good. Come along in." The old lady led her into the big white salon. Jennet was instantly aware of Iris, standing on the terrace just beside the open windows, but Lady Amanda was already introducing her to other people.

"Sir John Selham—Doctor Jennet Grey. Mrs. Carsdene—Mrs. Carsdene writes novels, my dear, but there is no need to be afraid of her. We're all afraid of Sir John——"

"Nonsense! Nonsense! Anyhow, the man was never born who could frighten you, Amanda." Sir John, small, grey-haired and moustached, laughed with unexpected pleasantness as he took Jennet's hand. "What do you mean by being a doctor—I simply don't believe it."

"It's too true," she told him.

"Dear me—I am beginning to remember that I have been thinking for some time back that I ought to consult a reliable medical opinion!" announced Sir John, staring very hard. "Doing any private practice, Doctor?"

"No; but I am sure you can always come to the hospital and consult—Doctor Sinclair," replied Jennet demurely.

Sir John stared harder than ever, then roared with laughter.

"Go away, John," said Lady Amanda severely. "I shall warn Doctor Grey against you—if she has not sized you up already."

"Too bad now—too bad!" he protested.

But Lady Amanda gently thrust him aside, and other introductions were made.

The ordeal was not as bad as Jennet had expected it to be. The room filled up, and she found herself talking to people quite gaily, and forgetting the feeling that she was here to be vetted. Lady Amanda took care that she was introduced to everyone who came in, with the exception of Iris Danvers, who had drifted into the room, and made a bee-line for Ivor.

Jennet did not know why she should notice that so particularly, or remain aware of those two talking, first in a distant corner and then going out on to the terrace, where certainly they were joined by others, but still seemed to remain the centre of the group together.

She found herself suddenly wondering if they were very friendly. Certainly Iris seemed to be doing most of the talking. And it was quite impossible to read from Ivor's expression anything that was passing in his mind.

Sir John Selham attached himself to Jennet, and demanded news of: "Bruce Ferguson—by Jove, we were at Cambridge together, don't you know? Hear that it was old Bruce who sent you out here. I could tell you some stories about him—still got an eye for a pretty gel, what?"

She was rather startled when, with a complete change of manner, he demanded: "Hope they're being decent to you at the hospital?"

"Oh yes—of course!" Jennet replied.

"I like Sinclair," announced Sir John, "but understand he's a devil to work with—fact, can't see him working with a woman at all. Hear he doesn't like 'em——"

It was not unpleasantly said, and remembering afterwards, Jennet could not understand why she should have felt so much resentment at the implied criticism. She found herself saying: "I think it will be a privilege to work with him. I don't think he cares two hoots what I am—so long as I'm competent."

Then, before Sir John could make any reply, Iris came up to them. "How do you do, Doctor Grey?" she greeted. "Sir John, how dare you desert me so completely?"

"Never could I desert you!" he assured her.

"You have ignored me all the afternoon." Iris shook a slender forefinger at him. "Doctor Grey, don't believe a word he says to you. He's the most unfaithful man in Mangtong." She was laughing, but Jennet had the fleeting impression that she was not very pleased. Then looking over the beautiful head, on which was perched a daring little white hat, she met Ivor's glance.

He raised his brows, and made a slight gesture towards the door. Jennet rose at once. "I think we must be moving now," she said.

"Surely the hospital is not waiting to swallow you up tonight?" Sir John protested. And to Ivor, who had joined them: "You must not let your new colleague overwork herself, you know, Sinclair. Duty's all very well, but all work and no play makes—what was the name——?"

"Jennet," supplied the owner of it.

He retained Jennet's hand just a little longer than was necessary, and obviously reluctant to part with it, let it go. "Now, if he illtreats you let me know. I'm on the committee and I will call a special meeting to deal with the matter!"

"'Bye, Doctor Grey," said Iris in her slow, insolent voice. "By the way, my brother was devastated not to be able to be here this afternoon."

She was insufferable! It was not what she said, but the way she said it—the way of somehow implying so much more behind the words, and Jennet was stung to drawl back:

"Really? Why?"

But Iris only opened her eyes, an amused expression in them. "*I* don't know," she replied. "Ivor, darling, don't forget what I asked you, will you?"

"Not if I have time to remember it."

Jennet felt her spirits lift. Gosh! how sublimely rude he could be. She felt that if Iris had got the best of the round with her, things were suddenly evened up!

A moment later she was saying to Lady Amanda, "Thank you so much for letting me come."

"There has been no chance to talk to you in this crowd," Lady Amanda replied. "What evening can you dine with me?"

"I——"

"Don't look at Ivor. You're entitled to one evening a week off, you know. What about Wednesday?"

"Of course she will dine with you on Wednesday," said Ivor calmly.

"Be here at seven, then. And if you find life too unbearable before then, ring me up. I have never heard that he actually ill-treats people—but don't stand any nonsense." And with her *gamin* grin, the old lady waved them away.

They drove out of the courtyard in silence, and to her surprise he turned in the opposite direction to that in which the hospital lay.

"No need to be back yet," he informed. "We'll go for a run. There's a temple along this road that's rather worth seeing—unless you want to go back for any reason?"

"You arrange what I want, don't you?" asked Jennet with ominous quietness.

"What do you mean?"

"I *am* capable of accepting an invitation myself—though you don't seem to think so."

"Oh!" he laughed shortly, and then in that strange, disarming way of his: "I say, I'm awfully sorry. But you didn't seem to know what to say, and—as I told you before, Lady Amanda's invitations—they're royal commands. Besides—naturally you'll have one evening completely off duty."

It was no use—she discovered that she could not be annoyed with him.

He asked: "Well, it wasn't so bad, was it?"

"This afternoon? No."

"Our Amanda has set the seal of approval on you."

"She's a dear," said Jennet warmly.

"I don't always think so! We're good friends, though, even if we don't always see eye to eye. You made another conquest——"

"Who? Oh!" Jennet laughed. "Sir John! He's rather sweet, you know—almost too much of a type to be true."

"The last of the gay Edwardians! He really ought to have been retired from his job by now—but with this upheaval all over the place I fancy the Foreign Office are glad of a really sound man. And he's a marvel at his job."

"I like him," said Jennet decisively. "He and Sir Bruce were at Cambridge together."

"I know."

They had reached the top of the hill, and the temple he had spoken of lay to their right. As the car stopped, Jennet sat in silence gazing at the strange shaped buildings, with their square towers and gilded roofs cascading down into fantastically curled eaves with a peculiar grace that brought her artistic sense a keen sort of satisfaction. She said:

"How lovely Chinese architecture is. Don't tell me that they are going to spoil it all with concrete and steel buildings——"

"You care for those things?" he asked.

"Frightfully. Don't you——?" And suddenly, sitting there in the car, they were talking eagerly of porcelains and jades, of dragon thrones and a vanished world, until the slanting crimson and gold rays of the setting sun reminded them of time.

"Good heavens!" exclaimed Ivor. "We must get back. You'll have to explore this place another time—it's worth it. The monks are quite amiable about showing their treasures. But duty waits for no man!" He braked the car, and as he turned it, Jennet knew that she had found another side of this complex personality. She noticed that some of the set, rather strained look which too often characterized his face in repose seemed to have gone out of it; and she thought: He needs to get away from himself sometimes—I'm sure he shuts himself up too much. And then rather defensively: Naturally I'm interested in him—I've got to work with the man, and it's all to the good of our partnership if he can be kept human.

They drove for two or three miles in silence; and then, his eyes still on the road ahead, Ivor said abruptly, "I am going to leave you to yourself for a month. If there's anything you want to be helped about, come to me. Otherwise run your wards in your own way."

"And at the end of the month, if I have killed off too many of my patients I suppose I'm fired?" asked Jennet.

"That's up to you." He gave her no answering smile, and she decided, regretting her lapse into facetiousness: How uncompromising he can be. For all that, she was suddenly amazingly happy. He was giving her the chance to show that she could make good.

She said, rather formally, because she did not want him to think that she was gushing: "I'll do my best to deserve your confidence."

"How do you know it is confidence?" he asked.

"Well, then—courage."

He laughed, and she was smiling too as a car overtook and passed them. In his mirror the occupant of that other car had already seen and recognized them, but they had not even noticed him, and Philip Devenham was frowning as he shot ahead.

The twilight was closing in when Ivor helped Jennet out of the car. She hesitated for a moment, and he found that he was curiously aware of her standing there with the light from the window behind silhouetting her slender grace.

She said: "Thank you very much, Doctor. And—I'll try not to kill off the patients."

He would probably snub her again, but she had to say something. To her surprise his eyes creased at the corners in a way she noticed they sometimes had, even when his mouth was not smiling, and he said:

"You'd better not, Doctor Grey! Good-night."

Without any more ado he turned and walked towards his own quarters, and entering hers, Jennet went straight to her bedroom. At the dressing-table she pulled off her hat and reached behind her to put it on the bed. Then, as she picked up a comb, she smiled at her reflection; then frowned and shook her head.

Don't forget! she admonished herself. You are not going to join the Noble Order of Ivor Worshippers. There are quite enough in this hospital already. Even Rose Hilton—sensible young woman though she appears to be—is quite besotted by the young man. But—drat him!—what is there that makes one feel at moments that it would not be a bit derogatory to lie down and let him walk on one?

And added indignantly: Rot! I'd like to see the man who would walk on me!

No, she did not mean to let her enthusiasm run away with her. He had accepted her, temporarily, at any rate, as his colleague and equal; the rest—as he had reminded her—was up to her.

For a fleeting moment she had a slightly scared feeling that that phrase might involve rather more than she cared to think about.

CHAPTER VI

AT the same time at which Jennet and Ivor Sinclair were parting, Philip Devenham was pouring himself out a drink in the dining-room of his house. There was no very tangible reason why he should be feeling so very disgruntled with life—except perhaps that an appointment made more than a week ago had kept him from accompanying his sister to call on Lady Amanda. Usually he would have been quite pleased to leave Iris to go by herself; there was not exactly any love lost between himself and Lady Amanda—the old lady's caustic tongue had made him wince more than once; though he had always appeared to humour her, and insisted—to her face—that he was her most devoted admirer. It was never pleasing to Philip to know that any woman, be she seventeen or seventy, saw through that superficial charm of his.

Squirting a rather smaller amount of soda than was necessary on to the whiskey in his glass, he stared at the amber liquid discontentedly for a moment; then, drinking half of it, went out into the hall, carrying the glass with him, and so upstairs, where he knocked sharply on the door of Iris's room.

"Come in," she called, and, as the door opened, turned her head sharply. "Can't you knock softly—— Oh, it's you!"

"It is, my sweet. What brings that peevish note into thy voice?"

"Your knuckles sounded like the last trump," said Iris fretfully. "I've got a beast of a headache."

"Two aspirins, followed at a respectable interval with one or more of the famille Bronx," said Philip, lowering himself into an armchair near the dressing-table at which she was sitting. "What's the cause—sheer boredom or annoyance?"

"Why should I be annoyed?"

"Search me, my pet." But perhaps he had his own ideas on the subject. After a slight pause he continued: "Well, what about our Mandy's tea-fight? Is the pretty doctor suitably launched?"

Iris shrugged her shoulders. "Oh, the seal of approval has been set upon her all right. I think it's going to be rather amusing," she added with elaborate carelessness. "People are really tickled to death——"

"And why?"

"Well—what a situation for poor Ivor. No wonder he hates it. A girl throwing her weight about all over his beloved hospital, and with the backing of the trustees. I should think they must be in their dotage not to realize how difficult it would make things. It isn't as if Ivor was middle-aged—or as if she were. Surely they could realize the gossip such a partnership would create in a place like this."

"Well, looking at the situation from their point of view," Philip found a place for his glass among the jars and pots and bottles littering the dressing-table, "I don't suppose they care two hoots about the inhabitants of Mangtong outside the hospital."

"But of course they'd care if they had thought about it. Any scandal to touch their marvellous institution——"

Philip lit a cigarette. "A word in your ear, old thing," he said. "And that word is—Amanda! There could be no more gorgon-like chaperon. And she seems to have taken the young woman under her wing. So—little Iris had better watch her step!"

"What on earth do you mean?" demanded Mrs. Danvers haughtily. "I'm not likely to say anything. I was quite willing to introduce the girl myself—— What the dickens are you laughing at?"

"I'm not. But tell me more," he urged. "What happened this afternoon?" He did not add "to give you a headache."

"Oh, nothing out of the ordinary. But, of course, that idiot woman Dania Carsdene started weaving romances. She's already planning one of her 'delightful love stories,' I'm certain, with a doctor hero and ditto heroine, ending up in marriage bells."

"Sometimes truth is stranger than fiction. Perhaps the trustees had something like that in their minds. Thought Doctor Sinclair ought to think of getting married, and sent him a hint!"

"Don't be a fool!" Iris went scarlet with an annoyance she could not control. "Ivor! Can you see him marrying anyone—least of all a woman in his own profession?"

"Stranger things have happened. And they looked extremely interested in each other when I passed them on the Fee Chang road just now." When he was disgruntled himself, it always pleased Philip to give someone else equal cause for annoyance.

"When did you see them?" Iris demanded.

"Ten minutes ago. Not more. I passed them, but they didn't even see me."

And it was over an hour since they had left Lady Amanda's! Iris caught sight of her face in the mirror opposite, and, aware of her brother's amused and rather cynical glance upon her, she rose quickly and walked over to the wardrobe.

"Get out," she said briefly. "I want to change."

"All right, my dear. No need to get all het-up," said her brother.

"I'm only warning you! Not for me to butt in on your concerns, or perhaps I should have told you during these last months that you weren't on—er—exactly the right road."

She had turned, and for a moment they looked at each other steadily. They understood each other only too well, these two; but this was one of those occasions when Iris resented the fact that her brother—in the light of the resemblance they bore to each other as far as the less pleasant sides of their characters were concerned—read her like a book.

She said: "Perhaps there might be some personal reason for you butting in this time."

There was a very slight pause. Then: "Perhaps!" he admitted.

"In that case, you might try and help, Philip."

For a moment he stared at her. "Why not? But—you're an extraordinary person, Iris. I can't say I admire your taste."

She laughed quite gaily. "No one asked you to, darling. Just do your bit—that's all."

When he had gone, though, the smile faded from her lips, and her face became almost haggard.

She thought viciously: If by any chance that's what Amanda's after, she will have to reckon with me. I've nothing to lose, she can't hurt me! And as she sat down to the dressing-table again: That old fool Selham! And that sentimental ass Carsdene! Ivor and—Jennet Grey!

And suddenly, again she was furiously angry; but under the anger was a swift, sharp stab of fear.

* * *

During that next week Jennet discovered how difficult it was to keep her mind on a coolly critical basis where the head of the Eldred Chambers Hospital was concerned. She admired and respected efficiency as much as Ivor Sinclair himself did; and this hospital was simply a model of smooth-running perfection. It was due, of course, to magnificent staff work; but while that work was born of loyalty to the hospital itself, she saw very quickly that it could never have been so strong if its roots had not been embedded in an even keener desire not to let "Ivor" down.

Very soon she was aware that she herself was in the grip of that same feeling. Whatever the doctor's faults might be, his work was marvellous, and there was little wonder that everyone should be keyed up not to fall below his standard.

It was all very well not to determine to be one of his slavish admirers, but already she found herself wondering if anything she did would fall below his exacting standard. She would have given her best in any case—now, without altogether realizing it, she was anxious to give more than her best.

But there was no sign of over-anxiety in the way she carried on. There were some difficult and interesting cases in her wards, and she dealt with them in a way which soon won Sister's approval; while her nurses, who at first had been dismayed at the idea of having one of their own sex to deal with, were very quickly ready to give more than lip service to her.

Jennet was secretly shocked to discover that if there had been slackness in any part of the hospital, it was in these wards it had occurred. Simon Barton had undoubtedly been slack over many things, and probably if his ward Sister had not been extremely capable, things would not have gone on as well as they had done.

There was one night out of every week when the whole medical staff met together and compared notes. That was the only occasion during those first days when Jennet saw Ivor for any length of time. Already she was very friendly with the rest of the doctors: the two younger men, Terence O'Dare, a blue-eyed Irishman, and David Macdonald, an equally blue-eyed but very red-haired Scot.

"The young ones are eating out of your hand, Doctor," Matron told her, with twinkling eyes.

"Well, they can go and find a meal elsewhere!" retorted Jennet uncompromisingly. Nevertheless, she liked them.

On that first night of what young O'Dare irreverently described as "The Old Man's Wake" ("Wakin' us up, you know, darlin'!") Ivor was in one of his most taciturn moods. He listened to what the others had to say, making occasional notes and very few comments; and Jennet felt rather as though she had once again become a student. There was one case in her medical ward that interested her enormously. She had some comments to make on it, and he listened with a quite expressionless face, merely nodding, or asking a brief question.

But when the meeting broke up she happened to be the last out of the room. She had lingered to gather together some papers, and Ivor came back and found her there.

"Oh, Doctor," he said, "I hoped I'd see you. About that girl. I suppose you realize she is improving every day? If you go on like that with her, there is every chance of doing rather more than patch her up. You ought to be pleased with yourself."

"Are *you* pleased?" It was not in the least what she had meant to say, but the words were out before she knew.

For a moment he stared at her; then he gave a quick, vivid smile.

"Why, yes!" he said. "I'm pleased. But your treatment is responsible for the improvement. Good-night." He went away without another word, and, waiting for a brief space before she also turned towards the door, she tripped and nearly fell over a soft object which was in her path.

There was an unmistakable swear word from the object, and she looked down to see Ming, the Siamese cat, stalking haughtily away, offence quivering in every hair of his tail.

"Oh, Ming!" Hastily putting down her papers she hurried after him, and, risking injury, picked him up. "I'm so sorry—I do apologize. Darling Ming—the very nicest cat I ever met!"

Ming relaxed, sheathed his claws, and purring rubbed his head under her chin.

"Come on, let's see if we can find some cream," wooed Jennet, and gathering her papers again, holding the cat close the while, went on her way. Just as she was leaving the hospital block she encountered Terry O'Dare.

"What are you doing with that animal?" he demanded. "Never was I in a hospital where an unhygienic cat ran around!"

"He's not unhygienic!" retorted Jennet. "He's Doctor Sinclair's cat."

"And that makes him germ-proof?" asked the irrepressible Irishman.

"Anyway, he's coming to supper with me, aren't you, Ming?" said Jennet.

"Lucky cat!" Terry gazed at her dreamily. "Wish I was him——"

"Nothing doing. You can come to tea tomorrow, if you like."

"Mavourneen——"

"Have some respect, young man!"

"A thousand pardons, Doctor Grey."

She could not help laughing. "Get along with you!" she told him.

A few moments later she put the cat down in the sitting-room, where he sprang on to the desk and sat like a fawn-coloured statue, his blue eyes shining like two pale sapphires.

He was still there when Jennet came back from the dining-room, where her supper was laid, with the promised cream.

"Nice cat," she said again. "Beautiful cat!"

Ivor Sinclair's cat. . . .

CHAPTER VII

THE following day, just before lunch, Jennet had reason to go into the laboratory for something. It was a long, low, white building standing by itself save for the fact that a narrow, covered-in passageway connected it to the main block.

As she pushed open the swing doors, and passed into the shining, white-tiled, glass and chromium precincts, she was aware of a figure bending over some test-tubes. A slender girl in a white overall, and hair of that shade of black which looks almost indigo, fastened in thick plaits about the small, well-shaped head.

A stranger.

Then as the other turned and looked at her out of slanting almond eyes, black as sloes against a face the colour of old ivory, Jennet realized the girl was a Chinese.

There was no reason for her to feel any shock, three of her nurses were Chinese girls—two of them American educated, the third a complete product of New China. But this one was not a nurse; and Jennet's shock was born of the startling beauty of the girl before her. If she had been asked she would have owned frankly that just lately she had acquired rather a prejudice against brunettes—but here was a loveliness of an entirely different type to Iris Danver's, though their colouring was so alike.

"Good-morning." The English was perfect, with just a touch of that something which makes English spoken by the educated Chinese so attractive.

"Good-morning," said Jennet.

"Doctor Grey, isn't it? I can't shake hands until I have washed. Perhaps you have heard of me—Lotus Ling?" There was that in the speaker's manner which only someone who feels that they have the right to be perfectly sure of themselves can show.

"I'm afraid I haven't," said Jennet frankly.

"Doctor Ivor has not told you that I work here? I have not been very well for a few weeks, and I have been away. I was so glad to hear when I came back that it was a woman doctor who had come. But I did not expect a girl like myself."

Behind the beautiful manners which chose those words, there was a sudden warm sincerity which it was impossible to mistake.

How lovely this girl was—just like a flower. Jennet said:

"How nice of you to be pleased. Will you tell me what you do here?"

"I was a research student at ——" Lotus Ling named a big Californian hospital. "When things became bad for China I returned. I wanted to help in the war, but my grandmother forbade it, and—though I would not have disobeyed—I had to come home. My grandmother had only one son, and I am his only child," she added simply. "She hopes that one day I shall give her a great-grandson, and she does not wish that I should be maimed or killed. You have perhaps not been to our house yet—the House of the Jade Gates and the Blossoming Courtyards?" She smiled. "There are Chinese words for those names, but perhaps you would not understand."

"I speak Chinese—mostly Mandarin," said Jennet. "I hope to learn a lot more——"

"Perhaps I can teach you."

"That is very nice of you."

"But I mean it. When I don't I can be anything but nice—in quite the Western way!" Lotus laughed, a delightful tinkling sound. "You must come and see my grandmother when she permits it."

"I should be honoured," said Jennet.

So this girl belonged to the big house behind the high walls where Ivor had told her "Old China" still lived. Though surely Old China had allowed this granddaughter to be very New China.

Jennet passed along, and attended to the business which had brought her here. It took a few minutes, and when she was through she found the Chinese girl waiting.

"I hope you don't mind," she said. "I thought I would like to walk round the flowers with you—if you have time."

"I have a quarter of an hour," Jennet told her. "We will walk as far as the gates, shall we?"

She was half-amused, half-intrigued by the other's evident desire to be friendly; and she felt vaguely that she ought to be flattered.

They walked along in silence for a minute, and then Jennet's companion said unexpectedly: "I knew the moment I saw you that the feeling I had when they first told me you were here was a true one. We were meant to be great friends—perhaps that sounds impertinent from a student—even," she smiled deprecatingly, "an advanced one—to an important doctor."

"I think it sounds very sweet of you," said Jennet, English enough to be just a shade embarrassed.

But Lotus went on calmly: "It is not the habit of the Chinese to give quick friendship, but I think that perhaps in some other life you were close to me, and it was meant that we should meet again. Does that sound odd—from a Bachelor of Science?"

"No." Jennet found that she was speaking the truth. "Not the way you say it." It might have done in England, but here in the Far East, with this strange mingling of East and West about her—the temple on the hill, the modern hospital here behind her—almost anything seemed possible. And she had never lost her inner sense of spiritual values. Being in contact with the starkness of life and death had never blinded her to the greater issues, as it did so many—even in these days when Science is beginning to shake off the shackles of materialism.

"Then——" Lotus broke off. "But we will talk another time."

There was a subtle change in her. Following the direction of her eyes, Jennet saw that a car had turned in at the gates, and was coming towards them, and instantly recognized Iris Danvers.

Iris caught sight of the other two as they drew to the side, and, slowing, stopped.

"Good-morning—or is it good-afternoon?—Doctor Grey. You're back, Miss Ling?"

"Yes, I am back, thank you, Mrs. Danvers." Never had Jennet seen a greater change. Lotus had no more warmth than a statue—a very polite little statue.

Iris addressed herself directly, almost deliberately to Jennet. "I'm gate-crashing in on Ivor——"

"Was he expecting you?" asked Lotus.

Iris gave her a quick look, raising her eyebrows slightly. "No." Tone and manner both asked: What the dickens is that to do with you?

Lotus smiled. "I was only thinking that he must have forgotten," she said calmly, "because Doctor Sinclair has gone out. He came"—she spoke to Jennet almost as though Iris was no longer there—"into the Lab. for a moment or so, and he mentioned to me that he had a lunch appointment in the city."

For an instant Iris's face was black. Then: "What a bore!" she murmured lazily. "I ought to have rung him. Oh, well—I'll see him later."

She bent forward to make sure in the driving mirror that her beautifully "put" face was quite in order. Then she backed the car, turned it and, waving her hand, drove out of the gates again at a speed which nearly knocked the porter over.

"I'm glad the road was clear," Jennet said, a little drily.

Lotus's face set. "I am not sure that Mrs. Danvers would mind being an inmate of the hospital as long as she was not too badly damaged," she said.

"I was thinking of the damage she might do to other people," said Jennet.

"But she would not think of that. How I detest that woman!" The Chinese girl's face was suddenly contorted with anger, and her hands clenched; the next instant the look had gone almost before it was there, and her face was inscrutable again as she added: "Never make a friend of her—never. She is evil."

Good heavens! thought Jennet. Another of them! Aloud she said: "I wouldn't flatter her so far. She is just shallow."

"Shallow bowls can still hold poison," said Lotus with Chinese metaphor. "I would not mind if I saw that one broken. And now you see I can be—not nice when I—dislike."

If she had said "hate," Jennet felt it would have been nearer the mark; and wondered why.

As she walked back to her own quarters a few minutes later she was thinking how strange it was that Iris should manage to get herself so cordially disliked. Was it jealousy?

She rejected the idea decisively. It was certainly not jealousy that made her feel she and the lovely Mrs. Danvers would mix about as well as oil and water.

* * *

In the mellow glow of the amber-shaded lights in his dining-room Ivor Sinclair ate his dinner in solitary state. There was a communal dining-room in the House where the Medical Staff fed. He usually graced it for midday "rice," but he preferred his own house most evenings. That was half the glory of his appointment here, that he was able to have some private life of his own. In those early days when he had been in turn house physician and house surgeon at big hospitals in England, although he had always got along excellently with his colleagues, there were several occasions on which he had been described as an unsociable devil! He supposed he was, though he had always felt that an irate houseman's description of him as "eminently damned exclusive" had been unfair.

But tonight he rather wished he had chosen to join the others. His solitary table seemed somehow very solitary—it emphasized the fact that a companionship that was very dear had gone out of his life.

His Chinese cook had, as usual, provided an excellent dinner, but it was only out of consideration for the cook's feelings that Ivor did not send it away almost untouched. He was thankful when he had disposed of the last course, and, having ordered coffee in his study, went in and shut the door.

There was a parcel of new books out from England. New copies of the *British Medical Journal* and the *Lancet*—a pile of interesting stuff to examine; but he felt oddly restless and disinclined to settle down.

Li, silent-footed as a ghost, brought in and poured out his coffee, and Ivor, leaning back in an armchair, closed his eyes.

The sharp ring of the telephone bell roused him.

"Damn!" He picked up the receiver, and after a moment the frown smoothed itself from his forehead.

"Good evening. Doctor Grey speaking." Very formal, and very formal in her apology for disturbing him; but the patient in which they were both particularly interested did not seem to be reacting so satisfactorily to the present treatment. Jennet proposed changing the treatment—rather drastically. "With your approval."

"And what if I don't approve? Your patient, you know——"

"Up to the present I have only been carrying out the treatment you ordered," she reminded him. "You said I might consult you if I felt doubtful. Frankly, I haven't had the experience with these cases you've had——"

"No. I realize that." He hesitated. "Do you want me to see her?"

"I don't think that's necessary if——"

"Look here," he said, "can you come across?"

"In about an hour—if that would do. There are some things I must clear up."

"That will do excellently. Come along in an hour then, and we'll talk it over."

He had thought that he did not want to talk anything over that night, but—oh, well, anyway it was his job. She would not have consulted him if she had not thought it necessary, he decided as he hung up. That young woman was not apt to make a nuisance of herself.

We are all self-deceivers. Ivor was not to be blamed for camouflaging the knowledge that he did not in the least object to the idea of talking to Jennet Grey under the severe cloak of duty.

He rose, and, drawing a chair forward, arranged the cushions, and, putting cigarettes on the small table beside it, went back to his own seat and began to read. Some time later he looked round with a start to find his number two boy at his elbow.

"Solly disturb you, sir," murmured the houseboy. "Lady to see you. Missis Danvers——"

"Mrs. Danvers!" repeated Ivor. "Tell her——" He was going to add "that I am urgently engaged." But a soft voice murmured from the door:

"You're not really busy, Ivor, and I'm coming in."

Ivor had risen to his feet, and without attempting to go to meet his visitor, remained where he was while she moved slowly forward.

Only a blind man could have been completely unaware of the picture she made, her white fur cloak slipping back from her bare shoulders. She let it slip, gathering it adroitly as she reached him, and paused, the cherry red of her low-cut dinner frock throwing into exquisite relief the cream of her skin and the dusky blackness of her hair.

She looked at him half-laughing and half-pleadingly from those great dark eyes. "Don't look as if you want to throw me out, Ivor. You were not busy."

"I was—exceedingly." He glanced at his watch. "And I am going to be very much busier twenty minutes from now—of which I can spare you exactly ten."

"Really!" she made a resigned gesture. "You are the rudest man. I came to see you at lunch-time, but you were out."

"I did not know that I had the honour of expecting you."

Iris bit her lip. "Couldn't you give me a cigarette, and try and be a little human?" she asked.

"Certainly I can give you a cigarette. There are some on that table—no, wait, have one of these." He took out his case.

She helped herself, and waited for him to give her a light. As she leant towards the flame of his lighter he was aware of the subtle perfume which always hung about her. He hated that perfume, and his voice was so hard that few people would have recognized it as he said:

"As far as your idea of being 'human' is concerned, I am afraid I am not likely to come up to scratch."

She sat down, the cigarette between her fingers. "Why are you so—difficult? You know that we must talk some time."

"Why?"

"Because—Ivor, I had to see you."

"What about? You saw me the other day at Lady Amanda's."

"Hardly the place to discuss personal relations."

He had moved across to the desk, and stood there, cold hostility in every line of him.

She sprang to her feet and, leaving her cigarette on an ash-tray, went nearer to him. "Ivor—what *have* I done?"

"What haven't you done?" he demanded with such concentrated bitterness that it startled even her. His eyes holding hers, he added: "Ask—Simon?"

"Oh, you are cruel!" she exclaimed. "You don't understand—I did nothing."

"Nothing that was new to you. The technique has been so perfected that you hardly noticed what was happening."

"I couldn't help it if Simon made a fool of himself over me," she protested, and then, seeing his expression, flung up her head. "Very well—if I did encourage him—you must know that it was only because I wanted to make you jealous."

"You flattered yourself!" he told her shortly. If she had been less concerned with impressing him she might have noticed how little surprise he evinced.

She went very white. "Oh! You're cruel. I ought to hate you; but—I'm crazy about you, fool that I am——"

"May I suggest," his tone was almost bored, "that you are merely piqued at failing for once to get your own way? And may I also remind you that you have already given a most convincing illustration of exactly what it means to be 'crazy' about me?"

She was very close to him now, a hand on his arm. "Ivor—haven't I paid enough? It was only because I cared so much—you knew that. It was you who ran away—my dearest. Nothing ever has been altered—it can't be." Her hand crept up to his shoulder. "Darling—please don't be so unkind. For the sake of everything——"

He continued to regard her in silence, making no movement.

Suddenly she burst into tears, clinging to him wildly; and at that moment the door opened; and over the bent dark head on his breast Ivor found himself looking straight into Jennet's amazed eyes.

CHAPTER VIII

"I'm sorry—I didn't know there was anyone with you—the boy said to come straight in——" Jennet realized that she was stammering like an awkward schoolgirl, and pulled herself up, furious with the situation which had suddenly caused her such acute embarrassment. Hang it all! Where was her training?—that hard training which teaches doctors never to give themselves away.

Iris had turned quickly, stared for an instant at the intruder and then, turning her back, searched in her bag for handkerchief and compact, and proceeded to repair the ravages of her recent emotion.

"Good-evening, Doctor Grey," said Ivor. "Yes, I told the boy to send you in as soon as you arrived." He spoke as calmly as though nothing out of the way had happened. "Sit down, won't you? And help yourself to a cigarette." He indicated the chair and open box of cigarettes.

As she seated herself, Jennet had no idea of how carefully that chair had been prepared for her; but she did sense that he was angry, and rather naturally mistook the reason.

Well, she couldn't help it! If he must make love to Iris Danvers, why couldn't he choose a more convenient time? He had known that she might walk in at any moment. But she supposed he had forgotten.

Iris, and Ivor Sinclair! Jennet decided that it was nothing to do with her what the R.M.O. did in his spare time, but somehow she would have banked on him being—more particular.

Iris snapped the flat gold compact shut, and turned. "Good-evening, Doctor Grey," she said coolly. "Don't take any notice of me; Ivor and I often fight with each other and make it up again, don't we, darling?" Her lovely eyes, quite dry now, were malicious as they met his; they dropped before the look he gave her.

"I'll see you out," he said briefly. "Won't keep you a minute, Doctor——"

"Good-night." Iris smiled brightly, but the smile faded as she passed out of the door Ivor was holding open for her.

The hall was quite empty, and she paused, facing her companion. "It's no use being furious with me," she said, half-defiantly. "How did I know that girl was going to walk in on us?"

"We won't discuss it," he replied evenly. "But please don't come here again."

"To interrupt your private interview with your attractive—colleague?" She was smiling, but her hands clenched tightly on the bag she held. "Is it really necessary for her to visit you as late as this?" And as he walked on, ignoring her, she followed, biting her lip. "You can be as angry with me as you like," she said, breathing quickly, "but I warn you, Ivor—there are some things I won't stand for. If you are going to fall in love with that girl——"

"I hoped I had been plain enough," said Ivor, with dangerous quiet. "You compel me to remind you that nothing I choose to do with my life is any concern of yours. Good-night, Iris; and—don't be a fool."

She went out quickly and, getting into the car, was aware that she was trembling from head to foot. She pressed the self-starter, and took hold of the wheel, steadying her hands with an effort—conscious of that tall form silhouetted against the lighted hallway, knowing that she had made an exhibition of herself and probably destroyed her last chance with him. But—if that Grey girl thought she was going to get him, well—they would both see! She thought, as the car shot recklessly away into the night: I won't let him go—I won't!

Ivor turned back into the house, his mouth set in a hard, straight line, his eyes full of distaste. What the hell! he thought. As if I haven't gone through enough without being made to look a fool before——

He found Jennet sitting exactly as he had left her, smoking her cigarette. She glanced up at him; and this time there was nothing in her look to which he could take exception.

"And now," he said, taking the chair opposite, "what was it you wanted to ask me?"

"I won't keep you many minutes," she replied. "It's only that——" She went on speaking, calmly laying her observation of the case she had come to discuss before him. He let her do most of the talking for the next few minutes, and, as she warmed to her subject, sat back in his chair watching her, conscious that something about her was acting as a sedative to his overstrained nerves. Heavens, what a relief to have a woman one could meet on one's own ground—who did not expect to be made love to, or admired.... Extraordinarily beautiful bone structure she had; the way her eyes were set——

"Do you agree, Doctor, or do you think the injections should be continued until the end of the week?" He was suddenly aware that that low, clear voice had ceased, that she was regarding him questioningly, and that the pause must have been rather a long one.

"I beg your pardon!" he exclaimed. "I'm afraid my attention was wandering. You were saying——?"

He listened attentively this time, reaching over to pick up a pad and pencil from the desk. Then, as he gave his opinion, she disagreed with it calmly, and saw his quick frown.

"There was a case in St. Monica's very similar to this," she said. "Bernard Felbridge sent it in, and we were particularly keen because it is such a rare thing. The R.S.O. was fearfully anxious to operate—but you may or may not know how against operations Felbridge is——"

"Yes, but he never waited too long—I mean, in my day he never left the surgeons to take on a completely forlorn hope——"

"Of course not. He's not hidebound. But I think you must agree these cases don't need operation, or you would probably have operated on this girl before."

"I never use the knife if I can avoid it," he said briefly.

"On the other hand, she is not responding as she should. I thought if we tried the other treatment?"

"Possibly. There's no harm in trying, anyway."

"I'll do it tomorrow, then."

"Good. Have another cigarette?" As he handed her the box she thought that he suddenly looked very tired, and refused with a slight gesture.

"No, thanks. I won't keep you any longer now. I—have some notes I want to make. And I want to look at that girl who was admitted this morning—diabetes case—before I go to bed."

They were both on their feet. "No need to overdo it, you know," he said rather curtly.

"I'm not."

"You were up most of last night."

"Oh, that was because——"

"I know why it was. But O'Dare was on duty," he interrupted. "He's quite sound, you know, when he's working."

"I'm sure he is. It was just that I was particularly anxious—and interested."

"Well, don't be over-anxious."

There was a sense of strain in the atmosphere, of which they were both suddenly aware; to Jennet it seemed as though there was a note of antagonism too. She thought with annoyance: If he thinks I'm a fusser—— Surely I can go into my own wards when I like.

She could. But she had come here to consult him. Still, that was over a rather particular case; there might have been trouble if she had gone ahead on her own and anything had gone wrong.

She said formally: "Well, thank you very much. I'll stay in bed tonight—unless I'm dragged from it. Good-night."

"Good-night." He followed her to the door and opened it for her. "You'll be all right? I mean, you can see——"

"There's a moon."

"So there is."

He had not noticed, thought Jennet. Too intent on his charming companion, when he saw her off! She walked quickly across the hall, and had reached the house door and passed through it before he was there. But he remained to watch her cross to her own quarters and hear the rather decisive click of a door as it shut behind her.

As he turned back into the hall, Ivor was aware of an odd sense of angry disappointment. Somehow he had looked forward to her coming over this evening, had thought that after their medical discussion was over she would remain to smoke a cigarette and perhaps discuss those books which he had not yet had time to examine properly; that he might get a fresh angle on this girl who interested him because she herself was so keenly interested in this work which they were sharing. He had almost forgotten how dismayed and angry he had been when she first arrived. He did not yet realize how completely he had put behind him any prejudice her sex might have aroused. In Jennet he had found for the first time that spark which was in himself—the love of their chosen work which the born healer possesses. He had hoped to find something like that in Simon Barton, but it had not been there because Simon's cleverness would have shown up equally in any other profession. He had become a doctor because his family wished it—he was the type who could have done anything well that he put his mind to, but he would never put his whole mind to anything.

This criticism was not in Ivor's thoughts; his floating remembrance of Simon brought a stab of pain. He so hated waste! It was odd, though, that he should find, or feel that he could find, what the man whom he had loved as a younger brother had entirely failed to give him—comradeship—in this girl who was filling the space Simon had left empty.

And now Iris had had to butt in, with her one-track mind, immediately pouncing on the obvious (as far as she and her sort were concerned).

What the dickens had Jennet thought when she walked in on that charming tableau! How dared Iris talk to him as if she possessed him!

But—hang it! there was no need for Jennet to have looked at him like that! He bit down viciously on the pipe he had put between his teeth. Did she imagine he had nothing better to do with his time than spend any of it making love to the Iris Danvers of this world!

Gosh! If she knew——

He only hoped that he had made Iris understand finally exactly where they stood. Even now the bitterness of what she had once done to him throbbed like a half-healed wound; but not because he any longer cared. Because she had taken something from him that he did not believe he would ever get back again—his faith in women.

> *"And sweare*
> *No where*
> *Lives a woman true and faire——"*

His lips twisted; and then an angry frown darkened his face as he seemed to hear again Iris's voice with that ugly note of jealousy in it: "If you are going to fall in love with that Grey girl——"

How like Iris to suggest such a thing. She seemed rather bent on chasing the impossible. . . .

*   *   *

It was nothing to do with her who Ivor Sinclair chose to philander with!

It did not seem quite necessary for Jennet to tell herself that so often while she got ready for bed, or to feel so angry and—yes, so disappointed.

Ivor and Iris—those two just did not seem to fit in. Then: "All men are alike!" she told herself impatiently. "From Ulysses onward!"

Only somehow she would have expected Ivor Sinclair to want something better than Mrs. Danvers could ever give.

And what in the name of Hippocrates is it to do with you? she demanded of her reflection in the mirror. Nothing whatever.

"Oh, damn!"

She had turned and knocked her hairbrush off the dressing-table, but it was not that which had called forth the brief little word which was so very expressive of her feelings just then; or that kept her awake, because every time she closed her eyes she saw Iris Danvers with her face hidden against Ivor's dinner-jacket and Ivor's arm around her. . . . And the picture did something to her that she did not understand at all.

CHAPTER IX

ON the Wednesday evening Jennet kept her dinner appointment with Lady Amanda. She was almost glad to get right away from the hospital for a whole evening, though, on the other hand, she did not feel like putting herself out to a lot of people.

As she was taken in a rickshaw towards Lady Amanda's house she wondered who else would be there. Not Ivor, at any rate; she was thankful for that, because—no matter how absurd she told herself it was—she still felt embarrassed when she remembered that scene in his study on which she had walked in.

She had not seen him alone since that evening, and they had hardly exchanged more than brief greetings as they passed each other in the hospital corridors. There had been a great deal to do during this past week. Being busy, she ought to have been happy, but she was vaguely aware she was not, though she could not have told why.

She had not seen Iris again, but she had come into contact with Philip, once, when she had snatched an hour to do some shopping in the city. They had met in the principal store, and he had insisted on taking her to tea. He had been particularly charming, and Jennet, whose sense of justice was strongly developed, felt that it was quite unfair to dislike him because he reminded her of his sister. He had begged her again to ride with him one morning, but she had put that off with the excuse that she really had not time just then, as she had quite a lot to do, preparing for the day, before she went on duty.

Then this afternoon he had called on her; but as she was just rushing up to the ward to see a case she had been able to spare him only two or three minutes, and he had gone away announcing that he would ring her up. She somehow rather wished that he would not—although she found him quite amusing she did not reciprocate his very obvious desire to be friendly.

When she arrived at Lady Amanda's, and having shed her wrap, was shown into the white-walled drawing-room in which the perfect pieces of red lacquer and the exquisite jades and porcelains would have made any collector green with envy (Sir John Frayne had been a famous collector) she found her hostess alone.

Lady Amanda held out a hand which, quite incredibly small and slender, seemed not only weighed down by the beautiful rings on it, but hardly to belong to its owner. Lady Amanda was inordinately proud of her lovely little hands, and, like that *gamin* grin of hers, they were curiously young. The clasp of that small hand was, however, as firm as a man's.

"Well, my child," she greeted, "sit down and tell me all the scandal from the hospital."

Jennet smiled back at her. "We don't have scandal in our hospital!"

The old lady raised her brows. "That's all you know. Or, in the idiom of my native land, 'you're telling me!'"

Before Jennet could find a reply to this cryptic remark the smiling number one boy came noiselessly in, and brought her a glass of amber wine.

"I haven't asked anyone to meet you this evening. Can't talk with other people around—so you'll have to put up with me."

"That's lovely of you," replied Jennet.

"Not keen on the social lights of the European set?" asked the old lady.

"I haven't had much chance to judge yet."

"Except when you have tea with ornamental lady-killers."

Oh, dear! This terrible old lady! Was there anything that missed her? Jennet wondered.

As though she read her thoughts, Lady Amanda chuckled. "How do I know? Elementary, my dear Watson! I happened to see you.

I should have come and spoken to you, but I am seldom in the mood for dear Philip, and he hates me like poison." She added as dinner was announced, and they rose: "You'll probably find him all right to amuse you in odd moments, though. And I don't think I need advise you not to take him seriously."

"No," agreed Jennet quietly, "I don't think so."

Lady Amanda took her guest's arm, and together they went through the sliding lacquered doors into the dining-room.

The old lady proved to be a most entertaining hostess, and to Jennet's relief she did not mention hospital affairs during dinner. She kept her guest constantly amused by her witty and mordant remarks; her wit was certainly drastic, but it somehow did not leave a nasty taste in the listener's mouth. Jennet guessed that though Lady Amanda could be a pretty ruthless critic she could be a very good friend.

It was when the sweet had been served that the elder woman asked: "You have met Lotus Ling?"

"Yes; several times. What a lovely little thing she is," exclaimed Jennet.

The old lady nodded. "Indeed she is. And I believe she is an exceptionally clever research worker."

Jennet agreed: "Undoubtedly, from what I have gathered."

"These modern Chinese girls—they are marvellous. If you knew the sheltered environment into which many of them were born," Lady Amanda told her, "you would realize how impossible it is to ever make time stand still. Lotus comes from one of the oldest and most conservative of families. Ling-Mai, her paternal grandmother, still refuses to change her mode of living. The House of the Blossoming Courtyard is a period piece! I'm going to take you to see the old lady one day."

"I'd love to go," said Jennet.

"You shall—one day quite soon. The Ling homestead always opens its doors to any of my friends," said Lady Amanda, "though there are certain people whom the head of it would as soon give a cup of poison to as a cup of tea!" She chuckled. "The beautiful Mrs. Danvers, for instance——"

Extraordinary how everyone seemed to dislike Iris! Jennet would have felt sorry for her if she had been anyone else.

It was when they were back in the drawing-room, and Lady Amanda had lit her first after-dinner cigarette, that she demanded abruptly: "And now—tell me how you are getting on with Ivor Sinclair, and incidentally exactly what you think about him."

Jennet knew subconsciously that she had been dreading that

question, though she did not know why; but she did know that she shied away from the idea of talking about Ivor, with those shrewd eyes fixed upon her.

She flicked the ash from her cigarette. "I—like him. He's brilliant. And," she smiled, "he has been quite nice to me since he got over his first terrific shock, poor man." That was good; her voice had sounded calm and casual. Why not?

Lady Amanda studied the end of her cigarette. "Good," she approved. "As long as you get on together I see no reason why he should be prejudiced. As a matter of fact I gather he thinks rather a lot of your work."

"Does he really?" Jennet glanced at her quickly. "Has he——?"

"Never mind. I have my ways of finding out things." Then, her smile fading, Lady Amanda leaned forward. "Be nice to him, Jennet! I am going to call you Jennet——"

"Please do," begged the owner of that name.

"He needs someone to break down that crust he's surrounded himself with. He's a lonely man——"

"Is he really?" asked Jennet. "I should have thought that he could be quite sufficient unto himself. And if he needs—companionship, there are plenty——"

"Plenty. But there's a link between you. Your work. And the fact," the old lady's face was smilingly innocent, "that you are the type of girl who has learnt to meet men without expecting them to make love to her. A woman friend is very good for a man like Ivor."

Jennet felt a thrill of something like panic; mixed with it was something else she could not understand at all. A sort of anger.

She said: "I think Dr. Sinclair would prefer friends of his own sex."

"He's lost the only one I ever knew of his making," replied Lady Amanda. "You've heard about Simon Barton?"

"Yes."

"I wonder how much? I'm not gossiping, my dear, but I have my own reason for wishing you to know certain things."

There was a brief silence.

The old lady helped herself to another cigarette, and tapped it thoughtfully on the back of her hand. Then: "Leaving friendships out of the question," she observed. "Iris Danvers would give her ears to get him. And about the worst thing that could happen would be if she succeeded. Not for one minute do I think she would; but—she followed him out here all right."

"Followed him?" Jennet thought her digestion must be really wrong, her heart did not as a rule behave so erratically.

"Yes; they knew each other in England, when Iris's husband was alive." And then, changing the subject calmly: "Are you interested in Chinese art? If so, you'd better look at these things." She rose and waddled across to a lacquered cabinet; and with the most amazing sense of relief Jennet realized that, for the time being at any rate, there was to be no more discussion regarding the affairs of Dr. Ivor Sinclair.

On her way back to the hospital she found herself remembering the things Lady Amanda had said. So he had known Iris in England —when she was married. And now Iris was in Mangtong, and she was free——

Didn't Lady Amanda realize that the last thing in the world she— Jennet—could do would be to be friends with Ivor? In fact, she had never met a man whom she thought it would be more difficult to be friends with. Even though she had liked him so much. She still liked him—or rather admired his work, in spite of the shock she had received on discovering that he was just as capable as the next man of being seduced by a lovely face and body, possessing no mind and perhaps even less soul. Something beautiful and synthetic—but something that wielded a spell as potent as Circe's.

Hell! thought Jennet. What's the matter with me? What do I care who he makes love to, as long as—as long as he doesn't let it spoil his work. But I can't be friends with him—there's something that stops me wanting to try.

What that something was she had not the remotest idea just then.

She got out of the rickshaw at the hospital gates and paid the boy off. She wanted to walk up through the courtyards. Thank goodness there was nobody about; she felt that she did not want to talk to anyone just then.

She sat down on the edge of the pool, and, leaning over, looked into the water. In the moonlight it was possible to see as clearly as by day the lazy, beautifully coloured fish which lay on the white surface bottom.

Jennet stirred the water with one hand, staring downward. Other people's business did not usually worry her, and she told herself that she refused to be worried now. She had enough to do to attend to her own work—there was plenty of worry and responsibility attached to it. Why should Lady Amanda suggest that she should expend any of her energies coddling a man who ought to be able to look after himself very well, and who certainly only expected her to attend to her job?

And yet—was he really serious? It would be ghastly if he were fool enough to marry Iris Danvers—dangerous if he got involved with her. She would ruin his work, because sooner or later wouldn't he be bound to find out how completely he had sold his birthright for a mess of pottage?

Iris loved herself far too much to ever let herself play second fiddle to a man's work. She would want everything, and what she would give in return was something he would tire of so quickly that one day he would hate himself for ever having been lured by it. It was all very well to tell oneself he was just like every other man. One had only to see him in the hospital—to watch him, especially with a sick child, to know how fine he was. If he was ever cynical— she was thinking of those marked lines of poetry again—it was the hurt idealist in him that made him so.

Jennet wondered why she should know all this so clearly. Why should she care? Of course she loved her profession—naturally, when (she had to own) there were so many misfits in it, one didn't want the finest and the best spoilt.

As she sat there the cloak she wore slipped back, leaving her shoulders bare. Above them, the firm, slender column of her throat rose, supporting her proud little head. Her hair was bright in the moonlight, and her lowered lashes threw a shadow on her cheeks. Against the marble coping on which she sat with such unconscious grace the turquoise and silver material of her evening frock seemed jewelled. The night and the setting made her a different girl to the efficient (if still too good-looking) woman doctor who walked her wards so competently in her white coat. There was no escaping from the woman in her now—and the man who came suddenly upon her realized it with a start.

For a moment or so he stood quite still watching her, his sense of beauty satisfied, but a strange reluctance to admit it awake in him. Then as she started and turned round he moved forward.

"Oh, it's you!" Thank heaven one had learnt to control one's voice—why couldn't one control one's heart too? Why must it beat like this—so that it seemed to fill the whole night? She looked up at Ivor as he stood looking down at her, sensing the hostility in him with a sudden burning pain; and then like a flash of lightning she knew——

Knew why she had dreaded the very thought of trying to be friends with him, knew that all the carefully laid plans she had made for her life were nothing, because, however clever a woman may be, however neatly she may arrange things, sooner or later the fate of every woman will overtake her, and—she will fall in love.

But not Jennet Grey with Ivor Sinclair. That was absurd— impossible. . . .

CHAPTER X

BUT absurd and impossible things—things which throw the whole of life off its balance—happen.

Never before had Jennet even glimpsed what it was like to feel real panic, but she knew it in that moment, and it was all she could do to stop herself from running away. If she got up now she was quite sure that she would make a bolt of it, and so she just continued to sit there, her hands pressed very hard on the marble edge of the ornamental pool; while Ivor stood there watching her for what seemed at least an hour of silence, though in reality it was only a moment.

Then: "I took you for a spirit of the moonlight," he told her. "Are you? Or were you only disturbing our beautiful fishes?" He spoke lightly, but she was quite certain that for some reason he was not pleased with the encounter.

She managed to make her own voice lightly indifferent as she replied: "I was admiring the beautiful fishes, but I wouldn't dream of waking them up!"

"That's good. I needn't report the matter to the Society for Prevention of Cruelty to Carp!" he said gravely. "Have you been having a very gay time this evening?"

There was a veiled mockery in his tone which annoyed her. "Not hilarious," she replied, "but very nice." And then: "You had, of course, forgotten that I was dining with Lady Amanda?"

"So I had."

Naturally he would have forgotten—though he had been responsible for arranging the date. No doubt, whatever leisure thoughts he had were adequately occupied. Jennet rose, drawing her wrap about her.

Seeing she was about to leave him, Ivor felt a reluctance to have her go which he did not attempt to analyse.

"Tell me how you got on with Lady Amanda," he requested. "She's a lamb, you know, when you get her at the right angle."

Jennet could not help laughing, and having done so was more at her ease. "She *is* a darling," she agreed. "But even at her best I would describe her as an amiable dragon rather than a lamb."

"At her worst, believe me, it would not be permissible to describe her at all," said Ivor. "You're still getting on well together, though?"

"Yes—I think so."

"Anyone else at the party?"

"No one."

"You are in favour!" He smiled down at her. If only that smile didn't make her heart behave so ridiculously. She had always been conscious of a little warm glow when he "unthawed," but now it was like something pulling at her heartstrings. That odd half-panic stirred in her again, and her voice sounded a little curt because of the watch she was keeping on herself as she replied:

"I hope so."

He fell into step beside her as she walked slowly towards the house. "I don't seem to have seen you for days——" That was not at all what he had meant to say, and not knowing quite what he would rather have substituted for those words he was annoyed again. What was the matter with the girl? he asked himself. She was extremely unfriendly. And then suddenly he too was remembering, and wondering if the last time they had encountered away from the wards was in her mind.

Hang it all! Even if she did think she had caught him out with Iris, what was it to do with her?

Answering his remark, Jennet said in her coolest and most casual voice: "You've seen me every day; but perhaps you were too busy to notice."

He ignored the observation, and after a moment's silence asked: "Everything all right still?"

"Quite, thanks. You've seen my reports?"

"Yes. I want to talk to you some time about—no matter now." He broke off as she paused outside the entrance leading to her own quarters. "You're tired, I expect——"

"I have a little work to do before I go to bed," she answered. "I shall turn in soon. If it's anything important you wanted to say to me——"

"It isn't. It will keep very well." His turn to be curt. As a matter of fact, anything he had been going to say could keep, because he had not the remotest idea what it was. And since it was quite alien to him to detain anybody who obviously wanted to go, he said even more abruptly: "Good-night."

"Good-night!"

Jennet disappeared, leaving him the moonlight in the scented courtyards, and the unusual but definite knowledge that there was something missing from the beauty of this perfect night. Hands clasped behind his back, he walked slowly back to the pond, and stood staring frowningly down into the silvered water, at the bottom of which the sleeping fish glimmered.

Damn silly things fish were! He experienced an almost vicious desire to get something and prod them awake.

What the dickens had Jennet Grey been doing—sitting there in the moonlight, looking more ornamental than any woman ought to think of looking?

She had not come out here to sit around, looking decorative. In fact, he was suddenly asking himself, again why she had come out here at all. What had really put it into her head to be a doctor?

And then, his new, illogical mood evaporating, though his irritation lingered, he thought: She's certainly a good doctor!

Only, it didn't somehow fit in.

He seated himself on the marble coping and, lighting a cigarette, stared into the water. After a brief space he had the strangest feeling that Jennet was sitting there beside him, her hair softened to a paler gold in the rays of the Eastern moon. Lovely she was—but somehow more than lovely. Beauty in a woman was a thing he had learned to distrust; brains a thing he was quite ready to respect, but, like many Englishmen, had no particular desire to make contact with in the opposite sex.

There were plenty of clever women in the world doing excellent work—good luck to them; but he had always preferred his own sex as friends—and to think of women in other terms meant disillusion if one expected more than surface things.

In spite of all his experience and his success he was still young enough to generalize. The truth was, he had met disillusion too early in life, and the scars it had left forced him to forge an armour against weapons which might open the old wounds again. It is not good for a young man who is at heart a very great idealist to see those ideals spattered with mud before he has had time to acquire the philosophy which teaches that life brings compensation to all those wise enough to wait for it—that in fairness and wisdom no man should set a woman on a pedestal and worship what he believes she is; and when that particular idol topples down, forget that what men really need in their sweethearts and wives are the blessed gifts of companionship and humour and friendship—things which Ivor had never consciously sought in the woman of his dreams.

And yet he was a man who, perhaps without realizing it, could appreciate friendship with Rose Hilton and Lady Amanda Trent. Was it perhaps because he would have liked to have been friends with Jennet Grey that he resented that sudden withdrawal into herself which he had sensed? And did he feel, as she had done about him, that friendship was something beyond his power?

Even if he had asked those questions, he could not have supplied the answers. Time alone would do that. But whether he would like the answers made yet another question. . . .

* * *

Sitting on the edge of her bed, Jennet stared at the opposite wall, facing this new and dismaying problem which had thrust itself into her life.

No use trying to look the other way. Always she had been ready to face facts, however unpalatable they were. Why begin now to lie to herself over the devastating fact that, however inconceivable it might be, she had fallen head over heels in love—like any ordinary young woman to whom love is the most important thing in life.

It was no use. From that first minute when he had come aboard the steamer to Mangtong, it must have been all up with her.

But why—why?

Why should it have been necessary for her to travel all these thousands of miles to meet a man who had the power to change the even beating of her heart to this breathless, frightening something which all in a moment threatened to change her whole life?

What a dirty trick for the Fates to play! But that, she supposed, was how these things happened.

If only she could think that it would pass—if she had been the sort who had fallen more or less easily in and out of love half a dozen times—or even once before! She had managed to keep herself so completely aloof from such entanglements. There had been flirtations, of course——

But this was something nearer earth, and since she was several years older, far more dangerous to her peace of mind.

In those first moments of discovery she told herself that the only possible thing to do was to throw up her job and go home. That, however, was not nearly as easy as it sounded. A second thought showed her that even if the times and circumstances had been different, it would have been mere cowardice to run away. She thought angrily: I'm behaving like a nitwit—emotion has nothing to do with work, the two things have to be kept entirely apart.

A theory which sounded very well, but, like many theories, unfortunately does not always work.

Above all, she concluded, Ivor must never guess. If he did, then she would really drink the dregs of humiliation; real panic gripped her at the thought that he might. After this, he must never even get a glimmering that she was interested in anything concerning him. She decided that she would keep away from him as much as she possibly could. At that moment the telephone bell rang.

There was an extension from her sitting-room to the bedroom, and she only had to reach out to pick up the instrument. As she did so, she wondered what was wrong. This could not be an outside call, it must be through from the main building.

But it was an outside call. She heard the operator tell somebody: "You are through to Doctor Grey."

"Hello!" said a masculine voice. "Is that Dr. Jennet——"

"Dr. Grey speaking." Jennet frowned. Who the dickens——?

"I stand corrected. It's that tiresome fellow, Philip——"

She had guessed already. If she had not been so concerned with other things she would have recognized the voice at once.

"Oh, it's you!" she said.

"Is it absolutely the wrong hour to ring up?" His confidence seemed rather dashed, and she answered more cordially:

"No—of course not."

"You hadn't retired to a well-earned rest?"

"Not as early as this," she answered crisply. "I've got some work to do."

"Listen," he coaxed. "I want you to come and see what the only peaceful spot in China looks like in the early pearly morning. May I drive you out tomorrow, before you start work, please, Doctor?"

"Don't be so absurd." Jennet could not help laughing.

"I'm really serious. You'll make a much better diagnosis afterwards," he urged. "I'll call for you at the crack of dawn if necessary."

She hesitated. It had suddenly come into her head that Philip Devenham might be very useful as camouflage. If she appeared to be interested in someone outside the hospital—— She knew that however he might feel towards Philip's sister, Ivor had no time for Philip himself. What did it matter what he thought of her (Jennet's) taste, as long as he never suspected the real trend of it?

"Hello! Hello!" said Philip anxiously.

"Hello!"

"I thought they'd cut us off. Were you only considering the kindest way to say no?"

"Not exactly. I was thinking that my only free time is before breakfast. I could be ready at seven, but I must be back here by eight-thirty—or just after. I go on my rounds at nine."

"Seven o'clock, then. I'll be at your courtyard gates——"

"You can be at the hospital gates," she said prosaically. "Thanks for ringing."

"Thanks for saying you'll come," he replied. "I'm most frightfully honoured."

"Seven tomorrow morning, then. I really must go now. Good-night." Giving him the barest time to repeat her last word, she rang off.

She knew that as long as she lived she would never succeed in forgetting the milestone she had reached that night. But she must not think of the inscription written on that stone, or the one that might have been written.

"At these cross-roads Jennet Grey discovered that she had lost her heart to a man who was—another girl's lover!"

That wasn't true. It couldn't be—just because she had found him holding Iris in his arms.

If it was, Jennet decided with a sudden new fierceness, it would be worth while trying to get rid of her for the sake of—his work. There was such a thing as competition.

But she knew so well that the last thing she would be likely to do would be to compete with Iris Danvers for the favours of any man— most of all for Ivor Sinclair.

Her future road seemed quite clear, however difficult it might prove; she must avoid Ivor as much as it was possible to do so.

CHAPTER XI

WHEN morning came, finding her heavy-eyed after an unusually disturbed and restless night, Jennet rather regretted her impulsive acceptance of Philip's invitation.

She supposed, however, that she had better keep her promise, and accordingly emerged from the hospital gates a minute or two after he had stopped his car.

"Punctuality is a woman's only necessary virtue," he told her.

"And wisecracks as early in the morning as this might be set down as a vice in any man!" Jennet retorted as she got into the car.

He laughed, showing his magnificent teeth. "I lay no claim to any virtues, lady."

"Well, please copy my punctuality," she requested. "I must be back here by half-past eight."

"O.K. You shall," he promised. "I'd hate to have the death of one of your patients on my conscience." And as she raised her brows: "Oh, I have a conscience!"

"We won't dispute the fact. I don't know you well enough." Jennet settled back as the car sped swiftly and smoothly along. She was suddenly glad that she had come. Philip was, after all, the best companion for her present mood. There was no need to take either herself or him seriously; he was so very much what he appeared to be—a gay philanderer. Perhaps it would do her good to philander a little also.

Philip said: "You haven't seen our famous temple yet, have you? I should think it's one of the few left in China whose treasures remain intact."

"No—that is, I've only seen it from the road," replied Jennet. Nevertheless, she added quickly: "But I'm afraid I shan't have time to see over it this morning."

"Oh, there ought to be plenty of time—or at least time to make the acquaintance of my friend the Abbot," said Philip. "By the way, I heard that you were dining with Lady Amanda last night—how did the dragon treat you?"

"She isn't a dragon—or if she is she must be the nicest of her kind," said Jennet. "Who told you I was dining with her?"

"One of those little birds that flit from twig to twig," he replied. "You would be surprised at the way information gets around in these parts." And seeing her expression: "Don't scorn the gentle art of gossip—what would happen to us if we ceased to be interested in each other's doings?"

Jennet shrugged her shoulders. "I would just as soon they did not concern themselves with my affairs. But I suppose that is asking too much."

"Much too much," he agreed cheerfully. "Don't you know that you are the greatest sensation that has happened since the war? You've no idea what a kick we've all got out of your arrival. The women are mad with jealousy and envy—the men don't know whether to be amused or annoyed at the fact that the somewhat superior Ivor Sinclair has struck it so undoubtedly lucky in his new assistant."

He had slowed down the car, and turned his head smilingly towards her; but the smile faded a little as he met her cold, angry eyes.

"Please don't try to be funny, Mr. Devenham," she said icily.

It was difficult to snub Philip. "I'm not," he assured her. "I'm merely stating something very like the truth. Hang it all! you don't expect not to cause any excitement, do you? If you were as ugly as sin, or one of those 'all boys together' young women, it would just be a matter for happy amusement at Sinclair's discomfiture. But as you are—what you are, isn't it natural that the—er—rather unusual situation should awake interest?"

Jennet bit her lip. She supposed what he said was logical, but she wished with a new fierceness that she had never come here—never seen Mangtong or Ivor Sinclair.

It was hateful to think of these people, who could obviously only think in terms of sex, watching with "amusement," speculating on how her arrival—not as a doctor and a partner, but as an attractive member of the opposite sex—was going to affect Ivor. Why hadn't Sir Bruce thought about all this sort of thing before he had persuaded the trustees to send her out?

She realized that it was no use getting into a rage—that would not convince Philip. She shrugged her shoulders.

"This is all so absurd that I find it difficult to understand. As difficult as you people evidently find it to understand that—shall we call it romance?—doesn't enter into the sort of relationship which our jobs have brought about between Dr. Sinclair and myself. So if the community expect wedding bells, or anything of the sort, they are going to be very disappointed. In any case," she added deliberately, "I do not find Dr. Sinclair attractive!"

"Good!" Philip approved, changing gear leisurely as they began to climb the hill. "Neither do I."

How surprised he would have been if he had known that she could have pushed him out of his own car with the greatest of pleasure for that; he thought he knew a great deal about women, but her impulse would have struck him as more than usually illogical.

He was looking at the road ahead. "That's between you and me," he said. "The rest of my family don't share my prejudice against the handsome doctor—that's an old story, and you'll probably hear it some day."

Jennet knew what he was implying; he meant to convey to her that Iris had a prior claim. Well, he needn't bother! She ignored his last speech, deliberately changing the subject with a remark about the temple, which was now clearly visible above them.

"It's supposed to be rather fine," he told her. "Can't say I know a terrible amount about these things—I'm afraid I'm rather a nitwit regarding ancient civilizations, and all that." There was a certain amount of charm about the way he made the confession, and Jennet smiled.

"How long have you been out here?" she asked.

"Only a year. I was in Peking before the Japs got possession. Then I went to Burma—longing all the time most desperately for a sight of Piccadilly. But beggars can't be choosers—I have to go where the bank sends me."

She had not even known that he was employed by a bank. "And now," he continued, "there's all this fuss and bother boiling up all over the world—and I'm tied here until it's over, I suppose." They had reached the top of the hill, and he stopped the car. "You're going to get out?"

She glanced at her watch. There was plenty of time. She nodded. "I mustn't be more than a quarter of an hour."

What followed was an experience she would not have missed. They were received by the Abbot; he was like a figure carved in yellowed ivory, and Jennet felt that he must be so incredibly old that he had been part of his temple for centuries. Today it was not possible for them to be shown the main hall; either some ceremony was taking place there or it was being prepared for one. The Abbot apologized with the most exquisite courtesy, and, summoning a monk, despatched them to see what they could with the request that they should drink tea with him before departing.

After a few minutes Philip contrived to get rid of their guide with the excuse that he knew his way about. He guided Jennet towards a terrace above which the splendid pile of the building rose, tier upon tier of richly coloured roofs, culminating in the magnificent, soaring height of the central pavilion, whose eaves curved in an architectural fantasy of beautiful tiles. Purple and blue and the colour of old rose gleamed in the deepening gold of the morning sunlight as they strolled beneath a tall gateway through the stone-flagged courtyards, past delicately carved symbols in bronze—storks, and lotus flowers and fierce guardians of the Chinese heaven and hell; past entrances to dark shrines where oil lamps glimmered and sticks of incense wafted blue spirals of sandalwood, and like fragrances, before the gracious, inscrutable statues of Kwan Yin, the Goddess of Mercy, who once lived in this world, and who turned back from the gates of heaven because she heard a child's soul crying for her love and protection.

Then they came out on to the terrace again, and Jennet was enchanted with the dwarf pines which grew in the most unexpected places among the rocks in the grounds just below, where a tiny stream flowed musically to lose its sparkling way amid a profusion of flowering bushes.

Away to their right rose the strangely shaped peak of the Mountain of the Flying Dragon, the foot of which was some ten miles from Mangtong. The green and purple slopes were still ringed with the delicate silver of the now rapidly vanishing mists of the morning; and before them lay revealed a view which seemed to show the whole province laid out like a many-coloured chess-board leading to the distant sea. Far away, the lovely, delicate green of the rice and millet fields stretched; and here and there little doll-like figures of the blue-clad workers, too small to be real.

"It's incredible that it should look so peaceful," said Jennet, "when there is so much horror—quite near, I suppose?"

"The distances are pretty incredible here," he answered.

Jennet rested her hands on the low, moss-covered wall in front of her. Philip watched his companion as she gazed at the panorama spread before them, apparently forgetting all about him. He disliked the idea that she had forgotten him, to a quite surprising extent, and felt an irritable desire to recall her, though at the same time it gave him the greatest satisfaction to look at her. He thought that if ever a girl was created to be looked at, this one was, and noting the lovely curve of her throat, noted also the firmness of the rounded chin it carried, the curve of the beautifully shaped mouth, and felt a perceptible quickening of his pulses.

After a few moments he reached out, touching her arm lightly. "Come back—you've gone much too far away!"

She turned with a start. "Sorry——"

He laughed. "A penny for them."

"You wouldn't find them worth it," she answered. "They were very prosaic." That was not true, for she had been lost in the beauty of the landscape; but she did not feel that he would exactly understand. One might give him the benefit of the doubt though, since he had brought her here.

"Lovely, isn't it?" she asked.

"Lovely!" But his eyes were on her face, and his meaning so clear that it deepened her colour, a knowledge which added to her annoyance. Then she became aware that his hand was still resting on her arm, and moved away, glancing at her wrist-watch. "I think we ought to be getting back——"

"You can't do that yet," he said quickly. "You've forgotten our rendezvous with the Abbot."

"But I'm sure there isn't time," Jennet protested.

"There will be. I promise I'll get you back—but you can't possibly refuse to drink tea with the old boy. I'll impress on him that you must be at the hospital in half an hour," he promised.

Jennet shrugged her shoulders, not too pleased at the way things were going.

As they continued along the terrace together Philip said: "It really is too absurd for you to be caught up in the hampering red tape of a place like the Eldred Chambers Hospital——" And as Jennet turned her head and looked at him, her eyes cool and amused: "What's the matter?"

"I was wondering why you find it absurd—and what exactly you mean by 'red tape'?"

"Well, having to be there to the minute, and all that sort of thing. Don't you hate it?"

"No, I don't hate anything about it," she replied. "Perhaps I've got a tidy mind."

"Oh, Lord!" he groaned. And then: "Do you know, if you were my sister, I'd simply hate to think of all the messy jobs you had to do."

"It wouldn't suit your sister at all!" Jennet spoke more drily than she had meant to.

He frowned, but not at her words. "It's no use—I can't help feeling you're wasting yourself. You weren't meant to deal with the sordid side of life—ugliness, and squalor, and illness."

"Ugliness there certainly must be in any hospital—pain is ugly," said Jennet. "Trying to do away with it is neither ugly nor sordid. In any case I don't feel at all flattered when you suggest that I am not exactly fitted for my job."

"Good heavens, I didn't mean that!" he exclaimed. "At least— hang it all! don't you realize that it is because I'm frightfully interested in everything concerning you, and I don't want all your interest to be centred in medicine."

"I assure you I'm not as limited as all that," said Jennet, not quite knowing whether to be amused or annoyed by this frontal attack.

"I don't believe you're limited at all. What I'm driving at, is that—you and I have got to be friends, and——"

"Here is the Abbot," said Jennet quietly. "I think he's waiting for us. And do make him understand that I must go in a few minutes."

The Abbot, who spoke excellent English, was most interested in the idea of Jennet being at the hospital, and spoke with enthusiasm of his "friend Sinclair." He also asked with quite affectionate fatherliness about her family, her age, her chances of getting married, etc. All at great length, while there was no sign of the tea they had been invited to drink.

At last it arrived though, and, having drunk it, Philip rose—and Jennet was on her feet at the same moment. More ceremonial in the leave-taking that followed, and she was aware that she had exactly ten minutes before Sister would be waiting for her in the ward.

She hated being late, and by the time Philip was able to start the car again she was seething.

"I'm awfully sorry," he told her. "Afraid for once you are not going to live up to your reputation for punctuality."

"I ought never to have come," she said shortly.

"You can't hurry a Chinese," he apologized.

"The thing is to avoid them if you are in a hurry. Please drive quickly——"

"As quickly as I can," he promised. "But I don't want to make you an 'orspital case, lidy——"

There was no answering smile on Jennet's face, though; and in spite of the fact that going down the hill and negotiating the rather twisty corners was not so easy as coming up, he drove at a much more dangerous pace than altogether pleased him—for oddly enough he was not a reckless driver.

Jennet might not have been quite so disturbed if she had not remembered that Ivor was due to see one of the patients whom he had transferred to her side of the hospital yesterday, and would have timed his visit for just after he knew she had finished her round.

Without asking what he should do, a little disturbed by his companion's anxious silence, Philip drove straight in and up to the hospital entrance.

And as the car stopped the first thing Jennet's eyes fell upon was the tall, white-coated figure of her chief, standing on the steps, his face set in unsmiling lines.

As Jennet got out of the car without waiting for Philip's help, Ivor came down to meet her.

"We have been looking for you everywhere, Dr. Grey," he said coldly. "Number seventeen had a relapse an hour ago, and as you were not in the hospital I was sent for——"

Could anything more appalling have happened—and to Jennet, who had never through her career failed to be on hand in any emergency! In that first moment she forgot her angry humiliation in her anxiety for her patient, a young Chinese girl in whom she had taken a particular interest.

"What happened?" she asked swiftly. "I must go at once."

Ivor, standing in her path, did not attempt to move. "There is no hurry now," he said. "She is quite comfortable, and fortunately no great damage is done—except that I shall be behind all the morning with my own work."

"I'm sorry." Jennet bit her lip. "I arranged to be back an hour ago——"

"Look here, this is partly my fault." Philip, who had alighted, and was standing by, cut in coolly. "I promised Jennet we'd be back in time, but we got all tangled up with the Abbot——"

Ivor interrupted curtly: "I'm afraid I haven't time to discuss who is or who is not to blame. I might perhaps suggest, though"—his eyes, cold and unfriendly, were on Jennet—"that it would be better to arrange your social engagements for the evenings. Meanwhile—the ward is waiting."

"I shall be there in five minutes," she said. "I must just change." She turned and began to cross the courtyard, and then on a sudden impulse retraced her steps, holding her hand out to Philip. "Thanks so much for the drive," she said, with her most dazzling smile.

"Thanks a million for coming," he replied, retaining the slender hand in his. "We'll do it again at a more opportune moment, won't we?"

"Rather. Au 'voir."

"Good luck. Hope nobody dies on you," called Philip flippantly as he got back into the car and, with a careless nod to Ivor, drove off.

Struggling into her white coat a few moments later, Jennet wished that she had dared look at Ivor again to see if her deliberately careless and friendly parting with Philip had added to his annoyance, as—knowing he disliked the younger man—she had meant it to.

I don't care what I've done! she told herself. How *dared* he speak to me like that!

But she knew quite well that he was capable of being even more drastic if he got the chance. It was infuriating that he should have had such an opportunity. That came of using Philip as a red herring——

Oh, damn! thought Jennet, as she hurried to start her day's work in anything but a scientific state of mind. . . .

Philip, driving home, decided that on the whole he ought not to feel dissatisfied. He was wise enough to know that it was probably only because she had been so annoyed with Ivor that Jennet had suddenly thawed and been quite sweet to him. Up to their parting it was true that he had felt the morning had not been a great success, or got him very far; but the fact that he found Jennet anything but easy to make headway with only made him all the keener to penetrate that cloak of reserve in which she had wrapped herself.

She was worth quite a lot of trouble, that young woman! he told himself, in spite of the fact that he had always run like the wind from "brainy" women. It was not her brains with which he was concerned. What the dickens did he care whether she was a good doctor or not? There were other and much more interesting things which he wanted to discover regarding her.

Taken as a whole, he could not feel that the future looked too black—she had promised to go out with him again, and he had every intention of seeing she kept that promise.

He was whistling as he walked through the house to his own room, and when he passed Iris's door she called to him.

She had danced late at the Club last night, and was having breakfast in bed, wearing a golden yellow satin bedjacket, which would have made most girls look as if they had jaundice, but with her only seemed to intensify the matt whiteness of her skin, throwing into marvellous relief the shining darkness of her hair and eyes.

"Well?" she enquired. "How did you enjoy your drive, dear brother? Did it turn out to be just what the doctor ordered?"

He laughed. "Perhaps not exactly—but I'm sure that in time I'll get the right prescription."

They exchanged a look of complete understanding. Then Iris shrugged her shoulders slightly. "Everyone to their taste," she observed. "And at least I take off my hat to your superb self-assurance. Take care that you are not disappointed, though—I'd say myself that she wasn't human."

"Oh, she's human enough!" he retorted. "She's got a devil of a temper. I don't think you need worry. If I'm not very much mistaken, her chief desire at the moment is to murder the charming Ivor. If he's ever been as rude to you as I've just seen him be to her, I wonder you can stand him. Unpardonable boor!"

As he explained what happened, Iris listened attentively, a glow of pleasure in her lowered eyes. To her mind, this was exactly as it should be. She had a pretty shrewd idea that Jennet Grey was not the type of young woman to put up with Ivor in his worst moods, whether she was in the wrong or not. If only he would be "impossible" enough to her, she would clear out. The more those two quarrelled, the better pleased Iris felt she was going to be.

CHAPTER XII

A DAY that begins badly usually manages to carry on in the same way, and as far as Ivor was concerned that particular day turned out to be just one damned thing after another.

When he finally found himself in his room, having first dined alone, he was about as fed-up as a man can be.

The stem of his pipe clenched between his teeth, he tried to concentrate on the paper he had picked up; presently, however, finding that he was not taking in a word, he put the paper down and remained frowning thoughtfully at the opposite wall.

He was fully aware that he had been unnecessarily curt and rude to Jennet that morning. Damn it! he thought, it wasn't her fault that poor, wretched girl had had a relapse—that might have happened to any patient any time when the doctor was off duty; and the worst of it was, Ivor knew he had not been nearly so annoyed at her absence as he was over the discovery that she had been out motoring with Philip Devenham. He asked himself why the devil should he care whom she went out with so long as she didn't neglect her work? It probably was Devenham's fault that they had been so late getting back, but—confound it—here was an illustration of how right he had been when he had objected to the idea of a woman in this sort of job.

She had seemed all right, he had almost been lulled into accepting her as a working partner in the same way he would have accepted another man, only—she was much too ornamental. Men like Philip were just naturally attracted like flies to a honeypot. And—like every other of her sex—she was ready enough to play the honeypot. Ready enough, it also appeared, to encourage the attentions of Philip. He always had disliked the other man, but it was strange how, during these last few hours, that dislike had deepened.

Hang it all! he mused frowningly, Jennet might be young, but she had gone through her medical training, been in contact with all sorts and types of men—she ought to have learnt to judge character; and, there she was, like any raw girl, ready to fall for a handsome face and the "pretty" manners of the sort of man who knew how to manage women because he had too much experience with them. Ivor told himself that he was the bigger fool ever to have expected anything different from her. It was rather startling to find that he had expected it, and to cloak the disappointment he summoned cynicism to his aid, telling himself that it was just another of those cases in which hope triumphs over experience.

* * *

Being deeply unhappy, unless one is the type who sits down under it, is apt to engender resentment against the cause of that unhappiness.

During the week that followed the morning of her unfortunate drive with Philip, Jennet was about as miserable as it was possible for anyone so busy as herself to be; and—angry with herself—she also became bitterly angry with Ivor.

She had avoided him deliberately, except on those occasions when it was absolutely inevitable for them to meet; then she was quite polite, but very businesslike. If they encountered outside the wards, or when any other of the staff was not present, they no longer paused for those friendly little chats which had been so pleasant.

And, straining every nerve to make a success of her cases, Jennet knew in her heart that the lodestar of all her hard work—and she was working hard—was just the approval of one man.

It made her angry with him, and more angry with herself. Once she had cared little or nothing about what other people thought of her work; the highest honour to be gained was the knowledge that she was relieving pain and suffering—making broken things whole again.

Love of the job, and glory of her own ability to do it well, was what counted, and therefore why should she be wondering all the time what Ivor Sinclair would think of what she was doing? It was the patients who mattered, and whether she succeeded or failed with them, not the opinion of any one man, even though that opinion could make or break her.

It just didn't make sense, wondering all the time if *he* would do it that way—and feeling always, even when her mind was occupied with other things, this ceaseless, gnawing pain at her heart.

She heard that Iris had gone away for a short time—too stupid it was that the thought that the other girl wouldn't be seeing Ivor, and *vice versa*, should give her the only thrill of pleasure she seemed to have felt for ages.

She told herself bitterly: I suppose my next pleasant experience will be to discover that I am actually jealous of Mrs. Danvers! But why be jealous of anyone when she was beginning to feel that she almost disliked Ivor?

Jennet told herself she was simply sick of hearing how wonderful he was—even Matron didn't seem to be able to open her mouth without singing his praises! Whereas, she decided, he is, after all, only one brilliant man in a profession in which brilliant and capable men are much more common, than the writers of novels which decry the medical profession, would like people to believe.

Having got so far she wished desperately she really felt that way, and was not merely "kidding herself along." Anyway, he owed her an apology for hauling her over the coals in front of an outsider.

But that first week slipped into a second, and the second into a third without his attempting to make an apology or, if he noticed her changed manner, giving any sign of doing so.

She would have had a shock if she could have guessed how much he did notice it, and how near he had come several times to making an attempt to break down the barrier which was spoiling what had once promised to be such a pleasant relationship. Yet whenever he reached the brink of doing so, Ivor told himself impatiently not to be a fool. Much better let things go on as they were—though he did not explain to himself just why; except that, seeing her having tea with Philip one day, he told himself she preferred other types of companionship to any he could have offered her; and went back to the hospital in a mood which was ready to find fault with everything and even reduced the volatile Terence O'Dare to a state of fury and despair.

That was an unfortunate encounter, for it was the first time Jennet had been out with Philip since their visit to the temple, and he had rung her up to catch her in a mood when she was too depressed to reiterate her eternal excuse that she was too busy. For all that how she hated to spend her few slack evenings alone! Lady Amanda had given her an open invitation to go to her house whenever she felt like it. She would have loved to avail herself of it, but the old woman's constant questions as to how she was getting on alarmed her.

It was not so easy to avoid Lady Amanda, who, having rung up once or twice to be met with Jennet's plea that she was so rushed it was impossible to get away, turned up at her young friend's quarters in person one evening.

Jennet thanked Heaven that Ivor happened to be dining at the Mangtong Club that night, otherwise she would not have been able to avoid asking him to come across for a drink, or Lady Amanda would have become much too curious.

Her visitor, seated opposite her, had smoked one cigarette, chatting amiably meanwhile, when, helping herself to another, she suddenly asked:

"What the dickens have you been doing with yourself, Jennet? You're losing weight, and you'll look absolutely haggard if you go on like this."

"Oh, I'm all right—I never was better," replied Jennet quickly.

"Rubbish." The old lady stared at her with disconcerting hardness. "You are heading for a breakdown, that's what you're doing. Don't contradict me; I've come across far too many doctors who have worked themselves nearly to death in my time. Not a scrap of common sense where their own health is concerned. Though I had hoped that a woman might not be such a darned fool. I'm going to ask Ivor what he means by letting you go on like this——"

"No, please don't—you are not to!" Jennet exclaimed.

"No use telling me not to, my child!"

"Please, Lady Amanda—I do beg you not to say anything. I may have lost weight, but it means nothing at all!" Jennet pleaded in a panic. And then desperately explaining: "You don't understand—he'll only begin to imagine I'm not strong enough for the work—and I'm as strong as a horse."

"It isn't a matter of strength—it's a matter of conserving it," was the obstinate reply. "If I don't say anything, you must promise me to let down a bit."

"I will—as much as I can," replied Jennet, and added with a laugh which she hoped sounded convincing: "I do assure you I'm not fading away. It's been rather warm, you know—and I'm not properly acclimatized yet." But she did not feel at all comfortable, though Lady Amanda seemed more or less satisfied, and changed the subject, saying:

"Anyway, one day next week you are going to have what I know you will find a unique experience." And, as Jennet looked at her enquiringly: "We are going to visit Ling-Mai."

"Lotus's grandmother? How exciting!" exclaimed Jennet with genuine pleasure.

"Yes; the old lady has consented to receive you. When I spoke of you, I gathered that Lotus had already forestalled me. Ling-Mai spoke of you as her granddaughter's friend."

"Lotus is very sweet," said Jennet warmly. "I feel really flattered to be described as her friend."

"You might be, I think." Lady Amanda raised her brows. "She is a queer mixture, that young woman. So very Oriental under that Western veneer."

"I never think of her as Westernized, in spite of her extremely advanced views," said Jennet. "That is why she is so intriguing. She is very clever, you know. It seems almost unfair that she should not have been allowed to spend the time necessary to take the degrees she wanted in America."

"There is the real Chinese," said Lady Amanda. "Her grandfather died, as you probably know—and she obeyed the command to return. Then of course all this trouble arose, and it was impossible for her to get back. I am glad Ivor allowed her to go on with her work here—though he was rather sceptical at first."

"Did you persuade him?"

"I think I helped." Lady Amanda gave her *gamin* grin.

Jennet laughed. "You've a way with you, haven't you? Anyhow, they seem very good friends."

"I'm glad she took a fancy to you," said Lady Amanda firmly. "She has very strong likes and dislikes."

So Jennet had already gathered. She was sincere in saying that she appreciated the Chinese girl's friendship; they had found a great deal in common, and Lotus was certainly a fascinating little person.

They met the following morning when Jennet was walking along the passage leading from the research wing to the patients' block, and Lotus stopped her.

"Doctor Grey, I am so glad that my grandmother is to have the honour of meeting you one day next week."

"Isn't it rather I who have the honour of being received by your grandmother?" said Jennet smilingly.

Lotus passed on, and Jennet was walking towards the swing doors at the end of the passage when they were pushed open, and she came face to face with Ivor.

It was impossible to beat a retreat, and she was filled with self-contempt at the knowledge of how much she would have liked to do so. He stood there, holding the door open for her, and there was nothing to do save continue to advance.

"Thank you." In another instant she would have passed, but he had already let the door shut, and stood before it, staring down at her.

Hang it! he was thinking, she *had* got thinner. She was looking much too fine drawn. How idiotic to go driving herself as she evidently had been doing! Lady Amanda's hint on the telephone that morning—it had been given half jokingly because of her promise to Jennet—was the second intimation he had received. Rose Hilton had said to him a few days ago: "I think Doctor Grey is working too hard; it isn't my business to tell her, but perhaps if you gave her a hint——" It had been Ivor's friend, not the Matron of his hospital, who had ventured so far. He had thought at the time: She's probably under the weather. And at the back of his mind had been the determination to see into the matter.

"You're looking tired," he said abruptly. "You had better take a week-end off. Lady Amanda would be delighted to have you."

And the hospital could do very well without her! Perhaps if she had been feeling less nervy her sense of humour would not have been in such complete abeyance; as it was, she felt a flare of humiliated rage. "Thank you," she said coldly, "I have no desire to go away for a week-end."

"Well, you look as if you need a rest," he retorted.

Now, no woman, be she young or old, likes that fateful suggestion that she looks tired, which is usually just polite camouflage for suggesting that she is becoming haggard and losing her looks!

"Besides," he continued, "we all take week-ends off occasionally. I shall probably go for one quite soon."

"I can't help what other people do." Jennet could be rude, too, if necessary. "I have no desire to leave my patients."

"Best thing for your patients if you're going to break down on them," he retorted. "Better think it over." And with a curt nod he went on and disappeared into the laboratory.

As the door closed behind him she heard him make a laughing remark to Lotus—a very different tone and manner to the one he had used to her.

She went quickly on her way, but she had to force herself to concentrate on the interview with Sister that followed. There was a lot of routine work to do that afternoon, and she had never felt it pall as it did.

When she finally found herself alone, she was aware of an intense weariness. As a rule she dined with the others, but this evening she had just ordered "something on a tray," and forced herself to eat it—for she knew that if she didn't, her cook, the number one houseboy, and Sing Li would all go into a huddle wondering if "Doctor ladee muchee ill." The news would then spread to Ivor's number one boy, and probably Ivor himself would be informed that his services were needed.

Afterwards, leaning back in her chair, she closed her eyes, conscious that her tired depression was something beyond mere body fatigue.

Of course, she had been driving herself hard, but it was not that which was wearing her down. Anyway, she thought bitterly, what the dickens was the use of putting everything there was of oneself into a job where it was not appreciated? Stupid to feel that way, perhaps—she knew the staff of the hospital thought she was doing splendidly, there was not a hitch between herself and one of them. If Terence O'Dare made himself rather a nuisance with his by now quite open adoration, that would have been something to laugh at and endure if she hadn't known—well, known that love was not a thing to laugh at. At least, some sorts of love robbed one of any sense of humour entirely; and if you lost your sense of humour you might just as well pack up altogether.

She roused herself. This had got to stop! Rising, she went over to the writing-desk. There were letters which she had been putting off writing for weeks—especially one to Sir Bruce. She must let him know how she was getting on; Lady Amanda had been enquiring whether she had done so.

She began.

"DEAR SIR BRUCE——"

What was she going to say to him? What could she say? *Thanks most awfully for giving me the chance to do this job—it's marvellous, but as I've been fool enough to fall in love with the head of the hospital,*

I can't possibly carry on. I've done rather well at curing people since I came here—but I can't somehow manage to cure myself of a disease which I believe quite a lot of people just catch and get over like they do the measles.

Supposing she wrote like that—what would he say?

Suddenly she seemed to see Ivor as he had been that afternoon, standing there in the white-tiled passage, looking down at her. She felt again the mad, quick beating of her heart. If only she could stop seeing him—if only she could forget this insanity.

The truth was, she had never fathomed her own capacity for giving—and it appalled her to discover how great it was.

She was doubly humiliated at the discovery that it was possible to long so desperately for even a kind word, an understanding look, from someone who didn't care anything about one.

If she left the hospital tomorrow, it would mean nothing to Ivor, except perhaps a little personal inconvenience, and a good deal more work, until someone suitable to take her place could be found. She thought: He isn't really capable of caring for anyone—he has just made himself into a machine, and if Iris thinks any differently she'll find out her mistake some day. But Iris would not want from a man the things which she—Jennet—would want. And in Iris he probably found all that he would ever ask from a woman.

I suppose if I knew the whole truth I should find that they were very well matched, Jennet told herself. And then, as the memory of that moment when she had seen them together swept back to her, something—the tensed tautness of these last weeks—snapped in her. An instant later her head went down on her arms and she was sobbing brokenly.

Doctor Jennet Grey, clever, capable, cool and calm in the face of any emergency, had suddenly ceased to exist for the time being—there was only Jennet, conscious of her own weakness, and most intensely lonely.

"I say, what the dickens is the matter?"

She started up and, grief smothered in dismay and horror, found herself looking into Ivor's amazed face.

"Oh!" She swallowed hard, and felt wildly for a handkerchief, which, as usual in an emergency, was not to be found. It must be in her chair; she walked blindly over, and felt ineffectually among the cushions with one hand, while she surreptitiously brushed the back of the other one across her eyes.

"Here you are—use this." A hand came over her shoulder, and a large, clean handkerchief was presented for her use.

"Th-thanks." When you have surrendered yourself with complete abandon to the blessed relief of tears, it isn't easy to pull up at once. She was still fighting for self-control as she used his handkerchief.

And though her back was to him, Ivor was still seeing her drenched eyes, and, as his surprise evaporated, anger began to take its place. He'd know the reason for this, he told himself grimly, and someone was going to get hell!

"What's the matter?" he demanded. "Who has been upsetting you?"

"No one——"

"Are you feeling ill?"

"No——" She wished he would go away. What on earth did he want here?

Summoning as much dignity as possible with a nose which still had to be blown, she said coldly, "It's nothing."

"That's absurd. You don't indulge in orgies of tears for nothing!"

"I was not indulging in an orgy!" She turned round indignantly. It was a foolish move. She had not regained so much self-control as she thought she had, and her words got somehow tangled and her lips trembled.

With her hair rumpled about her tear-stained face she looked so young and so forlorn that the only possible thing to do was to try and comfort her.

He put an arm about her shoulders. "What is it? You might as well let me help——"

Somehow that softened note in his voice was the last straw; she clutched her handkerchief desperately, and the tears poured down her face again.

"Oh, go away!" she sobbed. "Leave me alone——"

And then, before she knew what was happening, his other arm was around her, and as she raised her face blindly, his lips found hers. . . .

CHAPTER XIII

JENNET didn't know whether it was really a lifetime in which she learnt how perfect life can be, or just the length of that kiss. What she did know was that no matter what happened to her now, no price could ever be too big to pay for these moments.

Then he had released her, and she was back on earth again as his voice came to her:

"You see now why it is ridiculous to believe that a man and a girl can work together without complications arising! I suppose I ought to apologize for losing my head——"

Her heart, which had been soaring like a lark, crashed, suddenly weighted with lead again. That was all, then—he had lost his head, and of course in a moment she would be able to laugh it off. But above the dulling sense of miserable anti-climax, his half-exasperated voice went on: "Only I haven't any intention of apologizing—or of promising not to do it again!"

"Wh-what?"

"Unless you walk out of this place right away, the chances are about a hundred to one that I *shall* do it again. So we had better face the fact that for several weeks past I have been doing my best not to fall in love with you, and have completely failed."

She just stared at him, swallowing hard. And: "It's not the slightest use looking at me as if I'd fallen off a tree," he said irritably.

"I'm—not." She pulled herself together with a tremendous effort. "I—I was wondering if it is really true that you feel like that, why—didn't you tell me before?"

It was his turn to stare. "You see," she explained patiently, "I was quite sure that you were—interested in someone else, and it made me—quite uncomfortably unhappy——"

"Look here!" He caught her roughly by the shoulders. "What are you trying to say?"

Her eyes were fixed on a spot beyond his shoulders. "Perhaps I am trying to make you understand that you are not the only person to discover that—it is rather difficult to control falling in love."

"Jennet—look at me." He took her face between his hands deliberately; she met his eyes then, and in her own he read what she no longer had the pride or desire to wish to hide. Reckless of what might follow, in that moment she let him see right into her heart. And, looking beyond the door flung open for him, he was dazzled by the glory of what he saw. There was the key of something he had never believed it was possible to find—his for the taking.

"Jennet——" He, who had learnt to be so sure of himself, was in that moment overwhelmed, stammering, and half afraid. "Is it true? My darling, you don't mean to say you really care?"

"And I thought you were a clever man!" sighed Jennet. "I've been worried silly in case you should find out."

He caught her close, and once again the gates of paradise opened for them.

After a space he said against her lips, with a sigh of utter content:

"And so I've really found you at last—how stupid to fight the inevitable."

Her face turned, so that it was half-hidden against his shoulder as she answered: "I never even got the chance to fight. You just—stormed the defences, and that was that."

"I never even suspected the victory. I thought you had taken a violent aversion to me, you avoided me so successfully——"

"It's a pretty kettle of fish," murmured Jennet. "What are we going to do about it?"

"Get married, of course." The promptness of his response startled her.

She raised her head, and looked at him. "I don't think that's nearly so easy as it sounds," she said, a breathless catch in her voice. "We'd better begin to talk sensibly."

"All right. I love you. I want to marry you. Doesn't that make sense?"

"I'm not quite sure." She released herself gently, finding how difficult his nearness made it for her to think clearly—and to part of her it still seemed absolutely necessary for her to do that.

Heaven was in his arms—heaven would have been to be with him always, just to be a quite ordinary wife with the right to look after him. The girl Jennet Grey knew that—but there was another Jennet Grey who had dedicated herself with an ardour, which had not yet been diverted to any other cause, to the service of others. It was because she knew how great and almost overwhelming that dedication could be, and that the man she loved must have felt it, if possible even more strongly that she had done, that she was suddenly a little afraid.

"Ivor," she said.

"Darling——" She had moved away, but he followed slipping an arm about her shoulders.

"If you say that again," she told him a little breathlessly, "I shan't be able to talk to you seriously."

"Who wants to talk seriously? I've just become engaged to an absolutely marvellous girl—I want to be happy, not serious." He turned her face to him again. "Darling—darling, don't you understand that I've done quite enough serious thinking to last me over a considerable time?" This was a new Ivor—an Ivor she had never dreamed could exist. Laughing down at her with that little flame in his eyes he suddenly appeared years younger. And then his arms closed about her, and, the smile fading, his voice deepened, a half-pleading note creeping into it. "Jennet, I seem to have wasted so many years—when all the time you were somewhere in the world, and now that I'm in love for the first time in my life——"

"Is that true?" she demanded. "It isn't—quite, is it?"

"Yes," he answered, "it's true."

"But——" The question seemed forced from her. "Iris——?" Looking up at him she saw his face darken, and afterwards remembered the shadow of anger and distaste which had passed over it. There was a very slight pause; Jennet's heart was beating quickly while she longed to hear him utter the denial which common sense told her would be merely stupid to believe. Of course he had been "in love" with Iris—what she had to remember was that there are different grades of being in love, and all that really mattered was that whatever there had been between him and Iris was over now.

She was a modern, and her generation had learnt to face facts—no wise girl expected to be the first in a man's life. And, though she deliberately thrust the knowledge away from her, she knew she hated the thought of Iris Danvers, of all people, ever having had any possible rights over Ivor.

Then: "Look here," he said quietly, "this is about the last moment in my life when I want to talk about Iris. Perhaps—some day I'll tell you everything there is to be told. But will you believe me when I say that there never was anything between Iris and myself that you need mind about? If you—want to know about that night when you found us together——"

"I don't want to know anything you don't want to tell me," she interrupted quickly. "I don't want to—pry into your affairs——"

"Oh, my dear, I'd never suspect you of such a thing." He had released her, and he made a swift gesture of denial. "It's just—well, let's get that particular situation right, anyway. I didn't ask her to come. I didn't want her, then or at any other time. I was not encouraging her to weep all over me. No one knows better than she does that I had no desire to make love to her. If I ever had such a desire, it belongs to another lifetime." Jennet had gone across and seated herself, and moving over he stood beside her. One of her hands was resting on the arm of her chair, and he covered it with one of his as he continued: "I'm not going to tell you that I haven't imagined myself in love before, but I would rather not discuss my—hallucination, if you don't mind. What I do want you to remember is, that being in love and loving can be two entirely different things.

"At the present moment—vastly against my will, lady," his mouth was smiling again now, although his eyes were serious, "I am both in love, and I love. Oh, Jennet!" he knelt beside her, encircling her waist with his arms, his dark head pressed against her breast, and suddenly that voice which had the power to light all sorts of fires in her heart was unsteady. "I wonder if you will ever know how much

I love you? No wonder I was afraid of it, when it means giving so much, such a tremendously big part of myself——"

With a swift impulse which had all the strength of the tide of emotion he had set moving behind it, she put her arms round him, holding him close. In those moments when she bent to lay her cheek against the dark head resting on her breast, she knew all that strange ecstasy which makes a woman's love such a complex thing; that love which, even at its most intense, has still so much of the maternal in it, so that her lover is at once her child and her king.

And Ivor, feeling that wave of tenderness envelop him, knew a sudden strange humbleness and such happiness as he had never dreamed possible.

To each it seemed as if that moment gave them to each other, they could never belong more completely than they did in the silence in which their hearts alone spoke.

He said at last: "I've been looking for you all my life, Jennet—when I felt lonely and lost and disappointed, it was for need of you."

"How lovely that sounds." There was a little catch in her breath. "But have you ever been really lonely or lost or disappointed?"

"All those things." He stirred, without lifting his head. "Aren't we all?"

"I—suppose so," she admitted. "Those of us who want more than just the surface things." Her arms tightened. "I think I'd want to kill anyone whom I knew had hurt you." She was remembering again those marked lines in the book of poetry:

> "*And sweare*
> *No where*
> *Lives a woman true and faire*——"

And unconsciously she spoke the lines aloud.

"Hello!" he looked up at her quickly. "Old John Donne—how did you know?"

"That you had felt like that?" She smiled tenderly. "Darling, I saw that you had marked that poem when I opened the book one day. Did you really feel like that?"

"One feels all sorts of things in different moods," he replied. "But how does it go on?

> " '*If thou findst one, let me know,*
> *Such a pilgrimage were sweet;*'

I suppose," he looked straight into her eyes, "that I've been unconsciously making that pilgrimage all my life, and it has led me to —you." He rose, drawing her up with him; and then with a fierceness which was almost frightening: "Don't let me down, Jennet—don't ever let me believe that the pilgrimage was a vain one. How mad I am! As if you could—sweetheart."

His lips were against hers, and once again nothing mattered save that they had found each other.

But later, when they had said their last good-night, and, returning, he stood once again by the silver-lit pond where the fish lay asleep, he almost wished that he had told her that old, bitter story and broken down the last of his reservations. He hated it so much more now than he had ever hated it before—it seemed so unnecessary to drag the ghost of his sordid disillusion across the threshold of the lovely new house of life which had become his tonight.

For years the ghost had haunted him, and now the warmth of Jennet's lips and arms would shut it out for ever.

Besides, it would have meant saying so much more than a man can say in decency even to the woman who is closest to him—about another woman.

He forgot that the other woman still existed; no disembodied spirit, but very potent flesh and blood, capable of mischief as only a woman who has made up her mind to get something she wants and has no scruples about the means she will use can be. . . .

CHAPTER XIV

THEY had not planned anything further about the future that night—the present seeming the all-important thing. As she dressed the next morning, Jennet knew there was much to be thought of and arranged for. And it was not going to be nearly so easy as if they had just been two ordinary people with no responsibilities. If she and Ivor calmly announced that they were going to be married, she did not at all know how it was going to affect the trustees—whether they would agree to continue having her in her present appointment.

Some people might consider it an almost ideal arrangement, but trustees and Boards of Hospital Governors seemed to have all sorts of odd ideas about what was and what was not correct. Sir Bruce would uphold her; and—Lady Amanda——?

Lady Amanda! Jennet suddenly saw those shrewd, sardonic eyes screwing up in their wrinkles of fat—pictured the old lady shaking with mirth. And she had the awful suspicion that this was exactly what Lady Amanda had been waiting for. She might be pleased, but she would be vastly amused; and Jennet did not at all enjoy the idea of what to her was a miracle being a cause for laughter. Perhaps she wouldn't have minded Amanda Trent's so much if it had not been for her knowledge of the comment which would be rife among all those other people. She remembered her conversation with Philip, her cold denial that there was ever likely to be the least cause for coupling her name and Ivor's together (she had always prided herself on being truthful, but how she had lied to herself, deliberately blinding herself to what was happening to her!).

Suddenly she knew that she simply could not face ridicule—could not bear to have her love made into a laughing stock for these careless, shallow people who never would be able to understand the real meaning of the word.

And then there was Iris——

Curiously enough, she felt none of that sense of triumph which it would have been quite natural for many women to feel over a rival. Iris would never get Ivor now—never have the chance of spoiling things for him.

If she had analysed her feelings she might have discovered that the idea of anyone commenting on Mrs. Danvers' discomfort would have been distasteful to her, because there was something in her which, quite apart from her feeling for Ivor, made it almost humiliating to feel that there could ever be competition between herself and the sort of girl which every instinct told her Iris Danvers was.

No, she told herself determinedly, she was not going to have her happiness tarnished at the very outset. If she and Ivor had fallen in love—what an utterly inadequate description that seemed!—it was no one's business but their own, and there was no need to take the world into their confidence until they chose to—quite apart from there being other things besides themselves to consider.

What a heavenly world! She stood before the window gazing across the courtyards below, a little smile on her lips.

To be young, to be loved and to know oneself loved. Only the basest ingratitude could fail to appreciate that perfect trinity.

It happened to be a busy morning, and the usual round of the wards took longer than at most times. She was discussing a difficult case with Sister, her back turned to the swing doors, when someone came round the screen just inside them. She heard that light, firm step, knew at once who it was, and to her dismay felt the colour deepening in her cheeks, was aware of that quickened tempo of her heart.

Ivor said calmly: "I was told that Matron had come up here. Sister——"

"No, sir——" Jennet had always been amused at the way the

elderly and rather stiff Sister suddenly seemed to come to life whenever the young "chief" was about; just now, however, she was only too thankful that the other was merely interested in Ivor.

"Good-morning, Doctor," he said.

She turned, and their eyes met. His were sparkling with laughter, though his face was quite grave.

Beast! He was teasing her—guessing only too well how she felt. She could have slapped him.

"Good-morning," she replied, and, "I'll look at her again this evening, Sister." With a smile she turned and walked down the ward. By the time she reached the door he was there, pushing it open for her.

"Thanks." And as they both passed into the corridor, he said:

"Lady Amanda telephoned me this morning—she sent a message to you."

Jennet's heart missed a beat. "Yes——?"

"It is definitely arranged that you shall go to the House of the Flowery Courtyards on Wednesday afternoon—and you are not to let anything prevent you going. Royal Command!"

"I'll do my best to obey," said Jennet. Then, lowering her voice though there was no one about: "You—didn't tell her, did you?"

"Not over the telephone." And as she drew a breath of relief: "Why? Changed your mind?"

She looked up at him quickly. "No; have you?"

"Jennet," he said solemnly, "I have no desire to lower your prestige in this hospital, but if you ask questions like that, I shall have to chastise you!" Then: "Darling, please go away quickly, or I will *not* be responsible for my behaviour. And—wait a minute: will you please do me the honour to dine with me tonight?"

"Yes; thank you very much, doctor." Hurrying on she turned her head, and they laughed at each other with a sudden gay sense of intrigue.

She waved to him, and, turning the corner, ran into Terry O'Dare. He caught her by the elbows, holding her firmly. "Where are you going with the stars in your eyes at this time of the morning?"

"I'm going about my business," she answered, "and I've no time for poetry!"

"'Tis a sin a lovely girl like you should waste herself on prose—and care more about locating a Chinese woman's gallstones than accepting the heart a man lays at her feet——"

"What an idiot you are!" She laughed in spite of herself. "None of my patients have gallstones."

"Well, I thought of a respectable ailment," said Terry. "One I'd be liable to be able to treat myself. Would you be interested in diagnosing heart trouble now——I could give you some wrinkles if you'd like to specialize."

"Sorry. You'd better go to Dr. Sinclair," replied Jennet.

"Ah, what would he be knowing about it?—the man hasn't got a heart. Does he understand how the organ can ache and jump about, and get crushed under the little feet of——"

"Shut up!" Jennet freed herself. Then she added severely: "I wish you would keep your dalliance for out of business hours—kindly remember I have some position to keep up."

Mad Irishman! It was impossible not to like him; but hurrying on her way, those stars still in her eyes, she thought how little he knew.

"The man hasn't got a heart. . . ."

* * *

There were so many reasons for not taking the world into their confidence yet. Jennet was in no mood to have thought very seriously about them, but they were at the back of her mind.

Supposing that the idea of she and Ivor marrying should be looked on askance by the Powers That Be? If she had to relinquish her own job it would be bad enough, but if anything should go wrong with his——! That really was nonsense, she decided impatiently. There was no reason why Ivor should not marry——

Oh, but there was plenty of time to go into all that. They had only just begun to realize that they had found each other, and for once in her life Jennet wanted just to know that there was a lot of happiness in the world apart from any she had ever glimpsed before.

It was that secret happiness which lent something new and indefinable to her beauty when Lady Amanda called to take her for the promised call on Ling-Mai; a sort of inward glow which caused the old lady to give her one of those looks which made Jennet tremble inwardly with a superstition that those bright robin's eyes could find out anything she wanted to keep to herself, if their owner wished to.

But all Lady Amanda said was: "Humph! You're looking better. Hope Ivor has taken my advice, and prescribed for you."

To her horror and inward rage Jennet felt herself change colour. She turned away quickly, searching among the papers on her desk.

"Well, we had better get along—can't keep our hostess waiting," was Lady Amanda's only comment.

That afternoon's experience was one which Jennet always looked back to with a thrill of pleasure, for everything in her which loved beauty and appreciated the things which hitherto she had only become acquainted with in the pages of the many books on old and young China which she had read was fed to the full.

Behind the high walls which shut away the homestead of Chang P'o Ling was one of those homes owned by great Chinese families, of which in the Revolution, Civil Wars, and finally the great crime of the Japanese, many have vanished for ever. Here—head of the clan today—dwelt the grandmother Ling-Mai, ruling with a despotism which, while it had been on occasion and still could be ruthless, was mostly a benign despotism.

There were pathetically few of the family left to people the buildings in the flower-filled courtyards now, but the small great-grandchildren and nieces and nephews were dwelling in the ancestral home, also the wives of many other relatives and uncles who had no desire save for the peaceful arts, and to whom, growing old, the changing world beyond this remote and fortunate province offered no temptations.

The visitors were received by Lotus. A startlingly different Lotus to the one whom Jennet knew. This girl in her long, embroidered coat and wide satin trousers seemed far removed from the white-coated research student. She explained that she never wore Western clothes when her grandmother received visitors—Ling-Mai did not like it.

They visited in several of the courtyards, so that Jennet should be introduced to various members of the family. The girls received her with great ceremony and delight, very interested in her profession; the elders perhaps still a little disapproving. Many of the younger girls were already keen to be allowed to become nurses and go to the front with the Red Cross. No wall in China is built high enough today to keep out the worship of that great lady who is the wife of the man who is making his country into what she was always meant to be—one of the greatest civilizing powers in all the world.

And, even here, New China was making her way—anything else would have been difficult with Lotus bringing the changed world in her aura every time she came back through the outer gates.

And then at last Jennet found herself in the presence of Ling-Mai.

At sight of the great lady who was to the whole clan "Lady Of First Authority," supreme head of the family, Jennet's first thought was that she must be incredibly old. But when she met the dark, almond-shaped eyes set in that face of yellowed ivory, she somehow forgot to think of age.

Ling-Mai and the bare, beautiful room with its few pieces of exquisite lacquer—a desk, a low table, and some lovely chairs in scarlet and gold; a vase of the famille rose period which would have made a collector weep "tears of blood"; three beautiful paintings of flowers and birds on silk scrolls, and a few pieces of jade—this was her setting.

For a moment the hostess stared at her new acquaintance rather disconcertingly. Then she addressed her in Chinese. "I am glad to see the friend of my granddaughter, and of my other friend——" She bowed to Lady Amanda. "You are most welcome."

And then as Jennet replied, "I am more than honoured to be received by you," the long, dark eyes twinkled with approval; and when they had exchanged a few more sentences, Ling-Mai changed unexpectedly into English.

"Sit down beside me, here," she said. "I speak English—perhaps not as well as you speak Chinese."

"Much better!" replied Jennet with intense inward relief.

The grandmother laughed, a startlingly young and tinkling sound. "Oh, but I have not learnt to speak it properly for very long. Only since this bad little rebel of mine," she laid a tiny, jewel-laden hand on Lotus's shoulder—the girl had seated herself at her grandmother's feet—"went to America. But I have read it for many years. I like your poets and your storytellers—though I prefer the philosophers of my own country. But your Shakespeare, your Shelley—oh, many of your poets I know well! Ask Amanda here to tell you something of the discussions and arguments we have—two old women quoting poetry when they can no longer live it!"

"You're more highbrow than I am," said Lady Amanda; but it was obvious that these two, so like and yet so unlike, were the best of friends and understood each other perfectly.

They talked on, and presently her hostess began to ask Jennet about her work. She seemed even more interested in it than the old Abbot had been; and she explained that in spite of her "growing out of date" ideas that a woman's place was in her husband's courtyards, she approved of women taking up the profession of healing—that was why she had allowed herself to be persuaded to allow that granddaughter of hers to go out in the great world, and learn to use the gifts the gods had undoubtedly given her. She had, she admitted a little wryly, been very frightened after Lotus had gone, and but for the solemn promise not to do so, would have recalled her before she had the chance to even begin her training. Fortunately there were relatives in San Francisco—a maternal uncle of Lotus's who had become a brilliant doctor. Jennet had heard about this relative before, and had gathered from Lotus that the grandmother had never really brought herself to approve of those Westernized relations,

although in reality Dr. Huang was—like most of his countrymen—
merely Westernized on the surface. Although he had many friends
in California, and was greatly respected, his work lay among his own
people.

"I had," said Ling-Mai, "less objection because my granddaughter's betrothed had no objection—indeed, approved of all she
wished to do. It suited him to have his marriage postponed; in my
youth future husbands were not so eager to wait!"

Jennet was hardly conscious of the swift look she gave Lotus, but
the news the grandmother's words announced was new to her. There
was a slight smile in the Chinese girl's eyes as they met hers, but she
did not change colour, and, as usual, it was impossible to read anything that was passing in her mind from her expression.

At length tea was served, exquisite golden liquid, fragrant with
jasmine flowers, and accompanied by the most fascinating sweet-
meats.

As she looked down into the little, handleless cup of finest porcelain, which she had just received in the correct fashion in the palms
of her hands, it seemed suddenly as though a pair of eyes a shade
darker than that tea looked into hers—eyes that could be cool and
indifferent, inscrutable or warm, and ardently lit by a flame which
only she could kindle.

She had the sudden feeling that Ivor's thoughts were reaching out
to her in that moment. Then, happening to glance up, she found
Lotus watching her, and, as if her thoughts had been read, the colour
ran up into her cheeks.

Lotus thought quickly: She is beautiful—very beautiful. And
then with a fierce loyalty, almost as though she was contradicting
somebody: And she is good, and deserves every good thing the gods
may give her.

Even——! From the smile she gave Jennet no one would ever
have guessed that a knife twisted in her heart.

Aloud she said: "Are you looking for your fortune in the cup,
Jennet?"

Jennet laughed. "I couldn't find it if I was! There are no leaves—
perhaps that means there is no fortune."

Ling-Mai, who was talking in a low voice to Lady Amanda, broke
off to look round and say very decisively: "No—there is certainly a
fortune; but it is not to be read yet." Then she went on with her
conversation, leaving the two girls to talk to each other, Lotus
having risen and moved over to sit by her friend.

Jennet was getting a little worried, knowing that it was time for
her to be getting back to the hospital, but was unable to make a move

until Lady Amanda did—and Lady Amanda, contrary to the usual etiquette, did not seem inclined to remember that tea was the end of a visit.

But it appeared that she had not forgotten, for as Lotus took Jennet's empty cup the grandmother looked across at them again and observed:

"Amanda tells me that you must go back to your work. She will stay with me for a little, and you will take the car and send it back for her." It was graciously and simply said, and it was as much, and even far more, of a royal command as any Lady Amanda had ever uttered. Jennet and Lotus rose at once, and Jennet took her leave.

"It is very kind of you to have let me come. I really do appreciate the honour," she said. And her own simplicity was much more effective than all the flowery phrases she might have tried to find. And as the grandmother took her hand in a surprisingly strong Western handshake (this marvellous old lady was evidently not nearly as tied to convention as she had at first appeared likely to be), Jennet's appreciation was suddenly warmed to a real liking.

"I am very glad to have seen you. You will come some day again—and you will tell me your fortune!" It was a cryptic remark, but Jennet did not bother just then to analyse it.

Lotus went with her to accompany her to the outer gate. For a few moments they paced the stone paths in silence, and then Lotus half turned her head, giving her companions a sidelong glance:

"Well?" she said. "You may tell me how surprised you are—although I appreciate that you have not done so."

"I never thought of you as being—betrothed!" replied Jennet frankly.

"A Chinese girl who has reached my age without having a husband in view would be looked upon as a great failure—by a family like mine," replied Lotus calmly.

With anyone else Jennet would naturally have asked who the other girl's fiancé was, and all about him—knowing that her friend would be hurt and take it for lack of interest if she did not; but with Lotus one instinctively preserved a reticence which waited to be told, rather than asked. She wondered now, against the brief silence, if she was going to be told.

Then: "My future husband will return as soon as he has taken the final degree which he is working for," Lotus said. "He is in America now. He wished very much to return to fight for China, but those higher up to whom he is related preferred that he should finish his medical training, since good doctors—and he will be a very good doctor—are necessary to New China. When he returns—if other duties permit—we shall marry."

"Oh, Lotus, I'm so glad he's a doctor. You will have everything in common," Jennet told her. "You'll be able to help him."

"I hope so. I hope also that I shall make a good wife," Lotus said quietly. "Both our families are very well satisfied."

Was she happy? Was this future husband one whom she would have chosen if no family influence had been brought to bear on the match? If Jennet had been less keenly intuitive those questions might not have entered her mind. There was something so calm in the way Lotus accepted everything; but she knew enough of the Chinese girl to be aware that under that surface immobility a great fund of feeling lay. Lotus could love—and hate—rather better than the best. It was such a waste if she was making a marriage of convenience.

By now they were near the gate, and the old porter came out to open it.

Jennet paused to take her friend's hand, and impulsively clasped it between her own, looking down into that lovely, ivory-tinted face. "I do hope you will be very happy, my dear," she said.

"Thank you—the good wishes of a friend are surely bringers of good luck," replied Lotus in that charming, rather stilted way she sometimes had. "I hope that you too will some day find that great happiness you deserve."

"Thank you." Jennet's sudden instinct was to take Lotus into her confidence, but this was neither the time nor place for it, so she added instead: "I think your grandmother is wonderful—I'm not just saying so from politeness either!"

"She liked you too," replied Lotus. "I saw that clearly. You will come again to see her; she will insist."

"That will be lovely. I shall see you tomorrow? Will you have tea with me?" asked Jennet.

"I would like it so much."

They parted, and explaining his mistress's orders to the chauffeur, Jennet got into the car and was driven away.

Lotus, knowing that Lady Amanda and her grandmother would not want her to rejoin them, turned into the courtyard which surrounded her own quarters, passing through what was known as the Rose Door.

In Chinese households such as the Lings' each portion of the family has its own dwelling. And as Lotus paused, a tiny crease wrinkling her usually smooth brow, she saw nothing of the charming, low building with its jutting roof and curling eaves which rose, sloping away in gay-coloured tiles, or the masses of roses weighing down the bushes which filled the flower-beds.

She was thinking of other things—chiefly of Jennet. Jennet, for whom she had developed an affection as deep as that of a sister—an appreciation which was mingled with great admiration.

She thought now: She is altogether sweet—it would hurt me so much to feel any envy of her; any—jealousy. No, I must never feel differently towards her. Whatever may happen——

She shrank strangely from putting into any clearer image the thing she secretly dreaded, the thing which must surely push that knife which so often turned in her heart so deep that it could hardly be borne.

For Lotus also was very intuitive.

CHAPTER XV

JENNET, being driven swiftly back to that life which was so different to the one which she had just glimpsed, found herself occupied with nearer things than Lotus's future. She had only just glimpsed Ivor that morning. There had been an emergency operation on, and she had seen him hurrying towards the theatre, his face set gravely, his mind obviously on nothing but the task before him. The case was not in her wards, but from the private wing which had been opened a few months before Jennet arrived. The patient, she had gathered, had been rushed in by the half-French doctor who was the only private practitioner in Mangtong. She had been very rushed herself, and had had no time to find out any further details—but at lunchtime Terry O'Dare asked Macdonald if it was true that Sinclair was in a stew about his op case.

The anæsthetist, who was a man of few words, nodded acquiescence. "Should have been done days ago——" There followed some brief technical details, and, listening, Jennet realized with a stab of dismay that Ivor must certainly be having a tough time with his patient. She knew how he hated to lose a case, how determined he always was to deny defeat until he was ruthlessly forced to face it.

"If anyone can pull her through, he will," said Macdonald. "But he canna' work miracles."

She wondered now how things had gone—personally she had a great faith in Ivor's powers—but his success or failure was a very personal thing to her. She thought: It will rather complicate things if I'm going to worry about his cases as well as my own!

It was to her own cases she had to switch her mind during the next half-hour. Sister usually reported progress to her at this hour—and afterwards there was something she wanted to discuss with Matron.

She found Rose busy at her desk.

"Don't get up," Jennet begged. "I won't keep you many minutes—you look as if you were snowed under."

"My own fault," was the dry response. "I ought to have looked through these reports last night—but I regret to say that I was playing bridge, and got back at an hour for which I ought to have been reported!"

Jennet laughed. "Rather you than me! People who play bridge ought to be treated!"

"Unkind, Doctor! Matter of fact, I don't make a habit of it—haven't the time. But the company was amusing last night, and old Sir John Selham is a bridge fiend—though a nice one."

They discussed the matter Jennet had come along to talk about, and then as she was ready to leave, Jennet hesitated. "By the way——"

"Yes?" Rose asked.

"I was wondering if you knew what had happened about that case that came into the private wing this morning? They said at lunch that Doctor Sinclair was taking rather a poor view of it." She hoped that her voice sounded calmly interested, and never dreamt that Rose Hilton's quick thought was: And how you hate him to be worried over anything, bless you!

"He did the most marvellous work," Rose answered. "Never seen such surgery, but—I'm afraid it was love's labour lost. The patient died this afternoon."

"Oh, Lord!" Jennet looked at her in dismay.

Rose nodded sympathetically. "Too bad, isn't it? He hates to lose a patient—as our volatile Terry once observed, 'According to the Chief, you would think nobody ought ever to die in a hospital.'" But in spite of her light tone—that lightness in which nurses and doctors so often sound hard and cynical, but which is almost always just a protective armour—there was a troubled look in her eyes.

That shadow was reflected on Jennet's face as she entered her own quarters a little later, still without having seen any further sign of Ivor.

She knew that he was going out that evening, because he had grumbled to her yesterday about having to do so. She wondered if he would come and see her for a few minutes before he went out.

Going to her room, she changed quickly, and then sat down determinedly to write a letter. Once or twice her eyes wandered to the telephone, which in a moment would connect her with the one person in the world whose voice she was longing to hear.

He might have rung her——

Now, she warned, be careful! You ought to know him by now. You ought to realize that there are times when he prefers to be left alone.

Which was all very well as far as it went, but it was impossible not to be a little hurt that he should not want her; yet how well she knew the mood which, when anything has gone wrong, makes one inclined to avoid even the people one likes best. Only—wasn't the person one loved a little different? She knew now that if anything had gone wrong with her she would immediately have wanted Ivor.

Yes, but you're a woman—even if you have only just discovered that there are certain emotional weaknesses connected with that state! she told herself.

Nevertheless, it was rather hurting to be finally quite unable to avoid the fact that he must have gone out without getting in touch with her.

She only hoped no one else would disturb her solitude, and after dining in lonely state she took a book and began to read. It was a book she had been wanting to read for a long time, but it had only very recently arrived from England; and having read the first half-dozen pages she discovered she was quite unable to discover what they had been about. She set it aside impatiently. Perhaps she could concentrate on something heavier—but the something heavier was an equal failure.

Lighting a cigarette, Jennet rose and moved restlessly about the room.

How stupid to be at a loose end like this! There was plenty to do.

She went back to the book, and had managed by sheer force of will to at last discover what the first chapter was about, when the room door opened softly and Ching-Li announced:

"Doctor Sinclair!"

Her first instinct was to spring to her feet and rush across to him, but with great self-control she managed to sit where she was until the door closed, when she got up quickly.

"Hello." She held out her hand. "I thought you went out to dinner?"

"No. I made my excuses." He took the slim, narrow hand in his own, looked at it, and then lifted it quickly to his lips. The next moment she was in his arms.

"Darling," he said, lifting his head after a close, swift kiss, "I've been wanting you all day—but I wasn't fit to know. I suppose you heard what that fool Blanchard did on me?"

"I heard that a patient of his had come in, and—— Too bad!" She reached up, smoothing the deep, double crease from between his brows with her forefinger. "Don't frown! Aren't we supposed to take the ups and downs all in the day's work?"

"Damn it!" exploded Ivor. "I could kick these fools who won't call in another opinion until the patient's almost beyond help. Twenty-four—even twelve—hours ago I could have saved that girl. As it was, I had to take a sporting chance—and I loathe doing that. Behind the times, I suppose. I haven't yet learnt how little human life is worth!"

Jennet had never realized he could be so bitter; it was plain that he really had been upset.

"Try and forget it, darling," she coaxed. "It's the only thing to do. Sit down there." She pushed him gently into a corner of the settee. "I'll make you some coffee."

He gave a rueful laugh, taking a cigarette from the box she handed him. "I've been fighting mad all day." He let the unlighted cigarette fall, and caught her hand again. "Quite unfit to know! Marvellous person—to guess it, and leave me until the devils had dispersed."

She sat down next to him, her eyes teasing. "As much pique as tact! If you *wanted* to leave me alone——"

"I don't believe it." His arm slipped about her, drawing her close. "Have you found out what an impossible man you have promised to marry?"

"I like him!"

There was a rather lengthy pause in which words were totally unnecessary.

And then: "I love you," he told her. "In lucid intervals I'm rather startled to discover it possible to care quite so much for anyone. Do you think the day is likely to come when you can't stand me for another moment?"

She laughed, her face against his shoulder. "I may want to murder you—strangle you with my stethoscope!"

"How do you know I shan't knock you about?"

"It sounds too gorgeously Noel Coward—besides, that sort of thing went out in the 'twenties!" But it was good to have made him laugh. "It's no use trying to frighten me off," she continued. "You're a doomed man." She rose, and crossed over to plug in the percolator in which she always made herself coffee if she wanted it late.

His eyes followed her; the frown had gone from above them now: "And when do we tell the world of my impending doom?" he asked.

"Oh, Ivor—not yet! What the dickens is it to do with them?" And then rather defensively she asked: "Think of the chatter—let's go on keeping it to ourselves for a bit. Presently we might take Lady Amanda into our confidence, and see what she thinks about it."

"Do you contemplate her forbidding the banns?"

"No; but she'd be apt to want to advise. I wonder if I shall lose my job?"

"Would you be very upset?" he asked, with a sudden quietness which made her turn quickly and look at him.

"No—and—yes!" she replied. And then: "I don't want to give up my work, and—I don't want to interfere with yours."

He opened his lips, looking down at her, and closed them again, deciding that argument was quite unnecessary.

Drinking his coffee later, with Jennet seated beside him, he could be forgiven if he thought that there were few problems which the future was likely to hold that he ought to be scared about. After all, he had come through some pretty rough patches, and managed to succeed in most of the things he had undertaken. In that moment it seemed incredible that he should go wrong over the most important thing in his life; for, in spite of the fact that his work was so completely himself that he could never be detached from it, he was wise enough to know that the crown of his whole life was composed of the gifts which the girl beside him could bestow.

He had once said that work and health were the most important things in life—now he realized that the partnership to be perfect must become a trinity. Work and health and—love. And the greatest of these was love.

Jennet raised her eyes, and as they met his the colour ran up into her cheeks and her breath caught. Half unconsciously she moved a little nearer to him; and then with sharp shrillness the telephone bell began to ring.

"Confound it!" exclaimed Ivor. "Who the dickens is that?" He had risen mechanically and walked over to the desk; then, as he laid his hand on the instrument he paused. "Sorry—I forgot I wasn't in my own room."

"Do answer it," she begged; and as he lifted the receiver she leaned back watching him.

"Hello!" said Ivor. And then more sharply: "What? . . . Who is that?" He covered the receiver, and turned towards her frowningly. "Apparently Mr. Devenham wants to speak to you."

"Damn!" exclaimed Jennet. "All right." She crossed over and took the receiver from him. "Hello?"

"Hello, Mam'selle la docteure, and what have you been doing with yourself all these years?"

It was Jennet's turn to frown—there was no earthly reason why Philip should use that caressing tone to her, except that she supposed he used it to every passably good-looking girl of his acquaintance.

"Time must hang heavy on your hands," she replied acidly. "I think it's about a week since I saw you last."

"Dare I be flattered that you remember the exact time?"

She longed to retort: "For heaven's sake cut it out!" Instead she replied with a polite and frigid patience: "I hate to seem rude, but I'm extremely busy."

"So I gathered."

She bit her lip angrily. And he continued: "I won't keep you. I only wanted to remind you that you promised that I should take you out again—some time. Is the time any nearer?"

"I'm afraid it is not. I'm rather busy."

"But I must see you soon," he urged. "Couldn't you ask me to tea?"

"I'll think about it." Her one desire was to get rid of him. "Sorry, I must rush now. Good-night."

"Just a minute," urged Philip. "I've got a message for Sinclair. Perhaps you'd deliver it?"

"Certainly."

"Just tell him Iris is back, and sends her love. I'll be seeing you, then."

Jennet rang off, and turned back into the room. While she was speaking she had been aware of two things—that her own voice sounded stilted and somehow embarrassed because she was so annoyed, and that there was a sudden change in the vibration of the room behind her.

She glanced at Ivor, who was lighting a cigarette, his face inscrutable. She said: "Mrs. Danvers is apparently back. She sends you her love——"

And suddenly the whole lovely atmosphere which had been in the room before that bell rang seemed to be shattered.

"That's that!" As Ivor snapped his lighter shut Jennet forced a laugh, but if he had met her eyes he would have seen that they pleaded for understanding.

If Ivor had cared to analyse his feelings he would have been amazed at the strength of his desire to kick the absent Philip. It was a desire that had assailed him more than once—Devenham was the personification of everything that he most disliked in his own sex, besides there being other reasons which made him dislike to be in touch with the other man; and that Philip should have the impertinence to ring Jennet up with that calm assurance annoyed him intensely.

Stupid to be annoyed, of course! he told himself. But there it was —and he didn't see anything to laugh at. "Since when," he asked, "has Devenham been on Christian name terms with you?"

She flushed in spite of herself. "Isn't he on Christian name terms with everybody? I mean he's the type who calls a girl whom he has just met, Darling——"

"If he calls you Darling, you might let me know!" he interrupted grimly.

She stared at him for a moment, and this time her laugh was genuine. "Oh, Ivor, how exciting!" she exclaimed. "You're not going to tell me you're so unflattering to my taste as to be jealous of Philip Devenham!"

She had sat down beside him again, and as their glances met she saw the dawn of that smile which always began in his eyes, though his mouth was set.

" 'Is that Jennet?' " he mimicked. "Lord, I know I shall forget myself sufficiently to make it difficult for that ladies' darling to sit down, one day! What the hell's he doing, ringing my girl up and calling her Jennet as if he had every right——"

"Darling, do break it to me," Jennet begged. "Are you a Cave Man—every girl's dream of what she'd like her husband to be—until he starts throwing her around?"

He frowned. "He's got a nerve——"

"So has his sister, for that matter!" said Jennet calmly.

They looked at each other; and this time they both laughed. "Sending her love to you!" said Jennet.

"Heaven knows I don't want it."

"Well, I don't want him to ring me up."

He put out an arm, drawing her a little roughly towards him. "Listen to me. He has been much too interested in you from the first moment he saw you. I know his pretty little way, just as——" he broke off.

"Just as I know his sister's. Wasn't that what he had been going to say?" Jennet looked down, twisting a button on his coat. "Never mind his little ways. Give me credit for some intelligence. Supposing we decide to ignore the existence of both the fascinating Philip and his—relative?"

"All right." He drew her head down on his shoulder, leaning his cheek against her bright hair. And after a moment: "Sorry to be childish——"

A great tenderness welled up in her, sweeping away every lingering resentment; and she thought: It will be my own fault if I ever let anything spoil what only we two can find together. As if Iris matters! But all she did was to lift a hand and ruffle the dark head so near her own caressingly. She knew instinctively that he had something else to say, and she wanted it said and finished with.

"Only," said Ivor, "you see everyone out here knows Devenham's beguiling ways. They know also the minute a new woman arrives on the scene he makes a bee-line for her, and never rests until he has got her interested. And the poor fools certainly do fall for him."

"And you think I might have been one of those poor fools?"

"No, I don't—but I simply wouldn't stand for people watching and giggling and connecting your name with his in any way. That was why I was so livid when you went driving with him—at least, that was partly why."

"Thought it was bad for the reputation of the hospital?"

"I deserve that. I certainly didn't want to acknowledge that it was because I was disappointed not to have taken you to the temple myself. But," he continued hurriedly, "that's why I don't want you to —be seen about with him, or let him get too friendly. Of course you'll choose your own friends——"

"I expect to," she acknowledged serenely. "Surely you realized from the very beginning that I was not likely to fall for the fascinations of Philip?"

"How did I know?"

"Oh, I admit you hadn't an exactly exalted opinion of me——"

"You bowled me over, anyway." He took her by the shoulders, shaking her a little as he turned her to face him. "Do you think I ever imagined I should let any woman get her own way so completely? What I ought to have done was to follow my first instinct and pack you back from whence you came!"

She looked at him through her lashes. "Do you really think you ought to have?"

"No; I'm hanged if I do. Delilah!" He kissed her, and they both felt that was the end of the argument.

CHAPTER XVI

WHEN two people are very desperately in love it is all very well for them to agree not to take outsiders into their confidence—there are more ways of doing that than by putting a notice in the paper, or proclaiming the thing in so many words.

Ivor and Jennet both wrote to Sir Bruce Ferguson asking what difference their marriage was likely to make as far as the trustees and the Board of Governors were concerned. Jennet wrote that if it was likely, in Sir Bruce's opinion, to jeopardize Ivor's opportunities in any way, she wanted to be told so frankly. Ivor, with due respect to the great man he was addressing, did not suggest helping by any sort of compromise. As far as he himself was concerned, he knew that there was not the remotest chance of any suggestion of his resignation being put forward—the difficulty was whether the fact of Jennet getting married would not mean that "The Powers" would get it into their heads that she could give as much attention to her work as she could while single.

Meanwhile, the only thing to do was to wait for Sir Bruce's replies—which would probably take months to reach them in the present precarious state of the world.

Things being as they were, it was only natural that they should want to spend any spare minute together, and that where Jennet was Ivor usually managed to turn up sooner or later.

There were whispers both inside and outside the hospital. Inside, the first amused incredulity at what was happening under the eyes of the staff gave place to a wildly interested speculation and interest. Had anyone noticed anything? He spent rather a lot of time in her company, didn't he? Gosh, it wasn't possible that he had really got it at last!

Outside the gossipers merely smiled—and some of the smiles were not pleasant.

Jennet was much too attractive for the womenkind of the European colony to have altogether taken to her—and Ivor had been too much impervious to their charms for them to refrain from making acid comment; while Lady Amanda, not at all unaware of the whispers, and certainly not suffering from sudden short sight, like a certain Brer Fox, was content to "lie low and say nuffin'," until such time as she deemed it necessary to interfere.

Whatever others might guess, she was not yet at all sure that the two most important actors in the play were actually aware of what was happening to them.

If they were not, she had no intention of warning them—and, if they were, she knew that she would be told in time.

* * *

The high spot at this time of the year was the dance at the Mangtong Club. Everyone in the European colony who was not absolutely beyond the pale was expected to put in an appearance.

Jennet and Ivor would both be expected to do so. Jennet gathered that Ivor's appearance had usually been cut down to an hour, late in the evening.

"But this time," he told her, "I'm recklessly leaving O'Dare to look after things here—since the silly ass sprained his ankle he can't dance, so—as he is quite willing—he may as well make himself useful."

"Poor Terry—what a shame!" said Jennet, and happening to meet him in the corridor that afternoon paused to commiserate with him. He was still limping rather badly from the sprained ankle which he had managed to acquire by slipping downstairs.

"What a shame," she sympathized. "Wouldn't you have liked to have gone, anyway, and looked on?"

"No, thanks. I should probably have got tight out of sheer boredom," he replied with his wicked grin. "Besides, what fun do you think it would be for me, propping up the wall and watching you dance with other men? You wouldn't be singing—

" '*Dancing with tears in my eyes
'Cos the bo-ie in my arrms isn't yew;*'

And I couldn't bear it, darlint!"

"Idiot!" retorted Jennet.

"If I could sit out every dance—or even every other dance—with you, I might still let my wicked step-sister let me go to the ball—but failing that I'll stay at home, and kill my hated rival's patients off," he announced.

"Really——!"

His laughing eyes became suddenly grave as they met hers. "You'd never take me seriously now, would you?"

"You couldn't very well expect it," she replied. "You don't take yourself seriously."

"Ah, but I could! Jennet——" He caught her hand, his expression suddenly a mixture of pleading and pain.

There was not a soul about, and Jennet had the awful feeling that the thing she had been trying so desperately to avoid was upon her. She didn't want to hurt him, but—why *must* people fall in love with one when one did not want them to?

"Please——" she begged.

"All right—all right!" he retorted. "I'll give you back your hand presently. I know you haven't any intention of bestowing it on me:

"'*Although she saw all heaven in flower above
  She would not love——*'"

"Terry, dear, this is neither the time nor the place to quote Swinburne," she pleaded, her own sharpened intuition telling him how unhappy he was. "Seriously or not—you know you're one of my best friends."

"Friends?" He raised his brows. "Of course. That's the usual arrangement, isn't it?" And then, his voice and expression changing, he gave her that attractive, three-cornered grin: "Thanks for the crumbs! I'll treasure them. Bless you and—curse him, whoever he may be." Then, before she could prevent him—even if she had been unkind enough to be inclined to snatch it away—he raised her hand to his lips. At that moment a door at the end of the corridor opened, and Ivor came through.

Jennet withdrew her hand quickly, regretting the impulse a second later. Terry, quite unabashed, nodded to her and walked on.

It certainly was the oddest proposal and rejection that had ever happened, and Jennet stood her ground while Ivor came down the long corridor towards her. As he drew near she looked at him a little defensively.

"Really, doctor, if you continue to play ducks and drakes with the discipline of the hospital, I shall have to find you a safer job," he said, shaking his head at her. "Not done—not done!"

"What isn't done?" she asked innocently.

"Hand kissing between medical officers on duty. The fact is"—he took her arm—"you're about as good for discipline as Helen of Troy!"

"You'd better talk to Terry," she said. "I can't repress him." And then, "No—don't. He—he was rather upset."

He gave her a quick look. Not being unobservant, he had taken full note of what was happening to his junior. Poor blighter! he thought. And aloud: "He's due for a holiday, I think." Then smiling down at her: "Don't worry, darling—he's a volatile Irishman. He'll get over it."

It was sweet of him to be so understanding. She gave him a grateful look.

And yet, just for a minute when he came upon that little tableau, Ivor had not been at all inclined to be understanding. As a few minutes later he walked quickly through the white-tiled corridors, he was still just a little shocked at the memory of the anger which had gripped him at the sight of Terence O'Dare kissing Jennet's hand.

Hang it, it wasn't her fault if the poor young fool was head over ears in love with her—she didn't need to encourage that sort of thing to have it happen. Of course she didn't encourage it! Perhaps she might discourage it a little more, though—— He frowned. It would be absurd to let himself think for a moment that it amused or flattered her to have men fall in love with her; not only be absurd, it would be disloyal, and—definitely destroying.

She was everything he had ever dreamt a girl could be—to lose his faith in her by one iota would mean the end of all faith for him.

For the first time in his life, although he would not have owned it for worlds, Ivor was afraid. Also it was very humiliating to discover, as he was doing, that it was quite possible to know what jealousy meant. . . .

But he felt no trace of that most destructive of all emotions that evening. What he did feel was a very great pride in the beauty and poise and charm of the young woman who—by her own quite clear demonstration—was his. Far from objecting to the fact that Jennet was surrounded three deep the moment she appeared in the ballroom, he was sorry for the unlucky ones who couldn't dance with her.

Not for a very long time had Jennet felt in such high spirits. Why not? She was young, successful, superbly healthy; and in love, and loved by a man whom half the women in the room would have given quite a lot to attract.

Even the sight of Iris Danvers watching her from the entrance through which she—Iris—had just come, while she was dancing her first dance with Ivor, had no power to disturb Jennet tonight.

Ivor saw Mrs. Danvers, and nodded to her briefly as she waved to him. Then he said teasingly above Jennet's head: "Afraid your best boy friend can't be here tonight?" And as she looked up at him, her brows raised: "Pretty Philip has got a touch of malaria, and can't come to the ball!"

"Poor Philip," said Jennet. "I didn't know he was a subject."

"Gets it on and off since he was in India—where it's a pity he didn't stop!"

She laughed. "Really, you are unkind! I believe you honestly do detest him."

"I shouldn't be surprised," said Ivor drily.

Jennet thought: Surely he can't be really jealous of Philip; but because she was not in the mood for serious consideration of the matter, she dismissed it from her mind. As far as she was concerned Philip interested her so little that whether he was present or not cut no ice —a thing which it seemed quite superfluous to explain to Ivor after what had been already said on the subject.

If Iris did not matter to those two who were so supremely interested in each other, they mattered very much to her. As far as she was concerned, that evening which had been one of triumph for her last year, was a failure from beginning to end.

In the first place she hated illness, and was always furious when Philip went down with one of his attacks—particularly annoyed on this occasion because she had relied on him to "do his stuff" with Jennet. Then, although she always planned to arrive a little late so that her entrance got its full limelight of attention, Dr. Blanchard had turned up just as she was leaving home, and detained her so that she had arrived in the middle of the first dance. Added to that, the first thing registered on her was the sight of Ivor and Jennet dancing together and obviously interested in no one in the room save each other.

She did not lack a partner for the rest of the dance—one of her most devoted admirers had been patiently hanging around waiting for her—nor was there any lack of partners to follow. But among those who clamoured for dances there was no sign of Ivor, and it did not improve matters to have two or three people—Sir John Selham among them—comment on Jennet's looks.

Sir John, with lamentable lack of diplomacy, observed: "By Jove! —that girl is a looker. I thought you couldn't possibly have a rival, Mrs. Danvers—but it's a close thing tonight, what? Oughtn't to be any bad blood, though—wonderful foil for each other. You have all the exotic charm of the orchid, what!—and Doctor Jennet's like a water-lily!"

Iris forced a laugh, shrugging her shoulders. "My dear Sir John— do you think orchids and water-lilies go well in a bouquet?"

The little baronet's description was a poetically apt one, though— Jennet in a shimmering green frock through which a thread of gold glittered, with a chaplet of gold-tipped green leaves in her bright hair, and her transparent, milky skin, had something of the cool beauty of a water-lily about her; that flower which lacks the coldness of the other lilies, and has a strange, elusiveness about it.

Iris was wearing white tonight, with scarlet flowers in her hair and on her shoulder, and the otherwise unrelieved colouring of her dress served to deepen her own exotic tints. Inward anger and discontent gave her beauty a glow like that of smouldering fire.

By the time the evening was half over she was seething. If it had not been for the fact that it would leave the field to Jennet, whom she now realized she hated as only a jealous woman can, she would have cut the whole rest of the dance and gone home. But defeat was a thing which she had never acknowledged, and she told herself that she didn't intend to begin now. Although as a rule she had it under control in public, she had a devastating temper, and having watched Jennet through supper, and noted the occasional glance which passed between her and Ivor—although he was not her partner for the supper dance, as Sir John had bespoken it some days ago—Iris's self-control was wearing thin. She was in a brooding rage, when, deliberately cutting the dance that followed supper, she retired to smoke a cigarette by herself in the big palm court which led off the ballroom.

Something must be done about those two! It had to be. This simply could not be allowed to go on. Once Iris would have laughed at the idea of not being able to sweep any rival from her path; she had always managed to get her own way, and she had never been able to realize that in time she would not get Ivor. The difficulty with him had been that it was not another woman who had to be got out of the way, it was himself she had to fight—what she called "that cruel, unforgiving streak in him" which she had made up her mind was part of his pride. She had somehow never thought that he would look at another girl—it seemed so impossible that the flame which she had once kindled in him could be dead beyond all revival.

If Iris had been more intelligent she would have known that she must accept defeat—but she was not really very intelligent. Yet deep down in her, even she was forced to realize that Jennet, being what she was—having other things besides the lure of her looks and the promise of passionate fulfilment—was likely to establish a hold on Ivor stronger than any she—Iris—could ever have had. Without her realizing it, some of her rage was born of fright, and for once she was at a loss as to what move to make.

By the time she had finished smoking her cigarette she had calmed down a little. To make a scene—to let people guess how much she hated Jennet—would not only be undignified, but would only serve to make defeat more certain.

She rose, and as she stepped from the shelter of the big palm near which she had been seated she came face to face with Ivor. He was with another man, and they had come from the direction of the bar. He half smiled, and was passing on when Iris caught his arm.

"Ivor! You're the very person I wanted to see——"

The other man had walked on, and there was no one else in sight.

Ivor had no desire to remain, but it was difficult to shake that slender hand off, for she was holding firmly to his sleeve.

He said: "I haven't a moment, I'm afraid. Will it do later?"

"No, it will not." Her fingers tightened and she drew him back to the shelter of the palm. "What have I done now?" She was half smiling, half reproachful as she raised her great dark eyes to his. "Were you quite unaware that I was here, or didn't you think it worth while to ask me to dance? I've kept a couple for you——"

"That was awfully nice of you," he said formally, "and I'm afraid I'm very remiss. But you always had so many strings to your bow—or is it *beaux* to your string?"

"Well, one of the dances I have kept is the next one, and I think I deserve it," she replied.

He hesitated. "I'm awfully sorry, but——" Hang it! Why did she put him in this position? He began to feel angry as a man only can when he feels he is being chased into an embarrassing situation by an unwanted woman. But Iris, whatever her faults might be, was secretly aware of her own humiliation, and she began to feel her self-control slipping. How dared he put her in the position of actually having to beg him to dance with her? She was not logical enough to admit that it was she who had taken up the position.

Suddenly it seemed to her that it was the most important thing in her life that she should dance with him—that if she did not she would lose face completely. "Explain to your prospective partner that you booked me ages ago," she suggested. "Say you forgot, and I——"

"That wouldn't be very complimentary to you, and I'm afraid I can't do it, anyway," he told her. "When was the other one?"

"At the beginning of the evening!" She faced him, her lips white under their vivid lipstick. "Am I to understand that you are refusing to dance with me?"

"Look here, Iris, you're not going to make a scene, are you?" he asked.

"And supposing I did? Supposing I told the charming Doctor Grey that I had the prior claim? It's her you are going to dance with, isn't it?"

"I really have no time to discuss my arrangements——"

"Oh, you are cruel to me." She sank down suddenly on the seat beside her. "How can you humiliate me?"

He looked down at her, his eyes hard. How could she be so cheap? There was something revolting to him in the way she rang the changes on all the feminine wiles where he was concerned.

"You'd better let me get you a drink," he said curtly. "And pull yourself together."

"I don't want a drink." She looked up. Then she sprang to her feet again, barring his way. "Do you know that everyone is talking about you and that girl? Of course, she is so used to the seamy side —everyone knows the things that go on among hospital staffs! I don't suppose she minds——"

"How dare you!" He was livid, and for a second she shrank before the blazing anger in his eyes—but she was beyond controlling the vitriolic words which trembled on her tongue.

"I don't suppose she cares whether you are likely to marry her or not. That sort of enlightened young woman isn't particular about the conventions, is she? But I wonder what the Board of Governors would say if a real scandal started—not very good for the precious hospital would it?"

Ivor had been angry before, but in all his life he had never found himself gripped by such cold rage as he did now. If Iris had only been a man, she would not have remained where she was for a moment; but though she saw how angry he was, she had worked herself up to a pitch beyond being afraid. She was on the edge of an hysterical outburst, and she was quite reckless as to what happened.

And then, in that moment while they stood facing each other, the sound of gay voices and laughter broke the electrical silence, and a little group of people came surging in on them: Sir John, Lady Amanda, three other young people, and Jennet with the old lady's hand on her arm.

"There he is!" exclaimed Lady Amanda, catching sight of Ivor, whose back was towards her. "Neglectful person—flirting in corners while I wait patiently for the only dance I can get him to sit out with me."

Ivor turned, controlling his features with an effort, but already Jennet's instinct had told her that something was wrong, and seeing how white he was it was all she could do to check the instant impulse to ask what was the matter.

"Hello, Mrs. Danvers." Lady Amanda fixed her eyes on Iris. "Is anything wrong? You look extremely ill." The tone was quite concerned, but as Iris met that shrewd glance she saw amusement and understanding behind it. She knew that Lady Amanda guessed who was the cause of the agitation which she—Iris—was showing. She could have screamed in the elder woman's face, but, much as she hated her, she had still enough common sense left to know that to be rude to Lady Amanda in public would be the end of her socially.

Moistening her lips, she answered: "I—I'm not very well. I'm going home——"

"Too bad," said Lady Amanda softly. "Take my car. I shall not be leaving for quite a long time. Sir John, will you see that someone finds my car for Mrs. Danvers."

"Of course—of course. Allow me." Sir John offered his arm with a courtesy belonging to another age; and with murmured thanks Iris allowed herself to be led away.

She really was feeling ill now, and she was frightened. She did not want to have hysterics before all these people.

The old lady looked after her. She was not smiling, but if she had let her features relax, Jennet knew that it would have been in one of those mischievous grins of hers; and fond as she had grown of the elder woman, Jennet thought with dismay: She could be ruthlessly cruel if she felt like it. She could not help being sorry for Iris. What had happened to make her look so ghastly? She guessed that it was something to do with Ivor.

How could Iris humiliate herself, let down her sex so completely by continuing to throw herself at a man who had shown her plainly that he had no use for her? Jennet's pity was suddenly tinged with contempt, and yet—it must be pretty tough to love Ivor and fail to get him. And love was love, she supposed, even if there were different degrees of it.

"We're all dying of thirst," said Lady Amanda. "Come along——"

They found tables on the edge of the brilliantly lighted bar. Lady Amanda took possession of Ivor, and when Sir John returned Jennet found herself being monopolized by him.

"Too bad about Mrs Danvers," he observed. "She's usually the life and soul of this sort of thing—afraid there will be shoals of disappointed partners, what! She wouldn't let me go back with her—do you think she'll be all right, Sinclair?"

"Perfectly," replied Ivor briefly.

Lady Amanda changed the subject, but though Ivor appeared to be quite at his ease, Jennet knew that he had been badly upset.

He had already arranged to leave the dance early, because he did not care to be away from the hospital the whole night. Jennet wished she could have gone too, but felt it would look too obvious to leave with him. And so she remained dutifully to dance the last dance, and was grateful to know that Lady Amanda's car was there to take her home. She was dropped at the hospital gates.

As she went in and made her way through the courtyards it was still dark enough for the darting fireflies to show like coloured sparks as they flitted hither and thither. The moon, which had shone brightly earlier, was gone now, and the darkness had the depth which it takes on before dawn.

When she reached her own quarters a figure rose from the seat near the wall, and though she had half expected him to be somewhere about, her heart gave a little leap as Ivor spoke her name.

"You're very bad," she said. "You ought to be in bed."

"Shakespeare says something about a good divine that follows his own instruction," he replied.

She laughed. "I'm going to very shortly; but come in for a minute."

He followed her, because he knew that if he did not speak to her, he would not sleep at all.

She turned on the light in the sitting-room. The coffee percolator stood ready to be plugged in, and a plate of delectable sandwiches was arranged on a carefully laid table for two.

Jennet raised her brows. "Looks as though Li expected company!"

"Chinese servants think of everything." But his smile was gone in an instant, and in the light she saw that he looked tired and worried.

"Sit down and smoke a cigarette, darling," she invited. It was better not to ask him what was wrong. She hoped he would tell her presently, but she knew that he hated to be fussed—even if she had been the person to do the fussing.

He obeyed, lowering his long length into a chair and lighting a cigarette in silence, while she slipped off her evening wrap and busied herself with the coffee. Then he said abruptly:

"Jennet, we must announce our engagement."

She was startled enough for a little of the dark liquid to spill over into the saucer, but her hands were quite steady as she rectified the accident. Then: "Why?" she asked.

"It will—make things easier in the long run. And I particularly want people to know that we are going to be married," he replied. "People will gossip otherwise—the very fact that we danced together tonight——"

"Oh, Lord!" She made an impatient gesture. "Is this a small village?"

"Worse, my sweet."

"What *were* you and Mrs. Danvers quarrelling about?" she demanded. "Is it her suggestion——"

"Her suggestions don't really matter, but—I feel now that it's a mistake not to tell people," he parried.

She bit her lip. It *was* Iris. "We ought to wait for a reply from Sir Bruce," she reminded him.

He hesitated. "Perhaps. But—— Oh, hang it all, you've learnt something about the world, Jennet. You know how filthy people can be——"

"And are they being beastly about us?" she enquired coolly.

He felt that to repeat Iris's words would be as great an insult as the words themselves. He said obstinately: "I'm not going to have you gossiped about, that's all. And—it's only too true that we have got the reputation of the hospital to consider."

She stared at him, flushing deeply. Then: "I see," she told him. "At least, I think I do. Really, the beautiful Mrs. Danvers is a very unpleasant person. She evidently judges other people by what she would do herself—or, shall I say, would like to do?"

He saw that, quiet as she was, her anger matched his own, and he rose, taking her in his arms. "I'm sorry, darling. I'd forgotten what horribly obvious minds people have."

His nearness dispelled any dismay she had felt, and her laugh was genuine. "We should worry!"

"Not a bit—if we did not have to. But this is a devil of a profession we've chosen, darling," he reminded her. "Unfortunately if any scandal did start up, we couldn't afford to snap our fingers."

She frowned, knowing that he was right, guessing that Iris must also realize it, and had based whatever threats she had made on the knowledge.

After a moment: "I'll tell you what," she said, "we'll ask Lady Amanda's advice." And as he frowned: "Yes, I know you hate the idea of discussing our private affairs with anyone else, but don't forget that Lady Amanda is head of the committee—she's rather responsible——"

"You win." He kissed her again. "That's settled, then."

"Your coffee will be cold. Drink it up, and run along to bed like a good boy. We shall both be wrecks in the morning."

"What a selfish beast I am to keep you up." He emptied the cup she held out to him dutifully, and they went out into the hall together. At the door he bent his head to kiss her, and as she slipped into his arms again they once more forgot such considerations as time and space. Ivor was only aware of the yielding loveliness of the girl in his arms; the fresh, flower-like perfume which hung about her was intoxicating as wine, and almost against her lips he whispered unsteadily: "How I hate leaving you——"

Her breath caught; under his hand he felt the quick leap of her heart. "I hate you going," she answered. "But—you won't always have to."

"Darling——" Instead of kissing her again, he only pressed his cheek against hers and, putting her rather abruptly from him, whispered another quick good-night and went out.

As he crossed towards his own lonely quarters his blood was pounding swiftly through his veins.

No, thank heaven, he would not always have to leave her. And when that time came he knew that all that which he had ever sought would be his—the perfect blending of body, soul, and spirit which comes of a great love fulfilled. Companionship for his mind, solace for his loneliness, rest for the flame within him.

When he reached his door and opened it he glanced towards the east, and saw that the dawn was breaking; but he did not notice that in the western sky a flurry of dark clouds threatened the approach of a storm.

CHAPTER XVII

SOMEBODY else was watching that dawn, spent by the storm which had already overtaken her.

After a couple of enamel-backed hairbrushes had been flung at her, Iris's Chinese maid, outwardly as impassive as ever, had left her mistress to have hysterics by herself—a thing which she proceeded to do with considerable skill. For one hour, her temper quite out of control, she had raged about her bedroom, blindly throwing anything that came in her way on the floor, until it was littered with the glass of broken perfume bottles, the remains of a ruined dressing-table set, and various delicate silken garments torn to shreds. Not since she was a child, and, sent to bed for defying her elders, had proceeded to systematically wreck her bedroom, had Iris let herself go so completely. If only she could have got at Jennet she would have attacked her with the thoroughness of any woman of the slums.

The consequence was that dawn found her a shivering wreck, and though she slept from sheer exhaustion, when she woke she felt completely limp.

Anyone else would have been too humiliated to face the servants, but humiliation was not a characteristic of Iris's, who had always considered she was a law unto herself.

The tea on the bedside table had been put there without disturbing her, the room was quite tidy, though the usually littered dressing-table was rather bare.

Hang! thought Iris. I'll have to go out and do some shopping. It was a good thing her late husband had left her a comparatively rich woman—or perhaps it wasn't!

She rang for fresh tea, and seeing that it was not her usual serving woman who brought it, asked where the other was. She was informed that "Nai-Koang's mother plenty ill; she plenty solly, but have gone 'long slick mother."

The fact was that, not for the first time, the long-suffering maid had walked out. Iris frowned and shrugged her shoulders. It was a nuisance, because Nai-Koang was a marvellous servant. But she would come back—she always had done—though perhaps she had never had anything to put up with quite like last night.

For once Iris felt that she might have gone a little too far. But heaven knows, she told herself, I had reason. It was Ivor who was responsible; it was unthinkable that he should treat her in such a way.

Oh! he was maddening—like a stone wall. Nothing would move him when he had once made up his mind. It was cruel, horrible—but she felt she could have gone on standing that if it had not been for this new development. This Jennet Grey—how she hated her! If only she could do something to get rid of her altogether. But she knew in these saner moments that it would not be nearly so easy as it had sounded when she made that half-veiled threat to Ivor last night. She wished now that she had not done it—it would have been much easier to start a whispering campaign.

When she was dressed she went across the passage to Philip's room. He was sitting up in a chair by the window, very pale, the dark marks which fever had left beneath his eyes.

"You're better?" she asked perfunctorily.

"Yes. A bit shaky; but I'll be out again tomorrow." He looked at her a little sourly. "What the dickens were you doing last night?"

She had the grace to flush. "I was feeling ghastly. Did I wake you? I forgot——"

"You always do when it's a matter of consideration for anyone else's comfort," he retorted.

"Sorry." She moved forward and sat down opposite him, and as he caught a full view of her face in the light coming through the windows he received a shock. Though they quarrelled frequently, there was a strong tie between this brother and sister. They were both equally egotistical and selfish, both complete opportunists—perhaps it was their natural faults that held them together.

Philip was proud of Iris, of her beauty and of her reckless regard for anything that stood in the way of her own desires.

"Good Lord!" he exclaimed with a brotherly frankness. "What the dickens have you been doing with yourself? You look a perfect hag this morning!"

She bit her lip. "Thanks for the compliment. I feel one. That confounded girl of mine has walked out on me, and I shall have to go and get a facial."

"What—walked out on you again? Was it her you were flinging half the house at last night?"

"It isn't amusing," said Iris, her face darkening. "I was nearly off my head with one thing and another. I had a filthy time at that beastly ball."

"Wasn't the boy friend there?"

"Yes, he was. And danced half the night with that Jennet Grey creature—— I loathe her. I'd like to——"

"Steady," he cautioned. And then, really alarmed: "I say—I hope you didn't make a scene?"

"Of course I didn't. But I came home early."

"And left people to say that you were sick with jealousy!" He was really annoyed. "Hang it all, old thing—you might have had some sense of dignity! If Jennet was making a success, why didn't you do your stuff? I know you're not used to rivalry—but I didn't think you were the sort to sweep out on a defeat."

"I didn't care what I did," she replied sullenly. "You don't understand—I'm desperately unhappy—I can't bear it. He's in love with that woman—there's an *affaire* going on. You've only got to see them together to see that they're crazy about each other."

"Don't be silly!" he exclaimed sharply. "There's no *affaire*, or I'm a Dutchman! Jennet Grey isn't that sort. If they are in love, they'll get married and you won't be able to do anything about it." And as Iris covered her face, a little moan escaping her: "Good Lord alive, Iris! What has come to you? You can't really care about a stick like Sinclair—why, you've only got to lift your little finger, and all the men in the place fall on their faces."

She dropped her hands, staring across at him with haggard eyes. "I don't want all the men in the place—I want Ivor."

He watched her in growing amazement. "Are you really serious—isn't it just a matter of 'face'—you can't bear to think he won't be interested?"

"What a fool you are!" Her lips twisted contemptuously. "Don't you know that I'm crazy about him?"

"I can't see what you see in him," he confessed.

She made an angry gesture. "Perhaps I don't know myself—I know that I want him. I can't lose him to that yellow-haired cat. Not after all this time."

He continued to regard her curiously, as though he was getting to know her for the first time. "I often wonder," he said softly, "what exactly did happen between you two in England?"

She got to her feet, ignoring the question, and began to pace up and down the room. "I tell you, I can't bear it—I won't!" She turned to face him again, twisting her hands together. "You promised to help—it's your fault."

"My fault! I like that——"

"Well, it is—if you hadn't been ill——"

"Don't be silly, Iris—I didn't get malaria for fun. And, in any case, I can't make Sinclair love you. You've played your cards stupidly—nothing a man hates more than being chased."

"When I tried other methods," she said bitterly, "it only made things worse."

"Simon Barton, eh?"

"Don't let's talk about that." There were some subjects which even she was squeamish of dwelling upon. She said: "You can stop him from getting the girl—from marrying her."

He gave an amused laugh. "Afraid you overrate my powers."

"I suppose you're not interested any more. Talk about accepting defeat! You——" She broke off as Philip's boy entered to announce that the doctor had arrived.

Realizing that she was already late for her appointment at the beauty specialist's, Iris went quickly away, dashing into her own room in time to avoid Doctor Blanchard.

To Philip's relief the medical man was in a hurry, and did not stay long, though long enough to say that he had been most "desolated" that Mrs. Danvers had left the dance so early last night and that she had felt ill. Was she quite recovered, or could he——?

She was quite recovered, and had gone out, Philip replied, and so got rid of the voluble little Frenchman, who was openly regarded by his patients as being more socially than medically useful. No one quite knew why he had chosen to settle in Mangtong and decided to practise there for the rest of his life. There had been whispers that he had once been a ship's doctor, and had lost his appointment for some reason best forgotten.

Anyhow he was here, and though he was quite efficient at ordinary, routine things, the residents had cause to be more than thankful for that private wing at the hospital—when he chose to make use of it in time.

When he was alone, Philip sat frowning into space, the expression on his handsome face unusually concentrated.

He could not understand Iris, but he told himself that it was a darned shame she couldn't get what she wanted. Like Sinclair's impertinence not to be interested in her. By Jove! he detested that fellow. One would have thought, in decency and medical etiquette and all that (Philip was rather vague on what constituted medical etiquette), he wouldn't make love to the girl who was working with him.

Was it really true about those two? Or was it just Iris's jealous imagination?

Was that, Philip wondered, the reason why Jennet had chosen to ignore his overtures? To his surprise, he discovered that he understood his sister's feelings better than he had thought he did.

It must be hades to be desperate about someone and be ignored or snubbed by them.

Must be? It was!

With a sense of shock it came to him that Jennet caring for Ivor was as hateful to him as it was to his sister.

She had stuck in his mind more than any girl he had ever met. She had something—that elusive "keep-off" manner, which intrigued and tormented him. She was, in fact, wholly desirable, but it was not until now that he realized how much—how very much he resented her interest in any other man. . . .

* * *

It was Jennet who broke the news to Lady Amanda.

She had rung up in the morning and asked if she and Ivor might go to tea, but Ivor was prevented from accompanying her at the last moment, and she had to face the ordeal by herself. Not that she felt it to be a very big one; she was not in the least afraid of Lady Amanda, and knew that whatever advice she got would be sound.

If that shrewdest of old ladies had already partly guessed what she was going to hear, she made no indication until Jennet had "said her say." Then she announced that she had expected it for weeks, and was delighted.

"For all your cleverness, what a precious couple of babes you are!" she exclaimed. "What *do* you take people for? One had only to look at you last night to realize you were crazy about each other."

"Oh, dear!" Jennet looked at her in dismay. Then they both laughed.

"I'm truly delighted," Lady Amanda told her again. "It is the best thing that could have happened."

"But—do you think the trustees will think so?" asked Jennet. "I can't see how it can affect Ivor, but—shall I have to give up my job if I marry?"

Lady Amanda looked at her hard. "Do you mind?"

Jennet hesitated. It was not in her to be anything but perfectly honest. "I—don't know," she confessed. "My work means an awful lot to me—not just as a career, but because of the work itself.

And then—I suppose in a way I'd hate to be dependent, even on Ivor. Don't you understand, dear Lady Amanda?"

In spite of the big gap between their generations, the other did understand. In her young days American women had already set a far greater store on their independence than their cousins over the water. She had never wanted a career herself, had often said quite frankly that marriage was a big enough job for any woman to hold down. And now, sympathetically aware of Jennet's feelings, she said, more gently than the girl had ever heard her speak:

"I do understand, my dear. It's the old Eve and the new one in whom this in some ways blessed twentieth century has evolved. Doesn't the old Eve say that a woman has all she needs when she has the things she was primarily made for—love, a home, and children of her own; while the new Eve wonders if they are worth sacrificing work and career and personal independence for——"

"No, no; it isn't quite that!" Jennet exclaimed. "I'm not such a fool as to want to go on alone——"

"Only you do rather want to have your cake and eat it?" Lady Amanda's eyes twinkled. "It's only natural—however impersonal your ambition may be, there it is; there are your years of work, your dreams of all the good you can do to humanity. But you won't be the first medical woman who has married a man in her own profession. To me it sounds ideal—as long as you know when to let go. Supposing it is decided that you shall retire from your present position when you marry? Ivor won't always be out here. Personally, I should like to see him back in London when things settle down—and then what is to prevent you from practising too? You are young—you will be able to keep in touch with things through Ivor. Your career won't suffer in the long run, and your marriage will be all the better because in the first years of it you were able to give all your time and attention to it. And now that little sermon is ended for the moment, suppose you tell me why you suddenly decided not to wait for an O.K. from Bruce Ferguson before taking me into your confidence?"

"Please forgive us," begged Jennet. "I didn't quite know whether you would be pleased or not. We didn't want anyone out here to know but—people talk, don't they? And there seems a chance that unless we say loudly that we are going to get married, they might make some horrid little scandal."

"You mean someone *was* going to make a horrid little scandal? Who—Iris Danvers?" The attack was so unexpected that Jennet found herself without a weapon to parry it, but she had no intention of repeating what Ivor had told her.

"Ivor discovered that people were—inclined to say unpleasant things," she replied. "And I decided to ask your advice."

"My advice is, announce the engagement, and be damned to them!" retorted Lady Amanda. "I'll tell you what; I was already arranging to give a dinner party early next week. I *did* want a picnic, but I knew it would be useless to depend on you both for it. So we'll compromise on a dinner party, and I shall announce your engagement that evening." Which, she added mentally, will settle it once and for all. I don't think anyone will make any trouble after that. . . .

CHAPTER XVIII

HAVING once decided to do so, both Jennet and Ivor would rather have broadcast their news without those few days' delay. However, since they had put the matter into Lady Amanda's hands, it would have been tactless, to say the least of it, not to have left it there.

But, though she did not put it into words, at the back of her mind Jennet was troubled. If people were going to talk it would have been better to take action before they got well started.

Ivor might dismiss Iris's threat as something beneath contempt, but Jennet felt it might be foolish to underrate the other girl's power of mischief. She knew that Iris hated her, and that the other was not the type to accept any sort of defeat tamely.

If there was anything unpleasant going on outside, though, it did not reach the ears of the two concerned because during the next few days they were both particularly busy.

Although Sunday could not be looked upon as exactly a day of rest, as sick people in hospitals still have to be attended to on the Sabbath, there was always a certain sense of relaxation when the seventh day came round.

Ivor had been obliged to go out to lunch—the substitute for the dinner appointment he had broken on that fateful evening when he had found Jennet weeping by herself.

Usually Jennet lunched with the rest of the staff, but this week she felt somehow that she could not sit opposite Terry, knowing that in a few days now he was going to be dealt the final crashing blow. Of course he would get over it, but she was not foolish enough to try to persuade herself that because his disappointment was not likely to completely spoil his life, his feeling for her was not something far more serious than many people would have believed him capable of.

So, at the risk of being thought unsociable, she had lunched alone.

Afterwards she curled up in a big armchair with a cigarette and a book, and was lost in the printed pages, really enjoying herself, when, as she stretched out her hand to drop her cigarette end into an ashtray, another hand closed firmly about it, and annoyance mingled with the surprise in her eyes as she looked up and met the laughing, narrowed grey glance of Philip Devenham.

"Who on earth let you in?" she demanded, not attempting to hide her displeasure. Really, they were not on sufficiently friendly terms to allow of his walking in on her unannounced, as he undoubtedly had done.

"No one did," he replied. "I knocked on the window, but nobody answered, and so as it stood invitingly open I peeped round the curtain—and after that the temptation to come in and find out how long it would be before you discovered my presence was too strong to resist. Besides, I never really believe in resisting temptation."

Jennet frowned, annoyed at this interruption of her solitude, and in no mood to be amused. Philip reminded her far too strongly of Iris to be a welcome visitor.

"Next time," she said coldly, "you might take the trouble to get yourself announced. How did you know I was alone?"

The contempt in her tone, the knowledge that he was making no impression nettled him.

"Because I happened to see Sinclair lunching at the club," he replied. "And when you are not alone, it usually means you are with him—at least, I gather that is the popular belief."

"Like many popular beliefs, an entirely wrong one." Her voice was calmer than she felt. "I spend quite a lot of my life working, and with other colleagues and friends, you know."

He had not intended to say what he had, and he cursed himself for a tactless fool.

"You're not cross with me, are you?" he begged coaxingly. "Must I go? If you really hate the sight of me, I will."

It was rather difficult to turn him out in such a peremptory way, and she did not see how in common courtesy she could do it. "Don't be silly," she retorted. "As you've gate-crashed, you can sit down for a few minutes."

"Kind lady—if only you were always as kind as you are beautiful." He lowered himself into a chair. "And," he regarded her smilingly, "do you know you've been very unkind to me lately? My heart is cut by broken promises and——"

"Don't be ridiculous!" she interrupted.

"I'm not." He was suddenly serious. "You did make me a

125

promise, and instead of keeping it, you seem to have avoided me ever since."

She was the more annoyed because he had succeeded in making her feel just a little guilty. How stupid she had been to say she would go motoring with him again; it had only been on the spur of the moment, and to show Ivor that she did not intend to be intimidated. It really did not seem an adequate reason for Philip to sit looking at her like that. Of course, she decided, as she had done from their first meeting, he was the type. Love-making, or implied love-making, had become second nature. He could not be with a girl, and refrain from behaving as if she was the only one in the world who had ever interested him.

Can't he possibly give me credit for some intelligence? she asked herself irritably, and decided to put a stop to this once and for all.

"You know," she said frankly, "I should like you much better if you didn't think it necessary to do your stuff every time we meet. Couldn't we try a little intelligent conversation without your finding it necessary to imply that I am 'the only girl in the world, and you are the only boy' sort of thing?"

For a moment he stared at her blankly, and then as his eyes met the smiling mockery of hers, a little flame flickered in them. He had courted and found a lot of experience in his time, but he had never been laughed at like this before, and it gave his vanity a new and uncomfortable jolt—a jolt which was all the stronger because he had never thought her lovelier or found her more desirable than she seemed in that moment.

"And supposing," he said, "that I am really serious in thinking of you as the only girl in the world?"

There was something in his tone and look which startled Jennet in her turn. But she continued to smile as she answered lightly: "I'm sure you would never limit your mind to an only girl." And changing the subject determinedly: "Now suppose I give you some tea? Only you must remember Chinese etiquette, if I do."

She did not want to give him tea, but she did rather fancy seeing the politely immobile face of her Number One Boy coming in urbanely to break this unwanted tête-à-tête. Then the moment she had risen to cross to the bell she realized she had made a mistake. Philip was on his feet instantly, he passed her as if to forestall her, and then without ringing the bell, turned quickly so that she found him standing quite close to her—far closer than she wanted him to be.

She stepped back quickly, and would have fallen over the chair which she had not known was just behind her if he had not put out his hand swiftly and caught hold of her. Then, before she could prevent him, or even guess what he was going to do, he had swept her into his arms.

She was adroit enough to avoid his kiss, so that it only just brushed her cheek, but she was amazed at the sense of outrage his very touch roused in her. Her whole instinct was to drag herself furiously free, to tell him to get out and never dare lay a finger on her again. Then she discovered that he was holding her with unexpected strength. She had enough sense of dignity to want to avoid anything like a struggle, and controlling herself with an effort, she looked up at him coldly.

"Please let me go."

"Why?" His heart was suddenly beating very fast. If she had lost her temper he might not have felt exactly as he did now; it was her coolness which maddened him even more than her nearness; and her nearness was troubling him with unexpected fierceness. "Why are you so darned elusive?" he asked. "Why do you keep me at arm's length?"

"You are the most egotistical person," she retorted. "Why should I go to the trouble of keeping you at arm's length?"

"Heaven knows I've tried hard enough to be friends with you, Jennet. What have you got against me?"

"This sort of thing. Please let me go," she requested with rising impatience. "If you knew how I dislike being mauled about——"

The contempt of her tone, the knowledge that he was making no impression on her, stung him to anger. "I suppose that depends on who does the 'mauling,'" he suggested.

"Don't be vulgar!" He had relaxed his hold, and she freed herself with a jerk. "If you want some tea, you had better ring the bell, and if you don't want it, I'd much rather you went." This sort of thing was really hateful—she felt that sense of insult which a girl who is deeply in love with one man does feel when another has the audacity to make love to her. Not only that; there was something cheap about Philip's flirtatiousness. Even if she had liked Philip a little, and there had been no Ivor in the way, Philip's advances would still have roused her resentment.

He, too, was feeling resentful—not because of her repulse so much as because of the unusual sense of frustration which it roused in him. If he had been given to self-analysis, he would have been amazed to discover how vital it had become to something deeper than his self-conceit to make her respond to him. He stood watching her, his brows almost meeting.

It was absurd that after all his efforts he should not have succeeded in interesting her. If the young man had an exaggerated idea of his powers of attraction, perhaps it was not entirely his own fault; he had seldom failed to make a conquest when he had set out to do so.

"I don't see why you should treat me as a leper," he burst out. "You can't blame me for thinking that there is someone else. Is there, Jennet?"

She looked round. "I don't see that that is anything to do with you——"

"But it is. If it's true what they are saying about you and Ivor Sinclair——"

"And what are they saying?" She was facing him now, her head thrown a little back.

"What do you think they are likely to say, when a young and madly attractive woman is thrown into close contact with a man who had pretended to be uninterested in the sex until she arrived on the scene. You're always together—your behaviour at the dance the other night set a dozen tongues wagging." He was suddenly beyond caring what he said. "But you're a fool if you trust your happiness to Sinclair—if you think he's really serious. He is capable of doing irreparable harm to a girl, and when he's finished he will leave you high and dry as he has done at least one other. Believe me, I know what I'm talking about. His treatment of her has nearly smashed my sister's life up——"

"You can keep these charming revelations to yourself," Jennet interrupted, her endurance of the scene snapping. "I'm not in the least interested in anything that has happened to your sister. And for the rest, Doctor Sinclair and myself are quite capable of managing our own affairs——"

"Then there is something between you?" He was standing close to her again as he made the demand.

"That is our business. I fail to see why you should be interested."

"Interested!" He caught her by the shoulders. "Why shouldn't I be interested? I'm crazy about you." He swept her into his arms again. "Crazy, do you hear? Keep still, you shall listen to me." And then as he saw the dislike in her face: "Jennet, be kind to me. I tell you, I'm mad for you—I've fooled around, but I've never been in love in my life before. If you'd only marry me——"

She had to realize he was serious. This unhappy, pleading, half-frantic man meant exactly what he said—probably to his own surprise as much as to hers.

In spite of herself she felt sorry for him, but she knew that the only way of responding to his plea for kindness was to be quite frank.

"I'm sorry," she said. "I had no idea that you felt like that, but it is quite useless. I couldn't care for you—you see, I'm afraid I don't even like you. Now, please let me go——"

What he would have done next she had no chance of discovering. At that moment the room door opened, and with the air of a man who has a perfect right to expect a welcome Ivor walked in.

With a muttered exclamation Philip released Jennet, and swung round to face the new-comer. Between his now furious dislike of Ivor and the unusual strength of the emotion under which he was labouring he hardly knew what he was saying. "Oh, it's you!" he exclaimed. "I've something to say to you——"

"Then you can find some other opportunity to say it," cut in Jennet. "Please go now, Philip. Unless," she lowered her voice, "you really want me never to speak to you again."

For a second he stared at her. He was much more shaken than he realized, but he had just enough common sense left to know that to have a row with Ivor now would be to sign his own death warrant where Jennet was concerned. To live to fight another day was surely the wisest policy. And so, much as he hated leaving these two together, he picked up his sun helmet from the desk where he had laid it on his entrance, and brushing past Ivor went out without another word.

As the door closed behind him the other two were left facing each other.

To Jennet's dismay she saw that Ivor's face was set in that icy, expressionless mask which it always wore when he was very angry. She was aware of her own flushed cheeks and ruffled hair, and a sudden horrible embarrassment gripped her. She helped herself to a cigarette, and lit it with fingers which refused to keep steady. Then, breaking the silence, she looked across at Ivor, who had crossed over and stood staring at the bookcase.

"I'm glad you came in just then," she said.

"Are you? It struck me as being a particularly inopportune moment."

She could have shaken him, but to her dismay she did not know whether she wanted to laugh or cry.

"Don't be stuffy, darling," she begged. "I can't help it if young men will want to marry me. They'll soon know what a waste of time it is——"

"You don't mean to say that Devenham——" He swung round. "Of all the damnable impertinence! You!" He caught hold of her, drawing her towards him. "What did you say to him?"

"I'm afraid I was drastic. I was explaining that I didn't even like him."

His face relaxed, then darkened again. "He didn't dare try and kiss you?"

"Darling, to try is one thing——"

"I'll break his neck!"

"Ivor, you couldn't be jealous!"

"Couldn't I? I could be intensely resentful. Look here, this has got to stop. You've encouraged him far too much."

"I have not!" she exclaimed indignantly.

"Oh yes, you have! You've gone out with him—from the very first he has come here as if he had the right. Promise me it is going to stop now," he demanded.

"He'll know that it has to—after Lady Amanda's party. Do forget him." She laid her hand on his shoulder. "Dearest——"

"You're not safe to leave about." But his eyes were smiling now. "Good thing you haven't any male patients—Heaven only knows what would happen. Sir John hasn't by any chance asked you to marry him?"

"Not yet," she replied demurely.

He kissed her. "Loveliness! You are a dangerous female. What shall I do about you?"

"Marry me, and keep me in order!" She looked up at him smilingly. "Apparently you're not very safe yourself!"

"What do you mean?"

"Never mind. I won't drag up your horrible past." She felt that was the only way to treat what Philip had said—to laugh it off. She did not want to start "holding an inquest" on what had happened between Iris and Ivor; in fact, she felt a violent distaste at the idea of discussing it. How she wished those two had never known each other! . . .

CHAPTER XIX

On the Tuesday evening Jennet and Ivor arrived at Lady Amanda's together. As they followed their names across the threshold of the room, Jennet was conscious of the politely inquisitive glances of several of the people who were already there. She was not in the least embarrassed—only rather amused to know that they would soon have their curiosity appeased. After all, what did it matter what they thought or said? Then, as Lady Amanda broke off her conversation to come forward to greet them, Jennet saw, with a slight thrill of dismay, that among the group who stood at the other end of the room were Iris and her brother. It was clear that Lady Amanda was going to do the thing thoroughly!

"So glad you both managed to get here," their hostess told them. "I hope you have given orders that no emergencies shall arise in your absence, Ivor—or at least insisted that nothing short of an earthquake shall drag you away before dinner is over."

He laughed. "I've done my best. I should hate to be wrenched away in the middle of one of Ching's glorious dinners." Lady Amanda's cook was famed beyond this province. He had once been at the French Embassy in Peking.

"Oh, my dear, the most awful tragedy!" replied Lady Amanda. "Ching was taken ill this morning, and I'm afraid his number two is having to deputize for him. Now don't immediately go to the telephone and arrange to be called away."

"How dare you make such a suggestion?" he demanded. "Do you imply that all that brings me here is one of Ching's dinners? Seriously, though, what's wrong with him?"

She shrugged her shoulders. "A touch of the sun, I should think. Anyway, they said he was feverish, and seem to have shut him up in his own quarters. They are probably doing horrible magics over him—but his mother rules his household, and she's very Old China. You know what they are—one can't interfere. I shall be worried if he is not better tomorrow."

"Try and persuade them to let me have a look at him," said Ivor. "Matter of fact, I saw him on the waterfront two or three days ago, and I thought he looked a bit odd." He said nothing more just then, but he was annoyed with himself because the incident had gone out of his mind. What had happened was that he had been talking to a Padre who had recently arrived in Mangtong, when they saw Lady Amanda's cook. Ivor's companion had broken off to exclaim: "Why, surely that is Ho-Ching. I wonder what he is doing here?" And when Ivor had answered, "Cooking the most perfect meals that can be evolved, for Lady Amanda Trent," the Padre had said: "I suppose she knows all about him?"

When Ivor had asked if there was anything to know, besides the fact that the cook had been in the best service and was a wizard at his job, he had learnt with dismay that about five years ago there had been an incident in which Ching had run amuck and nearly killed one of the kitchen boys. As far as the Padre could find out, he had been detained for a time, and the story was a sad one. When Ching was quite young, Chinese bandits had descended on the village where he lived, and massacred his young wife and two children; he had become deranged by sorrow, but had been helped and nursed back to health by the medical mission, where he had been restored to mental health. Ivor, feeling rather disturbed, decided that he had better mention the matter to Lady Amanda, as it would not be very pleasant if the same thing happened again and Ching tried to carve up one of his fellow-workers.

He hoped devoutly now that the cook was not going off his head again, but this was hardly the place to mention it, especially as the last two expected guests, Sir John Selham and Lotus Ling, were announced just then.

Lotus was looking very lovely in Chinese dress, long strings of perfect pearls falling over the old rose brocade of her embroidered tunic, pearl and ruby-hilted dagger pins in her hair, and wonderful ruby earrings hanging from her ears.

Jennet's eyes were full of admiration as the Chinese girl moved across to speak to her, but she was unaware of the perfect contrast they made. Jennet in a white chiffon frock with a gold belt and slippers, with her transparent white skin and her bright, closely curling hair, her only jewels a string of turquoise matrix which fell to her waist—the loveliest thing she had ever possessed, because, apart from its beauty, it was Ivor's first present to her. He had given it to her that evening, just before they set out.

Against those two, Iris, in a close-fitting dress of her favourite silver lamé, with diamonds in her ears and flashing about her lovely throat, and diamond and emerald bracelets on her arms, looked somewhat overdressed. There was something a trifle flaunting, and decidedly challenging, about her beauty tonight. Lady Amanda, making a caustic mental summing-up, decided that the late John Danvers, whoever he had been, must certainly have been rich and done his wife well. An ornamental creature, but—theatrical. Never in quite perfect taste. Lady Amanda did not approve of young women covering themselves in diamonds.

Iris had put hers on recklessly tonight. She had been surprised and a little suspicious when she and Philip received invitations, her own covered by a gracious personal note from Lady Amanda saying that she was giving a rather special dinner-party and would be glad to see them. It was only the third or fourth time that they had been asked to dine at the Trent home. Iris knew her prospective hostess both disliked and disapproved of her. So what could be the meaning of this special invitation?

"You had better watch your step where her fat ladyship is concerned," Philip had warned his sister disrespectfully; but Iris was drunk with jealousy and misery, which made her even less of a sound psychologist than usual. She was actually foolish enough to imagine that perhaps Lady Amanda wanted to buy her silence by giving her a step up the social ladder. Though she did not attempt to speak to Ivor, she felt a thrill of triumph as dinner was announced and the party moved across to the brilliantly lit dining-room. Perhaps before the end of this evening she would get a chance to drop a hint to Lady Amanda which would put the old woman on her guard regarding "Doctor Grey." Lady Amanda was very interested in the welfare of the hospital. . . .

Though she had known that he was watching her in the drawing-room, Jennet had managed to ignore Philip, and she wished that he had not been seated exactly opposite her at dinner. The only compensation to that was that Iris was at the far end on the same side as herself.

It was a very gay dinner-party, and in spite of the absence of the far-famed cook, the food was remarkable enough to please the palate of any connoisseur. Jennet had given Philip a brief smile; she felt that it would have been stupid to cut him—awkward too, because nothing missed their hostess's eye; besides, what did Philip, or Iris, or anyone else matter?

Ivor was on Lady Amanda's right, Jennet next to him, with Sir John Selham on the other side of her.

As usual when she gave a party, Lady Amanda emitted a sparkle which seemed to be reflected in all her guests.

The meal swung smoothly to its conclusion, until the table was cleared of everything save the piled dishes of fruit, the perfection of the priceless porcelain dessert service, and the slender-stemmed wine-glasses, which, at a signal, the silent-footed boys began to fill with sparkling golden wine.

Lady Amanda leaned forward in her chair, looking down the table. Then:

"I'm going to ask you all to drink a toast with me," she said. "I am sure you will all be as pleased as I am when I tell you that I have great pleasure in announcing the engagement of my very dear young friends, Doctors Jennet Grey and Ivor Sinclair."

There was an almost imperceptible silence. Then a little murmur ran round the long table as everyone rose to their feet, glass in hand, eager smiling faces turned towards the two who remained seated.

They had not realized, those two, what a horrible ordeal it was going to be. Jennet would have given the world to run away; as she turned her head instinctively towards Ivor, he gave her a reassuring smile, and her shyness was swept away in a thrill of delight at the knowledge that now everyone knew they belonged to each other.

Sir John was smiling down at her, monocle screwed into his eye, his wine glass in his hand. "I say—too bad! You might have warned me!" he murmured. "Never had such a blow in my life——"

Congratulations were being showered upon them. "Only what we expected." "Lucky devil, Sinclair." "Heartiest congratulations." While the phrases were tossed about like flowers, no one noticed—except perhaps Lady Amanda—that two people remained silent.

Iris stood, staring before her, until, the health having been drunk, she realized that the others were resuming their seats, and sank back in hers, aware that her knees were shaking and her mouth quite dry. She had dreaded this news, tried to persuade herself that it would never get as far as this. She wondered now whether it was her own folly that had brought things to a head—but she was in no state to think very clearly about anything then.

In reply to the general laughing clamour, Ivor rose; taking Jennet's hand deliberately in his, he looked down at her, and then round the table.

"Thanks very much," he said. "You're telling me I'm a lucky man. Believe me, you don't know the half of it—I'm much luckier than your wildest flights of imagination could picture." And amidst more applause he sat down again.

Involuntarily Jennet glanced across and met Philip's eyes; they were burning intensely in the dead whiteness of his face, and he had the look of a man who had received a knock-out blow.

So that was that. Thank Heaven it was over. A few minutes later their hostess gave the signal for the ladies to leave.

Sir John had already opened the door for them to pass through, when there was suddenly a wild shriek in the hall outside, and pandemonium seemed to have broken loose. It was as though in an instant the wide hall was filled with screaming, gesticulating servants, while in the midst of it two figures, swiftly joined by several more of the men-servants, struggled wildly.

"Good heavens, what is it? Be quiet there—how dare you!" Lady Amanda would have stepped forward, but Ivor caught her quickly by the arm. "Keep back, please," he said authoritatively. "Keep the women in here——" And passing swiftly through, he shut the door.

"What on earth——" Lady Amanda stared at her guests in horror. "I must find out what it is. Let me pass, Sir John——"

"No; please obey Sinclair, and stay where you are," Sir John begged. "I do think one of us should go, though."

The noise in the hall had already subsided, but as Sir John opened the door again, Jennet saw that Ivor was struggling with a small, yellow-faced figure, and her heart turned over as she caught sight of the Chinese man's face. In an instant she guessed what was wrong—only the insane looked like that; only the insane would have such strength against what would otherwise have been far superior weight. Then, even as she looked, the struggle was over. As the other men emerged from the dining-room, Ivor was saying: "Better tie him up. I'll telephone for a strait-jacket—why was the devil ever allowed in——?"

Jennet was beside him. "I'll telephone," she said.

"Tell them to get a couple of strong men and a stretcher. He'll have to be sent straight away, poor little beast," ordered Ivor. And to Lady Amanda: "Too bad! But I'm afraid Ho-Ching has lost his senses. I ought to have warned you that I'd heard he'd been under detention before——" He broke off, biting his lip, staggered, and would have fallen if Lotus, who had made her way silently through the crowd, had not flung out her arm and supported him.

"You are hurt!" she cried. "Let me help you."

"All right. It's only my shoulder——"

At that moment Jennet reappeared at the door of the library, in which room she had been telephoning. Lotus, from whom Sir John and another man had taken Ivor, beckoned her imperatively. "Doctor Sinclair is hurt. I think it must be a knife wound——"

"It's—nothing," protested Ivor; and, sagging forward between his supporters, fainted dead away.

It was the doctor in Jennet that got her through what followed.

Leaving the now unconscious Ho-Ching to be dealt with by the others, they moved Ivor into the library and laid him on a sofa, where, his blood-soaked coat being removed and his shirt cut away, the deep flesh wound he had received could be attended to.

It was a strange scene: Jennet in her white evening dress, and Lotus in her beautiful brocade and jewels, working as calmly and efficiently as though they were in a hospital ward. Sir John had offered to take his car and hurry post haste to the hospital and back, but Lady Amanda had everything necessary for first aid on the premises, so Ivor had been attended to without the necessity of Jennet accepting the elder man's offer. She had hardly finished before Ivor's lids lifted, and she found herself looking into his puzzled eyes.

"What the dickens——?" He tried to rise, and fell back, his face contracting.

"Keep still!" she ordered, taking his wrist and putting her finger on his pulse. "I've had quite enough trouble with you for one night!" It was the only way she dared trust herself to speak. He was a stranger—she was his doctor; if she thought of things in any other terms she had the awful dread that she might break down.

Too weak to do anything else, he obeyed, watching her face; and then slowly everything came back to him.

"What have they done with the man?" he asked.

"He has been taken away." It was Lotus who answered.

He turned his head, and looked at her. "Hello! You there——"

"Quiet!" warned Jennet. "You mustn't talk—and you are not going back to the hospital or anywhere else tonight. I'm going to arrange with Lady Amanda for you to remain here."

"Good Lord! I can't——" But he found that he had a strange disinclination for argument, and when she went out of the room he lay back, his eyes closed, and almost at once sank into unconsciousness.

Lotus came silently forward, and stood looking down at him, her dark eyes fixed on his face as though she could never look long enough. After a few moments she bent to draw the light blanket which had been thrown over his feet a little higher.

Ivor moved, and, without opening his eyes, murmured: "Darling——"

The Chinese girl straightened as though she had been shot, and, turning, walked away, white teeth pressed hard down on her lower lip. With a sudden surge of bitterness she wondered why one should be sent into the world to be tortured. Life had seemed so easy, so clear cut, before duty had recalled her to her grandmother's side. She had counted herself exceptionally lucky to have been allowed to study the things which interested her most, and to have been able to choose the man she was to marry. That was one of the things which during these last months she had forced herself to remember—no one had forced her betrothal on her, and though her attachment to her fiancé had never been in the realms of high romance, she had been sure that they would be very happy, and between them be enabled to do a lot of good in the world. The young doctor believed firmly in the emancipation of women, and looked for a friend and companion in his wife. But that he loved her with a strength and devotion which far exceeded her feeling for him she had always known.

To ask him to give her her freedom was a thing that could not be done—it would be unprecedented, and her grandmother would die of rage and shame even if she had dared suggest it. Besides, what would she do with her freedom? There was one thing which, even in her maddest moments she had always known she could never do— even if Ivor Sinclair had ever shown the slightest interest in her. He had been so kind—too kind, but only as a teacher and a colleague, and Lotus knew that marriage or even love between a girl of her race and a Western man could, as the world stood today, only bring disaster. She told herself that it was her foolish, disloyal, mad heart which had betrayed her. She had tried to discipline it, almost believed she had succeeded until this evening, when she had heard Lady Amanda make that announcement at dinner.

She covered her face with her hands, shamed, and hating herself, until the opening of the door warned her, and she turned again as Jennet came back into the room.

With Jennet was Macdonald, who had just arrived from the hospital, and Lady Amanda, who looked decidedly pale.

Ivor opened his eyes, and, seeing his hostess, grinned at her rather ruefully. "Shame to spoil your party," he said.

"Don't be silly!" she retorted. And then, dropping all attempt at her usual crispness: "When I think what might have happened!—why on earth didn't you leave him to murder the other servants?"

"Because I didn't know who he'd start on next. Look here," he glanced at Jennet, "I shall have to get back to the hospital. A night's rest, and I'll be as right as rain in the morning."

But here he was firmly put down. He was going to remain here—for tonight at any rate; to go to bed; to have, in Macdonald's words, "a wee shot of morphia," and if he was strong enough, he could return to the hospital tomorrow.

Both Jennet and his other colleague were certain that Ivor would have little inclination to exert himself the next day, and they thought they could leave it at that.

And so with the help of Chang, Lady Amanda's Number One Boy, who was very strong, they got Ivor upstairs and into bed, where Jennet left him in the hands of the sometimes dour but always devoted David Macdonald. She was glad that it had been the Scotchman and not Terry who had been free to come along—somehow she did not feel like facing Terry tonight.

Until, having washed, and tidied her rather dishevelled appearance, she descended the stairs again Jennet did not realize how shaken she was. It was only when she reached the hall that the full force and shock of what had happened came to her. She stood still, aware that she was trembling, and that it would take very little to smash up her self-control.

Meeting the politely sympathetic Chang waiting in the hall, she paused to ask: "Chang, can you bring me brandy and soda to the library, plenty quick?"

"Can do," replied Chang smilingly, and obviously approving, departed on his errand.

Entering the library, Jennet had got halfway across it before she discovered it was not empty.

Lotus sprang to her feet, but not before Jennet had realized the attitude of utter despair in which she had been sitting. Nor did she move back quickly enough to hide the startling fact that there were tears on her cheeks.

"Lotus——" Jennet took a swift step forward, but already the silent-footed servant was in the room, setting down the tray on which there was a decanter, syphon, and glass.

Jennet asked calmly for another glass, recovering from her first shock sufficiently to see that what was the matter with Lotus had better be ignored, because the other girl would be so dismayed at having been discovered in tears.

"I'm making free with Lady Amanda's hospitality," she said. "I —don't feel quite like facing a lot of questions without something to steady me. You'll have some too——"

"Oh, no; I never do."

"Doctor's orders! Just about a tablespoonful." And having seen that Lotus obeyed, she took her own glass and sat down.

Lotus said quickly: "You look so ill. Cannot you go straight to bed?"

"As soon as I've seen Lady Amanda. I——" Jennet closed her eyes. "I'm beginning to think about what might have happened. It's only a flesh wound—the knife glanced off his rib. But do you realize that if the thrust had been a little lower, an inch or so further to the right, it might have gone right through his heart. Why, Lotus——!"

The glass Lotus had been holding had slipped from her fingers to the carpet, and she stood swaying a little, her eyes closed.

"If he had been killed—I can bear anything better than that." It was as though the words were wrung from Lotus's stiffened lips. No training, no self-control was strong enough to keep them back. Then, like someone coming out of a drug, she opened her eyes again and stared at her companion in horror. "What have I said——?"

"Nothing, my dear." Forgetting herself completely, Jennet went to the other girl, taking her hands in a firm, close clasp. "Nothing that I shall remember if you don't want me to—— But oh, I wish I had known! I would never have let Lady Amanda ask you to be here—I'm so sorry."

She knew now—the carefully guarded secret which would be Lotus's eternal shame ever to have betrayed. For a moment dark eyes and blue ones looked into each other.

Then: "I wish you every happiness in the world," said Lotus. "I mean it. I'm so glad to mean it. You are my friend, and a friend understands and—forgives."

"My dear—what is there to forgive? Unless you have to forgive me," said Jennet. "I wouldn't have hurt you for the world——"

"You have no blame, Jennet. She who picks the rose, forgetful of the thorns, deserves to be wounded."

Lotus's philosophy had centuries of wisdom behind it. But philosophy has never really healed a bleeding heart.

CHAPTER XX

It was hardly surprising that Jennet slept very little that night. She kept seeing Ivor again, as he had lain there on the divan in Lady Amanda's library—so pale and still with that horrible red patch on his white shirt front. Lying in bed, she found that she was shaking from head to foot with the knowledge of what might have happened. Although, as a rule, she had it very well in hand—in her profession it would have been fatal to fail to control it—she was cursed with a very strong imagination.

Tonight, after the shaking up she had had, it was not so easy to control—she found herself wondering what she would have done if Ivor had been killed. What would life have been—what would it be without him? She drew back before the question as she would have done if she had found herself looking down into a dark, deep abyss. She was suddenly incapable of facing the horror of it, and her very incapability frightened her.

How helpless we are! she thought. Women! If I died tomorrow, his heart might nearly break, but his life would still be very full, as it was before he met me. It's only a woman who can never be complete without love. It will take thousands of years to free us from the chains we long for, and if it ever really happens, that will be the end of the race. But it won't happen. It's what we are here for, perhaps, the spiritual link. . . .

And thinking of the love of women, she felt a fresh pain in her heart as she remembered Lotus. Poor little Lotus! Why on earth didn't I guess it before? she asked herself.

How could she have done? What chance would Lotus, who controlled any outward show of her inmost feelings so rigidly, have ever given her to find out that most vital secret? It was only the shock the other girl had received which had caused her to give herself away—and Jennet was half ashamed of having unwittingly trespassed.

She had the strangest feeling, though, that the knowledge had drawn herself and the Chinese girl closer, instead, as it might so easily have done, of dividing them.

Dawn was already breaking when she fell asleep, but that did not prevent her from being up even a little before her usual hour. It was difficult to wait until she was bathed and dressed before ringing Lady Amanda's house. One of the hospital nurses who could be spared had been sent along there last night, Lady Amanda having begged: "Please send someone with some authority, or I'm sure that I shall never be able to prevent him walking out."

However, to everyone's relief, Ivor was not inclined to walk out. He was very weak from loss of blood, and, however his mind might chafe at the enforced inactivity, it was clear enough to tell him that in the present state of his body a few days' rest was essential. He might be able to direct things, but he certainly could not take any active part in them.

The news Jennet received from Nurse was that he had slept well. "He is a bit irritable," she added, "and he would like to see you— or someone 'intelligent' as soon as you can spare the time."

It was difficult for Jennet, her fears of the night dispelled, not to laugh. Poor darling, how he was going to hate this! "Tell him I shall come during the lunch hour," she said.

* * *

Jennet could not help feeling that those next few days while Ivor was forced to knock off any active work were very much worth having. It was so lovely to have him there "at her mercy" as she teasingly told him. There was nothing to prevent her going to Lady Amanda's on the three evenings for which he was there. On the fourth day he was to return to the hospital. His wound was healing up nicely, and though he was still strapped up he was fit enough to work again.

Meanwhile, the news of their engagement was, of course, common property by now. Lady Amanda had recovered both from her own shock and the loss of her superlative cook, whose place was already adequately filled.

"I suppose poor Ching couldn't help going out of his head," she said. "But really I wish he had not chosen quite such an important party to do it at—stealing all the limelight for himself."

It took more than a mad cook to frighten Lady Amanda, and she waived aside the suggestion that she might have been in considerable danger herself.

"I suppose I ought to have been told at the beginning that he had been under detention, but after all we did have some good dinners," she said calmly. Not that either Jennet or Ivor was in the least deceived—they knew their friend (if she had no care for her own safety) had been badly shaken at the idea of what might have happened to Ivor.

It was on that third evening before Ivor was due back that Jennet returned to the hospital, having firmly refused Lady Amanda's offer of the car, her thoughts on the hours which were just behind her. Their hostess had gone out to dinner that evening, and she and Ivor had been alone. It was always lovely to be with him—but somehow being there in Lady Amanda's beautiful house had brought a closer sense of being together.

For a brief time it had almost seemed as though they were in their own home—Jennet sighed. Lovely, if that illusion could ever become reality. She was suddenly realizing that she would want a home some day—a real home.

She remembered what Lady Amanda had said about Ivor not always being here. He was doing marvellous work, but it was only a phase of his career, and it might even become a cramping one. Yes; surely some day they would go back to England—to London, and there in the very centre and hub of the Empire he would be able to find full scope for all that was in him. . . .

As she passed through the hospital gates she noticed half-mechanically a car drawn up in the shadows by the lodge. Reaching her own quarters, she let herself in, still half a-dream. She did not encounter a servant, and it was with a little shock that, as she opened the door, she found that the light was on. The next moment her shock was more definite, as the girl who had been sitting in one of the deep chairs rose, and Jennet found herself confronting Iris Danvers —the last visitor she had either looked for or wanted.

For an instant Jennet found it impossible to control her expression of dismayed unwelcome. Then: "I didn't know there was anyone here," she said.

"Your boy didn't want me to wait. I'm afraid I gate-crashed," Iris replied. "I—wanted to speak to you." She spoke without her usual self-confidence, and noticing the nervous opening and closing of her hands, Jennet realized that she was in a state of intense nervous strain.

She was looking extremely ill, and against her extreme pallor her over-painted mouth was like a scarlet stain.

"What is the matter, Mrs. Danvers? Are you ill?" asked Jennet.

"Ill!" The twist of Iris's lips was almost a snarl. "Not in a way that medicine can cure—at least, you have the prescription, but I don't expect you to give it to me."

"Hadn't you better sit down and tell me what is the matter?" Jennet requested; but her calmness was assumed. She knew with inward dismay that she was in for a scene of some sort.

She sat down, motioning the visitor back to her seat, and after a brief hesitation Iris reseated herself.

"I don't know why I've come," she said. "Except that I couldn't stop away any longer. I suppose Ivor *is* getting better?"

"Oh yes, he'll be back here tomorrow." Jennet thought: If she really has come here to discuss Ivor, she has got a nerve! Her eyes met the smouldering dark ones calmly.

"I suppose you would be very shocked," Iris spoke a little breathlessly, "if I told you I almost wish he'd been killed; that I believe I would rather know him dead than that he was going to marry you—or anyone."

"No, I shouldn't be shocked. I should think it a pity you had brooded yourself into such an exaggerated state of mind," said Jennet.

Iris made a fierce, impatient gesture. "Don't come the doctor over me," she said. "I'm not your patient—Heaven forbid that I should be. We're just two women who happen to be in love with the same man." She stared shamelessly and challengingly across. "It can't be any news to you that I love Ivor?" And, without waiting for an answer: "If he had told you the truth about us, you would know that I have the right to love him—to feel that I've been most abominably let down."

"Ivor and I have never discussed you," said Jennet. "Please don't say any more." It was not anger, but humiliation for the way Iris was letting herself down, that made her voice unsteady. "I am—truly not interested."

Iris mistook her hesitation. She thought that she had touched her rival on the raw, and the furious desire to really hurt took hold of her. She said: "If you don't know what happened in England, it is time you did. It was not either of our faults that I happened to be married—neither was it my fault that when I was free he was more interested in his work than me. Oh, I could endure that. Ivor's the sort—whether you believe it or not—in whose life a woman will always take the second place. I was quite content to—go on as we were. Everything would have been all right if you had not come——"

"Please!" Jennet rose. "This is all very unnecessary."

"From your point of view, no doubt. You naturally hate the idea that he was my lover——"

"I don't only hate it—I simply don't believe it," replied Jennet contemptuously. "If it ever was so, it was so long ago that it doesn't matter——"

"If I told you that I only came to China because of him?"

"It wouldn't make any difference." Jennet did not try to keep the contempt from her eyes and voice. "You are just wasting your time. What Ivor did before he met me doesn't concern me."

Iris had not quite known what kind of reception she had expected her "revelation" to be met with—perhaps she judged Jennet by herself, had hoped for a scene in which recriminations could be bandied backwards and forwards, had hoped to rouse the other to a frenzy of the same type of jealousy which was torturing herself. But, as she faced that calm figure, she suddenly knew she had failed, and abruptly changed her tactics.

It had always been the same with her since she was a child—when she could not get her own way she had recourse to the one weapon which had again and again helped her to succeed. It had failed with Ivor—but then Ivor was like iron, she told herself, still clinging to the belief that sooner or later she would melt him. Poor Iris—perhaps she had never really grown up; as a child she had got her own way when she cried, and even now she could never quite believe that tears would fail her.

She had risen from her chair, but she flung herself down into it again and burst into a storm of weeping.

"What do either of you care that my heart is breaking!" she sobbed. "He's mine—you have no right to take him." She turned, clutching Jennet's dress. "You don't know how cruel he can be—if he tired of you he would be exactly the same——"

This was rather too much! Jennet disengaged herself firmly. "Listen," she said, "what you need is a sedative. I'm going to give you one, and then you had better go home and go to bed——"

"I don't want anything—I won't have it——" Iris was working herself up, but already she was alone in the room. Her hands clenched so that the nails bit into the soft palms. Jennet was back in a moment, a small glass in her hand.

"Drink that!" she ordered; and to her own surprise Iris found herself obeying.

"Now relax," Jennet told her, putting a cushion behind her head. "I must look over these——" She sat down at the desk, and began to glance through the papers which had been left in readiness.

She had to thank Heaven that she could shut her mind to everything except what it was needed for at the moment, and five minutes passed in which she had forgotten the other girl. Then she was recalled by Iris's voice:

"I'm going home now." And, as Jennet looked round and rose: "I was a fool to come. I might have known that all you cared about was getting him. But at least you know now that he was mine first——" Drawing her wrap about her, she walked to the door. Jennet saw her to the outer door, and with a quiet good-night, to which she received no reply, shut the door behind her.

So that was Iris's car she had half noticed when she came in? Well, she ought to be able to drive herself back quite safely after the strong dose she had given her.

She went back into the sitting-room, and going over to the chair in which her most unwelcome visitor had sat, mechanically straightened the cushions.

The gardenia perfume which Iris always used a little too freely hung in the air. With a gesture of distaste Jennet walked across and opened the window wider behind its shrouding of fine net. Then she lit a cigarette, and prepared to finish her work before she went to bed.

But, for once, all her powers of concentration failed her.

Iris and Ivor—was it true? And why should it be so hateful to hear it put into words, even though she was certain that Iris had lied. From the little Ivor had said, it was surely clear that whatever had happened to break what there had been between them had been Iris's fault. For a few minutes Jennet almost made up her mind to ask him what really had happened. Then she told herself: I'm hanged if I will. That's what she wants—to make some sort of controversy. And of one thing at least she was certain—Ivor would never take another man's wife away from him. He was not the sort to carry on an under the rose affair. And for the rest—it was more hateful than ever to think he had ever cared for Iris. But she was not going to ask him to vindicate himself, because she loved him, and because she trusted him. . . .

CHAPTER XXI

AND so she did not mention that curious and unpleasant interview with Iris.

Ivor was very busy after his return, and by the end of another week was able to resume all his usual activities.

Meanwhile, the news of his engagement to Jennet being now common property, congratulations showered upon them, and everybody seemed eager to entertain them. People were kind, and it was not ingratitude for that kindness which made them both glad that neither of them had enough spare time to enable them to accept many invitations.

What Jennet did wish was that Ivor could take a holiday. She knew he needed it badly, and he had said a little while ago that he might be going off for a week. She remembered amusedly how she had resented the suggestion that she could be spared.

It was illogical, though, to feel a qualm of such utter dismay as took hold of her the evening when he told her that he would have to be absent for four or five nights.

He had come into her sitting-room to smoke a cigarette, as he nearly always did at the end of each day, and, leaning back, watching her face through the spirals of blue smoke with that feeling of complete satisfaction which being with her gave him, he said suddenly:

"Do you feel capable of taking full charge of this place for a few days, Lady Doctor?" And, as she looked at him quickly: "There's a very important person organizing some sort of committee to make a better job of co-ordinating medical supplies for the Chinese soldiers and my presence has been requested at——" He named a place in the interior, which was about a day's journey down the river.

"They want some help, and I feel have every right to it," he continued, "and I think I ought to go. In fact, I've got to. Things are running very smoothly here just now. And"—his eyes narrowed in that delightful way they had when he was pleased or amused—"I don't seem to have noticed that anything dreadful happened while I was *hors de combat*. So I think you will be quite capable of carrying on."

She knew that it was a tremendous compliment; nothing would have induced him to leave the hospital unless he had believed it would be absolutely safe in her hands, whatever emergency arose.

"Thanks," she said briefly. "I'll do my best." If it was a little curt, Ivor, who was very intuitive, knew exactly what it meant.

"Good," he approved. "That's settled, then."

"When are you going?" she asked.

"Day after tomorrow."

"And you'll be gone——?"

"Four days at the most."

She crossed over to pour herself another cup of coffee, and he rose and followed her. "Glad to get rid of me?"

She turned, looking up at him; and with a swift, impulsive movement, caught hold of him, hiding her face against his shoulder.

"Hate the idea—most surprisingly."

"Blessed one! So do I." He kissed her hair. "I love you—you're dreadfully demoralizing. But four days isn't really a lifetime. What will you do while I'm gone?"

"Work hard, and go and see Lady Amanda. She seems to like talking about you——"

"Odd taste." There was a brief silence. Then: "Will you think me an awful fool if I ask you to promise me something, Jennet?"

She looked up at him quickly. "Of course not—what is it?"

He hesitated, surprised at his own impulse, half inclined to suppress it. And then: "I want you, as far as it is possible, to avoid seeing anything of Devenham while I'm away. I mean, I don't want you to receive him here, or—go driving with him or anything like that." He was half laughing at himself as he said it; but as she laughed back, he gave her a little shake.

"But, darling!" she protested. "I don't make a habit——"

"Don't you?"

"You are the end! I went out with him once!"

"Well, you can avoid that happening again. You can't deny that he had acquired a habit of dropping in on you." Then, his smile fading altogether: "I know the breed. They can be importunate when they want anything."

"Philip knows it would be quite useless now," she reminded him.

"Bet you the minute my back's turned he'll be after you again. And I resent his chasing you, to a most extraordinary degree," he admitted frankly. "I don't think I'm jealous—that wouldn't be complimentary to either of us; but I just object."

"All right. 'Objection sustained,' as they say in the American courts," she laughed. She did not mind his asking for the promise, and gave it willingly—not only because she had no desire to see Philip, but because she loved the idea of pleasing Ivor; and if he was human enough to be a little jealous, she did not find it unflattering.

But when he had said his final good-night, and she was getting ready for bed, she found that though she tried to shut both Philip Devenham and his sister from her thoughts, they lingered there. How she wished those two would leave Mangtong. It wasn't that she really cared about anything Iris had said, and Philip was quite negligible—but she was honest enough to own that she hated the other girl's claim on Ivor, however fictitious it might be——

Oh! she told herself impatiently, forget them! And then, as she sprang into her bed and turned out the light: They can't do a thing to hurt us now.

For all that, deep down in her heart there was a rather unhappy wish that Ivor was not going away—it was not only that she was going to miss him abominably, but she had the strangest feeling that without him she would be more vulnerable—though she did not know to what.

* * *

The great thing to be said for the Eldred Chambers Hospital was the complete lack of jealousy among its staff. And that ideal which put the hundred per cent. efficiency running of the place first, made it quite all right that Jennet should be in full charge, and that men like David Macdonald and Terry O'Dare should serve under her without any question of their longer service. It was a compliment, too, that no one in the nursing staff felt any qualms.

But even Jennet had not realized what an enormous amount more there would be to do. There was hardly any chance to miss Ivor, much less time for anything outside the hospital in those first two hectic days.

Things were complicated by the fact that a mild epidemic of an unpleasant sort of gastric influenza broke out without any warning, as such things are apt to do. There had been perhaps half a dozen cases in the week before Ivor went—some Chinese who had come to Out Patients, complaining of pains, and one of the nurses had been laid up. It was more uncomfortable than dangerous, and seemed only to last for two or three days. But on the day Ivor left for his conference another whole half-dozen cases broke out in the hospital staff and wards, while news came from outside that there was a lot of it in the town.

"Drat the bug!" said Jennet to Terry. "I do hope Ivor hasn't taken it away with him."

"Of course it doesn't matter if the whole of Mangtong goes down with it as long as that doesn't happen!" he teased. He had taken the news of her engagement with admirable outward philosophy; if it went deeper than he showed, he was generous-natured enough not to want to spoil her happiness by showing his hurt.

But, as David Macdonald was among the victims, it complicated things by making them extremely short staffed.

Jennet felt it was incredible the way those first three days sped by. On the fourth, or the fifth at the latest, Ivor should be back.

On that third evening she leaned back in the chair into which she had thankfully flung herself, a cigarette between her lips, her eyes half closed. It was the first time she had been able to relax since she got up that morning. But at least she had the satisfaction of feeling that things had gone pretty smoothly. Thank Heaven for the efficiency of the nursing staff, which, even if they were depleted, still functioned smoothly.

She had meant to ask Rose to have dinner with her tonight, but there did not seem to have been any time for dinner.

It was pleasant to sit there, the smoke curling upward from her cigarette, letting mind and body relax—pleasanter still to think that perhaps this time tomorrow Ivor would be back.

A sudden wave of longing swept over her. Without him everything seemed to lack an essential meaning. How lovely to see him coming in at the door again, to see that quick smile trace the tired lines away from his face—that little flame spring to life in his eyes. How dear he was; and—how difficult he was apt to be! She had no illusions on that score. She loved him all the more because of his faults, while—her lips curved in a smile of tender amusement—she had no intention of encouraging them. He had such a tendency to work himself to death, forgetting, when he expected other people to do the same, that what might be a tonic to him was the pace that kills to people who lacked his fund of nervous energy.

That awful habit of wiping the floor with anyone he thought had slacked, or done the wrong thing. She had heard him "let fly" more than once; the amazing thing was, no one ever seemed to hold it against him—and all those round him did their jobs well, not because they were afraid of him, but because they really hated to fall short of what he expected—knowing well that where he asked an inch of them, he would give a yard himself. Jennet found herself wondering how she would feel if he were really to have her "on the carpet"— and knew that she would hate it.

Thank Heaven he had never had to reprimand her for anything to do with her work—except that once when she had been late. She knew quite well that he would be as frank and unsparing with her as he would be with any other. She told herself that she would not expect anything else, but she could not help feeling that it would be too devastating to have him look at her as if she was the veriest brainless idiot.

I suppose we are bound to have a good fight some time! she decided. If we were destined always to say "yes" to each other, how dull life would be. And however angry he is he soon gets over it. Unless, of course, someone had outraged his whole design for living.

There were things which, she guessed, he could be quite unforgiving over. For instance, whatever Iris had done must have been pretty bad, because it had so obviously set her beyond the pale where he was concerned; and when he disliked people, how he could dislike them! Pressing out the stub of her cigarette, Jennet laughed softly to herself. Philip as a second instance (she would rather remember Philip than Iris) and remembering him, she wondered how he was really taking the fact of her engagement. Except at Lady Amanda's, she had seen nothing of him since that unfortunate interview when he had asked her to marry him. Jennet was not flattered at the remembrance; looking back, she could not take that proposal seriously. It was pique at not being able to get beyond her defences which had made him lose his head like that. There was nothing permanent enough about Philip to make him a marrying man. For all that she could not quite forget the look in his eyes when they had met hers across the dinner table just after Lady Amanda had made her announcement.

She was not wasting sympathy on Philip, though; she was quite sure he must have hurt a lot of women in his career, and if for once he was even slightly pricked himself, it might do him good.

She sighed. The very last thing she had looked for or wanted when she came out here was a train of young men losing their hearts to her; the very last thing she would have hoped for, if she had ever thought about it, was that in one of those young men she would find so much of that secret ideal which, almost without knowing it, she had set for the man who could be hers.

She stretched and rose, and at the same moment the telephone rang. Frowning, she reached for the instrument, hoping that she had not deemed herself safe too soon, and it would not be Philip's voice she heard.

Instead, the soft tone of an unmistakably Chinese voice came across.

"Please allow me speakee Number One Doctor Lady——"

"This is Doctor Grey," replied Jennet.

"Thank you. This Su-Li—Amah b'long Ladee Amanda. My ladee catchee plenty pain. Wantee stlong medicines welly quick. I no wantee my ladee die——"

"Is Lady Amanda ill?" demanded Jennet with a pang of alarm.

"Welly ill. She wantee you come quick 'long her—plenty quick——"

"All right, Su-Li; tell her I will be there immediately."

Jennet rang off hastily. If Lady Amanda had asked her maid to ring, she must be feeling very ill. It was probably only the same trouble so many people were suffering from, but she couldn't possibly be left without anyone to see her. Jennet knew that nothing would induce her to send for Dr. Blanchard, whom she hated, and had called an incompetent nitwit to his face. She did not doubt that Su-Li, who if her mistress had a pain in her little finger expected her imminent demise, had exaggerated; nevertheless, she would have to be attended to at once.

Jennet glanced at her watch. It was just nine o'clock. There was hardly a chance that she would be wanted again that night, but in any case she would not be gone more than an hour—or half an hour longer than that at the most. It would take twenty minutes to walk to Lady Amanda's house. If she sent for a rickshaw it would make it a little longer before she got there. She decided to walk, and having slipped a wrap over her frock—the nights were always amazingly chilly in contrast to the heat of the days—and collected what she wanted, she rang for the boy and told him where she was to be found if she was needed.

The moon in its last quarter was shining brightly as she passed through the gate and took the road which would lead her to her destination, but there was an ominous halo round it, and in the direction of the river great banks of dark cloud were rolling up. On and off there had been a storm threatening all day; she hoped it would not break for a few hours—she certainly did not want to be caught out in it.

She thought: I hope the beastly thing will keep off. But she decided there was really nothing to worry about as Lady Amanda would doubtless insist upon sending her back in the car.

When she arrived she was admitted by the Number One Boy, who greeted her with the great respect due to the fact that she was the Number One Doctor Lady called for, and with a very evident relief. Lady Amanda still had "plenty bad pain," but before she could learn more from him, Su-Li was there, and she found herself being ushered upstairs into Lady Amanda's bedroom.

A fire was blazing merrily, and, wrapped in a brilliant peacock-coloured Chinese coat, exquisitely embroidered with birds and flowers, the old lady was huddled in a chair beside it. She looked extremely ill, but she managed to smile at her visitor, and greet her cheerfully.

"Good-evening, Doctor. Brought your little black bag?"

"Why aren't you in bed?" asked Jennet severely.

"Because every time I move I get a pain——"

"Then the best way is to lie down and keep quiet," retorted Jennet. "Anyway, let me find out how bad you really are." She smiled as she produced a thermometer and placed it in the patient's mouth.

A few moments later she was aware that there was a decidedly odd pulse and a temperature below normal—which was exactly what she had expected. Having administered a dose which would allay the pain and internal discomfort, she superintended the amah getting her mistress into bed.

"And you will please stay there until further notice," she admonished.

"Depends how long that is," grumbled Lady Amanda.

"Two or three days. You're only being fashionable, and you haven't got it very badly," said Jennet, and explained how things were going at the hospital.

Lady Amanda appeared to be feeling better already. She grinned. "It would happen! And I suppose you have been worked half to death. I'm ashamed of myself—wouldn't have sent if I'd known."

"Then it is just as well you didn't know," Jennet told her affectionately. "Now you are not to talk—try to get some sleep. Have Su-Li give you another dose in three hours—or when you are awake. And someone is to telephone me first thing in the morning."

"Fancy taking orders from you!" The old lady gave a ghost of a chuckle. "Too bad Ivor isn't here—he would have me at his mercy. All right, child, I'll be good." Then with a stronger flash of her usual energy: "By the way, Su-Li did explain to you why I couldn't send the car? That fool will drive more carefully when I have finished with him."

Realizing there was a story behind that ominous threat, and not wanting her patient to talk any more, Jennet nodded. "I must run away now," she said, "in case I'm wanted."

"Thanks for coming, my dear—glad to know I'm not an imminent inmate of your hospital. Good-night——" Lady Amanda was already drowsy, and as she left her, Jennet knew she would be asleep very soon. She beckoned Su-Li to follow her, and on the landing outside gave her some brief and clear directions, which she had no doubt would be followed to the letter.

As she was going downstairs she turned back. "What happened to the car?"

The Chinese woman replied in her picturesque pidgin English that Fu—the chauffeur—had taken the car to a big garage in the town which was run by two Americans, to have some adjustment made; on the way back another car had been driven into him, and the Rolls was now back at the garage "plenty sick!"

Of course, if Lady Amanda had not been ill, she would have taken care to find out how Jennet had got there. As it was when she emerged from the house again, she couldn't help wishing that the unknown careless driver had been somewhere else when the grey Rolls was on its way home from the garage. For the sky was very overcast now, and there was a nasty, ominous little wind blowing across the silence of the night.

Leaving Lady Amanda's house behind her, she quickened her pace, but she was not halfway back to the hospital before the wind had dropped, and in the distance the grim sound of thunder rolled.

Hang it! thought Jennet, I'm not going to behave like a scared kid. But if storms in England were trying, storms here could be devastating, and even if she had enjoyed the idea of one, wisdom would have urged her to hurry.

She began to run, and had gone about a hundred yards, when, turning a bend in the road, she found herself half blinded by the glare of the headlights of a parked car. She moved to one side, and stood quite still, very angry at the carelessness which could so easily have caused an accident. Then as her sight cleared she realized that not only had the headlights been left full on, but the car, instead of being drawn to the side of the road, was pulled halfway across it. Without a moment's hesitation Jennet walked up to it and opened the nearside door, determined to give its occupants or occupant a piece of her mind. As she looked in, the headlights threw back enough illumination to show her the man who was half slumped over the wheel. She recognized Philip Devenham at once, and in those first moments thought that he was drunk; she took him by the arm, shaking him roughly.

"Philip! what do you think you are playing at?"

He opened his eyes and groaned. "Oh, Lord—I feel so damnable——" And then, raising his head: "Is it you, Jennet?" He shivered violently, and as he moved, trying to sit upright, his hand touched hers and she found that it was icy cold. "Tried to turn the car," he explained hoarsely, "and nearly ran into the blasted wall——"

She needed no explanation, having guessed what was wrong— here was another victim of what appeared to be the spreading epidemic. She hesitated, thinking rapidly. Philip would never be able to get that car back by himself—and just then there was another roll of thunder, and a few heavy drops of rain fell.

Drat it! thought Jennet. I hate this day! Nothing has gone right.

"I feel damnable," Philip groaned again. "I——"

She cut him short. "Get into the other seat, please. I'm going to drive."

"Oh! Thanks awfully——" Obviously incapable of discussing the matter, he moved over and leaned back, his eyes closed, while she got in and took the wheel. It was the first time she had driven a car since she came to China; the road was narrow in that particular place, and she had some difficulty in turning. While she was doing it, she was aware of the lightning flickering in sheets of flame across the horizon. But once the car's lamps were pointing in the right direction, the thing seemed to be simplified. Her eyes steadily on the road, Jennet had time to curse the situation in which she found herself. She did not know how she was going to avoid seeing Iris. Hang it all! how these two seemed to make complications. Well, she would have to take this car on, that was all—and send it back to its owner in the morning. Philip certainly would not have any use for it tomorrow.

Philip's house was on the lower road, and it meant rather a detour; keeping her mind deliberately from those ominous rumbles and flashes, Jennet drove steadily, and in just over ten minutes had drawn up before the porch of the ornamental villa (modern style) where Philip and his sister lived.

She leaned over and touched her companion. "You're at home, Philip. Can you get out?"

He nodded, but there was an anxious expression in his eyes as they met hers. "I say! I do feel cheap——"

"Stay where you are," she commanded. "I'll get some help." But though she rang the bell three times there was no reply. The house was dark, and there was no sound within. Frowning, she went back to the car. "Do you know where your servants are?—they seem to have taken a holiday."

"Oh, Gosh!" he exclaimed faintly. "I forgot. We've a new lot—rotten, and all related to each other. There's some sort of family celebration on, and I had to let 'em off. Iris is away—until tomorrow——"

"Well, you had better give me your key," requested Jennet with the calmness of exasperation.

Of course they had impossible servants—it was common knowledge that Iris could not keep decent ones. As she took the key he produced, and opened the door, Jennet was remembering that Lady Amanda had told her a few days ago that Su-Li had a new assistant—a woman who had been maid to Iris, who had thrown things at her, when the woman had very properly walked out, and being Su-Li's niece was now under the same roof as her aunt.

She helped Philip into the house, and as she turned the light on in the hall and shut the door, the storm sounded nearer.

However, there was not really time to think about that now. Fortunately, she had her case with her, and having got Philip into the sitting-room, where he collapsed on the divan, she proceeded to go once again over the monotonous but necessary job of checking pulse and temperature. He was worse than her last patient had been. She gave him the usual dose, bidding him lie still.

He obeyed, his eyes on her face. For the first time he was able to realize clearly that she was here with him.

"What's wrong?" he asked.

"With you? Influenza of a sort—everyone's getting it."

"Darned lucky, aren't I? On top of that dose of malaria. I don't seem to have picked up from that yet." Philip was the type of male who felt terribly sorry for himself when he was ill. "What an angel you are!" he murmured. "What should I have done if you hadn't come on the scene——?"

"Someone else probably would have if I hadn't," she replied practically. "But you ought to be in bed—and I must get back to the hospital. I'll ring Dr. Blanchard, and see if he can come to you."

"Right. You'll find the telephone in the room opposite."

She rose at once and went out. She was halfway across the hall when there was a flash of lightning which filled the place with blue fire and a reverberating clap of thunder that seemed to shake it. Jennet shrank back, involuntarily leaning against the wall behind her, every nerve tingling.

The telephone bell had rung in a tinkling sort of jingle, and then stopped. Outside the skies had opened, and a veritable deluge was descending.

Philip called out rather weakly: "By Jove! That struck something. You all right?"

"Of course." She pulled herself together. This was not the time to give way. A moment later she was at the telephone, but the instant she put the receiver to her ear she knew something was wrong; and try as she would for the next five minutes, in which there appeared to be some sort of promise that the storm had receded again, she could get nothing but an intermittent buzzing out of the instrument—a buzzing which told only too clearly that the line was out of action. . . .

CHAPTER XXII

OF all the maddening things to happen! Knowing that it was no use continuing to stand there, Jennet hung up the receiver again and went back to the room where she had left Philip.

"Oh, Lord!" He looked at her pathetically. "How rotten I do feel!"

"Poor man." But if he had expected her to "lay a hand upon his fevered brow" he was disappointed. To do him justice, it could only have been a faint expectation, because he really was feeling ill. As she stood looking down at him he asked:

"Did you get your call through?"

"No—the storm has busted the wretched instrument," she replied, with a calmness she was far from feeling. "I was just wondering what time your servants are coming back."

"Heaven alone knows! Probably not before morning. A dog couldn't live out in this." He spoke with his eyes shut.

"My goodness—I can't stay here until the morning!" exclaimed Jennet.

He grinned faintly. "You're quite safe, darling—I can't even make love to you——"

"Don't be a fool!" she retorted sharply.

But that had evidently been the last sally of which he was capable for the time being—and as she studied his pallid face, which appeared more ghastly in contrast with the black cushions against which it rested, her sense of trouble deepened. What on earth was she going to do about him? He ought to be warm in bed. Here he was in evening dress—he had evidently been dining out—in the last sort of apartment one would ever dream of choosing as a sick-room.

It was impossible in the present state of the weather to open a window—the whole room would have been wrecked in a few minutes. The only thing to do was to try to make Philip as comfortable as she could on the divan.

Jennet proceeded to take off his collar and tie—fortunately he was wearing a soft silk shirt—and having done that she went upstairs in search of something warm and light to cover him with.

She felt an increasing distaste for being in this house at all, and as she opened the first door she came to and, turning on the light, realized it very obviously belonged to Iris, she shut the door hastily. Her second attempt was luckier—an obviously masculine room faced her. She went to the bed, and, collecting some blankets, took them downstairs again.

She was glad to have to think of something besides the storm, which was still raging, flashes of lightning and claps of thunder seeming to race each other, while the rain poured down. In spite of her nervous tension, Jennet still found room in her mind to be grateful for the fact that Iris was not here—because she knew that under no circumstances could she have dared to go into that storm.

Philip complained hoarsely that he had a mouth like a lime-kiln, and she went away again in search of a drink for him. She found a siphon of soda-water in the dining-room. The servants must really be exceptionally bad, she thought. There was nothing left ready in case he should have wanted it when he came in.

As long as she lived Jennet never forgot those next few hours. Philip dozed and groaned intermittently. And it became obvious that he had something more than the symptoms she had noticed in the other 'flu victims.

His temperature went up, he became hot and cold by turns, and presently he became a little delirious. If only she could have got him to bed—but strong as she was in spite of her frail appearance, she did not feel capable of attempting the task.

It was well after midnight before the storm abated altogether. The rain seemed to have stopped, and seeing that her patient was sleeping restlessly she went out to the front door.

The night had a curiously calm, washed look—clouds were still scudding in the sky above, but patches of stars and the evening moon showed between them. The car stood where they had left it, water was still running off its roof but apparently there was nothing wrong with it. If only she could risk driving it quickly to the hospital, she could send some help back——

At a sound behind her she turned swiftly to find Philip standing in the sitting-room doorway, his eyes bright with fever, fixed upon her.

"Jennet—I was coming to look for you. Let's go to the temple—want to show it to you by moonlight," he said.

She hurried to his side, taking his arm. "Come back and lie down, Philip."

"Lie down? Why? Don't be s-s-silly." His teeth were chattering. She led him firmly back to the divan. "You must keep quiet——"

"No. Sinclair's not going to stop me from taking you——"

"Of course he isn't," she soothed. "But it's much better for us to stay here."

She compelled him to lie down on the divan again, and covered him up. "Now try and go to sleep—you are not well." He closed his eyes obediently, while she kept her fingers on his wrist. When he opened them again he studied her face intently, a puzzled expression in their depths.

"Jennet—what the devil——?"

She smiled. "You know that I drove you back. Keep quiet now. You'll be all right soon——"

"Feel rotten now," he reiterated, like a child.

"Then drink this, and go to sleep," she told him firmly; and, supporting his head, held the glass to his lips.

He swallowed the medicine and turned his head against her. "Lovely person——"

She did not move, and a few minutes later he was sleeping again—this time more quietly. He looked suddenly young and rather desolate, and for the first time she felt a sort of pity for him. Poor

Philip—there wasn't very much to a life like his; one never really knew who was to blame when people turned out wrong. He was so different to Ivor—Ivor, who would be strong in the face of any circumstances.

Perhaps it is inevitable that a woman—if she has any heart at all—should feel softened towards a man who loves her hopelessly. Jennet wondered if there were perhaps some redeeming points in Philip Devenham's character; he was shallow, selfish, much too sure of himself and he meant absolutely nothing to her, but he must have been a very good-looking and quite sweet little boy. Perhaps it was because he had been too spoiled then that he was all he was today.

She drew away from him very softly. . . .

She must have dozed off, for she was awakened by a sound in the room and sat upright, to find herself looking into the face of a Chinese whom she instantly guessed to be the truant houseboy. He was standing a yard or so away, staring at her; for an instant she stared back. Then, as a full sense of what was happening came back to her, she rose to her feet, passing a hand over her hair.

"You Mr. Devenham's Number One boy?" she demanded sternly.

"Yes, missee——"

"I am Doctor Grey," she informed, and proceeded to explain briefly and concisely what had happened. She added that someone was to go for Doctor Blanchard at once, that Philip was not to be left alone, but must not be disturbed until the doctor came. Then, having written a hurried note which she left for Blanchard's arrival: "Now listen carefully," she ordered. "I am going to take Mr. Devenham's car, and I shall send it back later——"

It struck her that the servant was not very intelligent, but she could only impress on him again that he must go to the doctor at once. A few minutes later she was in Philip's car, speeding towards the hospital.

Dawn was already lightening the sky, and she wondered anxiously if she had been missed. If it had not been for the storm, she knew she would still have been unable to leave Philip alone even for a short time, and have gone back to let them know that she was all right. What with the thunder and her patient she had not had the chance to worry about anything else. But now, driving in the dawn light, she was gripped with apprehension; she hoped desperately that everything was all right.

The gates were locked, and she had to stop the car, get out, and ring for admission. The night porter came out after a brief interval—he had evidently been dozing—and for a moment he stared at her blankly. Then:

"Doctor Grey!" There was relief in the man's voice. "You wanted up at hospital—plenty quick——"

She was already back in the car, and without waiting to ask any question she drove swiftly through the open gateway.

She stopped in the main courtyard and, leaving the car, ran up the steps into the building. As she entered she came face to face with Rose Hilton. The Matron was as perfectly starched and coifed as usual, but seeing her about at this hour advertised the fact that something was very wrong.

Catching sight of Jennet—who realized afterwards that she must have looked decidedly ruffled after her long night—an expression of mingled surprise and relief crossed Rose's face. "Doctor Grey! Thank Heaven——!"

"What's the matter, Matron?" Jennet asked quickly. "I couldn't possibly get through that storm——"

There was no time for questions or explanations now. Rose herself was feeling curiously tired and keyed-up. "Doctor Blanchard brought in a case," she said briefly. "The usual delay. Doctor O'Dare had to take the decision for an immediate operation, as you were not there——"

Jennet's heart was suddenly like lead. "Did everything go all right?" she interrupted.

"We got her off the table and back to the ward, but she took a sudden turn for the worse. I think she had all but gone, but, thank God! Doctor Sinclair arrived back in the middle of it all. Do I believe in miracles!" Rose heaved a deep sigh of gratitude. "He pulled her round, with us all working like heck. It will be touch and go for a few days, but I hope we shan't lose another patient!"

"Doctor Sinclair!" Jennet stared at her, wide-eyed.

"Yes; he arrived in the middle of the storm."

"Where is he now?"

"Gone to tidy up, and get a rest, I hope—poor man," Rose replied. "Are you all right?"

"Yes—I got held up."

It was not for Rose to ask how or why or where, and she hurried on her way while Jennet turned and went out of the hospital again. As she walked in the direction of her own quarters the knowledge that Ivor had arrived back in her absence was filling her with dismay. What evil fortune had made things go awry as they had gone that night? Of course she would be able to explain—but already she knew that explanation was going to be more difficult than she cared to contemplate. That she, of all people, she, whose devotion to duty was as strong as Ivor's own, should have failed to be on hand when she was needed!

But she was no coward; however difficult it might be, the thing had got to be faced out, and mingled with her half dread of their meeting was joy and relief at the knowledge of Ivor's safe return.

Suddenly she felt that she must see him at once, and turning off towards his house, reached the door almost at a run. It yielded beneath her hand, and she was in the hall almost before she knew it. Although it was getting broad daylight outside, the electric light was still burning in Ivor's study.

He was sitting at his desk, facing her; he had evidently been making some notes. The pen lay idle on the desk beside him, and his face was buried in his hands. Never before had she seen him in an attitude which suggested weariness and defeat. She ran forward with a swift exclamation, but at the same moment he glanced up and she stood still. He looked tired and drawn, but there was no softening in the eyes which met hers. So for a moment they regarded each other.

To her horror, Jennet felt herself go scarlet and then white. What had happened had not been her fault, and yet she knew she both looked and felt guilty.

She was half aware of an almost childish longing for the shelter of his arms; if only he could have taken her into them first, shown that he was glad to see her. She knew it was no use to expect it; all these months of working beside him had taught her that when it was a matter of work, or anything to do with the hospital, he was not likely to spare time for anything else.

She did not realize that even in the stress of that desperate two hours after his return his mind had for the first time been divided— between the vital task on hand and the gnawing anxiety of wondering if she was safe, what could have become of her. Then, back in his own room, tired out mentally and physically, he had faced the bitter disappointment not only of her failing to be on the spot to welcome him, but in the realization that at a time when her skill and authority had been badly needed she had been absent from her post.

He got to his feet. "Jennet! I was just going along to Lady Amanda's. Was it the storm that held you up?" He spoke without anger, but his eyes were stern and uncompromising.

"Yes—partly," she replied. "And——"

"Why did you go out? Surely it would have been better for you to stay here in case you were required?"

Thank Heaven she could begin to explain: "Lady Amanda rang up and asked me to go—she was feeling really ill, and I didn't like to refuse. Besides, it was so near I thought they could get me at once——"

He frowned. "I see. Nothing serious, I hope?"

"'Flu. There has been a lot of it about since you left. I expected to be back within an hour."

"Was she worse than you expected, then?"

She loathed the feeling that he was putting her in the position of having to defend herself. "No. I was there only half an hour," she answered.

His face softened, though it still remained grave: "I see; you had to shelter from the storm?"

If only she could have left it at that; she despised herself for the weak longing to do so. With an effort she kept her voice steady while she explained: "I walked there, thinking she would send me back in the car—but the Rolls was out of order, and I had to walk back again. I was halfway here, when I met Philip Devenham—he was ill, too, and I had to drive him home."

She saw his face darken. "You are not telling me that you have been with Devenham all this time?" His tone was icily incisive.

"I'm afraid——"

"Are you aware," he demanded, without giving her a chance to finish her sentence, "that when I went away I left you in charge of the hospital—that the whole running of it rested in your hands?"

"Of course——"

"Listen!" he commanded, white with anger. "You are probably still unaware of the fact that while you were with your friend Devenham, Doctor Blanchard chose to send in another of his forlorn hopes."

She nodded. "Yes; I know. Thank Heaven you got back. I expect it would have been just the same if I had been in the hospital. I mean, Terry O'Dare——"

"Did his best—and had to rely almost entirely on his own judgment. We all know that O'Dare's strong point will never be surgery. I doubt very much if you would have considered the patient in a fit state for operation—you would have rightly taken the risk of waiting rather than the risk of operating. In this particular type of case O'Dare has neither your experience nor mine. It speaks well for his skill—or luck—that she came off the table alive. You know the rest."

She nodded, feeling like a whipped child. "But she came through all right. I mean, you——"

"Helped to pull her together for the present. The rest will depend on what the combined efforts of the nurses and myself can do.

What I want you to understand is," he said coldly, "that if she dies there might easily be an enquiry; some sort of fuss which will bring this hospital into unpleasantly strong limelight—and Blanchard, who doesn't love us, though he likes to send us his dirty work to do, would have quite likely pointed out that it was the second of his cases we had lost in the private wing, within a few weeks of each other."

"I know," she admitted unhappily. "I don't want to make excuses, only I couldn't possibly let Philip go back alone. I tried to ring, but the beastly telephones were out of order. He really was too ill to be left——"

"Surely the servants could have looked after him?"

"He was quite alone in the house." She might have explained more clearly if he had given her time—except that just then her brain was not at all clear.

His anger, which had been cooling to a reasonable temperature, suddenly boiled. If she had been with Lady Amanda he would have been ready to accept the fact as something regrettable but finished with—later on, further explanations would have helped him to make excuses for her; but that she should have neglected her duty and the sacred charge he had laid upon her, to spend hours doctoring Philip Devenham was more, in his present mood, than he could bear.

"Don't bother to explain!" he begged, with a biting sarcasm more potent than any blaze of anger. "I quite understand that 'Philip' was more important than any promise you made to me——"

"You don't understand." Her lips trembled, and she clenched her hands tightly. "It was impossible to leave him—and then the storm came. Ivor, I'd have given anything for this not to have happened. I know I ought to have been here, but——"

He made an angry, frustrated gesture. Then: "I suppose I ought not to blame you," he said. "I am the person to blame. I ought never to have left you—to have expected the same clear-headed loyalty I could have looked for from a man——"

"Oh——!" She drew back as though he had struck her across the face.

He did not see the stunned hurt in her eyes. Although he would have insisted that his anger against her was just because he had trusted her and in a moment of emergency she had let him down flat, what he was really thinking was that she had forgotten everything else and remained with Philip—Philip, whom in that moment he could very comfortably have killed. And because he was madly and inconsequently jealous, he wanted to hurt her as she had hurt him.

He continued, with dangerous quietness: "You may remember

that from the very beginning I told you that I disliked the idea of women in executive positions in a hospital. I think this has proved how right I was—they are much too apt to let their emotions cloud their judgment."

There was a moment's dead silence.

And then: "Of course, if you feel like that, there is nothing more to be said." Jennet hardly recognized her own voice.

There remained a lot to be said, but she knew she dared not trust herself to stay and even try to say it.

She must get away—she must be alone, or else she would really prove to him in a much more humiliating way that women failed to stand up to certain situations! Anger, bitterness, hurt pride at his unjustness—all these emotions were warring in her, but none of them caused that aching, searing pain in her heart.

She turned and walked towards the door, her head high. And, watching her, he did not guess that she was moving blindly.

Just for an instant he had the impulse to call her back, or follow and take her in his arms; it was buried under his anger and disappointment. Just then she was not the girl he loved, but the partner who had let him down—caused him to make what he now felt to be the greatest error of judgment he had ever been guilty of.

Besides—why the devil should she care what happened to Devenham? . . .

CHAPTER XXIII

JENNET did not remember anything afterwards between leaving Ivor and finding herself staring blankly about her own room.

She had been in the grip of that blinding mental pain which makes one quite oblivious of where or how one moves from one place to another.

Even now she only knew that since she had last seen this room something had happened to change the whole world, but she was suddenly too utterly worn out to analyse what it was—all that she wanted to do was to sleep.

Undressing was a completely mechanical thing. For the first time in her life she left her clothes where they fell, and when finally she slipped in between the sheets she was asleep almost as soon as her head touched the pillow.

It was some hours later when she began to dream uneasily—vague, disastrous dreams. She was in the midst of that horrible one in which the dreamer has to get to a certain destination at a certain time, and finds herself in the wrong train, when the soft click of a raised blind woke her, and she found her maid in the room, and her morning tea on the table beside her.

In an instant she was fully conscious, and with her wakefulness came memory of all that had happened last night.

She had never thought it possible to dread seeing Ivor as she dreaded seeing him now, and she summoned all the pride of which she was capable to see her through.

If he had metaphorically wiped the floor with her—raged, stormed, even threatened to write to England and have her removed from her post—she felt that she could have coped with it all. What she could not fight was the cold, incisive statement that she had let him down simply and solely because she was a woman—and she could not forget the statement, because in her present mood of self-accusation she actually suspected that he might be right. Her heart was wounded beyond words—but so was her pride. She knew that things could not possibly be left as they were now. She and Ivor would have to have this thing out.

But apart from a distant glimpse in the corridors, there was no chance of getting near him that day. After the usual swiftly taken early round of his wards, he spent the whole day in the private wing.

For the first time Jennet found it really difficult to concentrate on her own work, and was grateful that no complications arose in the usual routine. All the time her thoughts were with Ivor. She knew that he was putting up a big fight—and in that fight was his pride for the prestige of the hospital; a prestige which he felt had been imperilled by his action, his mistake in delegating his responsibility to someone who had failed to deserve his trust.

How galling that thought was! As the day went on, she tortured herself with it, until it became like salt rubbed into a wound. However, she had schooled herself to wear a mask almost as unrevealing as Lotus's, and of all those with whom she came into contact that day, only Rose Hilton guessed that something was wrong.

It was easy for Matron to guess what that something was. She knew Ivor too well not to be aware how what had happened last night affected him. She still knew nothing of where Jennet had been, but whatever the explanation was, she realized it would have to be a hundred per cent. alibi to get past Ivor. Rose had a generous heart, and she was very fond of those two—she hoped devoutly that nothing would go wrong with that part of their lives which was—whether they realized it or not—quite apart from their work.

It was Rose who rang through on the house telephone to Jennet some two hours after dinner that evening, and told her that the patient who had been operated on last night was now definitely out of danger. "I just thought you would like to know," she said laconically.

"Thanks a million," replied Jennet; and to her relief, for she did not feel very much like making conversation just then, Rose bade her "Good-night, Doctor," and rang off.

Jennet hung up the telephone and sat looking at it. The fact that the relief she felt did not lift an iota of the heavy weight at her heart did not take from that relief. Neither did it alter the decision she had come to—a decision which would once have come very near to breaking her heart; but now there were other considerations which were even more certain of doing that. Once before she had sat in this room, trying to write a difficult letter, but on that occasion Ivor had come and made it quite unnecessary. If he came now it would make no difference at all, though, she told herself.

And then, as she turned to pick up her pen, she saw that he was there.

He had come in so quietly she had not even been aware of his entrance.

"Oh!" She stared at him.

He said: "I'm sorry if I startled you. Do you mind if I sit down for a few minutes?"

"Of course not. Please do." She would have given so much to be able to go to him in the old way, but his conventional apology seemed to strengthen the barrier which had been built last night.

Then she noticed his pallor, and the weariness with which he lowered himself on to the settee.

"Cigarettes beside you," she said.

"Thanks. I don't think I'll smoke——"

It was almost incredible that that awkward silence should fall between them. He had turned his head to look at the bookshelves, but he did not see one volume on them. And as he looked round again their glances met.

For a moment they regarded each other intently, but it was Jennet who was afraid of sustaining that glance. For the first time since he had hurt her so bitterly, she felt the sting of tears at the back of her eyes, and was filled with terror lest she should break down.

"Shall I make you a cup of coffee?" she asked, turning towards the percolator.

"I'd love one." He watched her as she bent over the thing—the firm, beautiful hands as they measured the coffee, the lovely lines of her profile; some of his tiredness slipped from him in the peace of her presence, even though they seemed so far apart. In that moment his desire to bridge the gulf between them was stronger than anything else in him. But he was not very sure of himself when he spoke.

"Jennet," he said, "I'm afraid I was—rather drastic last night. I was tired and—frankly, disappointed."

She answered without turning round: "You had every right to be. I certainly ought to have been here——"

If she had wanted to take the wind out of his sails she certainly could not have chosen a better way; only such a thought was not in her mind. After hours of misery and anxiety she was simply intent on castigating herself. Then suddenly—now she had started—common sense came to her aid, telling her not to be a fool, above all, not to justify his taunt by really letting her emotions cloud her judgment. She smiled slightly into the surprised question of his look. "Only you see—it was circumstances and not my muddled feminine thinking that did me! I'll confess right away that I'm scared stiff of thunderstorms, but I don't think that would have kept me from coming back if I had not been equally scared of leaving Philip to walk out into the night and get himself really damaged. You see, his malaria bug came back to complicate his other symptoms; and, after all, as a doctor I don't see how I could have left him."

"Will you tell me exactly what happened?" he asked.

She told him, as briefly as possible, but clearly enough for him to understand the whole thing.

When she had finished there was a moment's silence. Then:

"You know, I've been disliking myself pretty cordially all day," he told her, "and now I'm——" He rose, and stood looking down at her. "What can I say to you, Jennet?"

She said steadily: "You thought I had let you down, Ivor. You had a perfect right to rate me, but—you hadn't any right to put down my shortcoming to my sex."

"I know. I'm ashamed."

Those four brief words healed her wound as nothing else could have done. Whatever his faults might be, he was generous—and since he was ready to sacrifice his pride, how could she be foolish enough to be miserable behind the wall of hers?

While she talked to him she had gone on with her task, her hands had not been quite steady, but she had made the coffee and filled the cups.

She left them where they were now, and, taking a step forward, walked straight into his arms. However she had resented the comparison he had drawn last night, it was the woman in her that swept aside all resentment now, made her determined not to be outdone in humbleness.

But that had to wait for a minute. He was holding her close, and for those moments of reunion nothing else mattered.

"I'm every sort of a swine," he told her. "I don't know why you have anything to do with me."

"Oh, dear!" She drew back to look at him, laughter in her eyes. "I'm afraid I adore you! . . ."

It was some minutes later when they remembered the cooling coffee, and sat down side by side to drink it.

Though that load had lifted from her heart, Jennet was grave again, and, noticing her gravity, presently he asked: "Anything else the matter, sweetheart?"

She hesitated. "I—hate inquests. I'm afraid we'll have to hold one, though. Ivor——"

"Yes?"

"I know you were angry—disappointed——"

"And jealous!" he confessed. "Don't let's leave out the human element!"

She frowned, allowing herself to be diverted from the main subject. "How could you be? I had told you——"

"The human element again, darling. I expect I secretly hated the thought that Devenham had got the better of me the moment my back was turned—I told you he would try to do so! Of course," he added hastily, "I don't mean that even in my maddest moment I really believed you had deliberately gone to spend the evening with him."

"And stayed the night?"

"Jennet! You didn't imagine——"

"I don't think I imagined anything. I was too miserable. That's apart from—the main issue, though. We've got to face it. You didn't mean to say what you said—but it was something which has lain at the back of your mind all the time—anger just brought it out. You've been afraid all along that I might do that—let you down, I mean. Make some error of judgment. You never would have been afraid of that if I had been a man——"

"If I had been afraid, do you think I would have left you in charge as I did?" he asked.

"Yes, my dear; to try and prove to yourself that you were wrong."

He was silent for a moment. Was she right? Had his first prejudice really been so deep-seated that it had still been there? Then he shook his head. "No—honestly. I have had no fault to find with your work since you came here. My taunt last night was as stupid as it was ungenerous—you have done your work with that mixture of skill and imagination which is the perfect combination needed to make something more than just a good doctor. You are born to the job, Jennet—you need never doubt that. And you're capable of going so far that some day it would not surprise me in the least to hear myself described as 'Jennet Sinclair's husband'!"

If it was slightly exaggerated it was certainly the most generous tribute. And she knew that he was far too sincere to—even loving her as he did—have made it if he had not meant every word of it.

The curious thing was that, with her pride able to fly its flag again, she was able to see quite clearly for the first time the road that lay ahead of her—and that road was not the one he indicated. It was a road which she had once believed she could never contemplate, but now the thought of taking it gave her no pang.

"Darling," she said. She was smiling and her eyes held his steadily. "Thanks a million. I shall remember that as long as I live."

He took her hands. "It is far more important that you should forget last night."

"Please let's both forget it," she begged. "And now"—she tucked her feet under her, curling up beside him—"tell me about your journey—I'm longing to know how you got on."

"Tomorrow," he promised. "I'm awfully tired, and I just want to be tired like this, near you." He leant his cheek down to hers. Presently his head turned, and he found her lips.

CHAPTER XXIV

Ivor finished addressing a final envelope, added it to the little pile of letters which had to catch the morning's mail, and screwed the top on to his fountain pen with a sigh of relief.

Those were done with. In a few minutes he would be free to go across to Jennet.

Wonderful to think that the time was not far off now when he would not be obliged to cross a courtyard to find her waiting for him. As he reached for a cigarette and lit it, his eyes were curiously soft. They were going to make a success of things—the two of them. He knew that he was not lying to himself when he told himself that the thing which was going to matter most in the world to him was Jennet's happiness. That, bless her! could never be quite complete without her work.

After all, she had as much right as he had to the career for which she had worked so hard, and to which her gifts entitled her.

He loved his own profession enough not to wish to rob it of talents which were bound to bring it fresh laurels—even if, as a man, he would so much rather have had the undivided allegiance of the girl he loved.

Although he was still filled with angry regret for the things he had said on the night of his return, he had the curious feeling that that misunderstanding had cleared the air.

And yet he had not explained to her fully what had really lain at the bottom of his disappointment—the sudden memory of his old bitterness rising again, making him ask himself how much of a fool he had been to trust a woman once more—not with his work, but with his heart. He had actually asked himself last night if she *had* encouraged Philip; did a man, even a man like Philip Devenham, persistently hang round a girl without any encouragement?

> "*And sweare*
> *No where*
> *Lives a woman true and faire.*"

Behind his anger something like panic had risen in him; though he had hardly known it until afterwards. He could laugh it contemptuously away now, asking himself what sort of a fool he had been to let the doubt exist—the doubt of the burnt child who dreads what the fire may do to him a second time.

Well, it was over; Jennet didn't know about it, and in her generosity she had forgiven the rest.

He started from his reverie as, with a soft thud, Ming the Siamese cat landed on the desk beside him.

"Hello!" said Ivor severely. "Where were *you* last night?"

The cat rubbed itself against him, purring loudly, while his master stroked him behind the ear; he had no intention of answering that question, which he probably considered indiscreet. "Not even here to welcome me when I came back," said Ivor reproachfully. "Just as well probably—I wasn't fit to know."

Ming butted him gently under the chin with his sleek, firm head, and then, indulging in another favourite trick, flung himself full length across the blotting-pad and lay there, his strange blue eyes half closed, emitting that ecstatic noise which the French so picturesquely describe as "spinning a purr."

Ivor was just reaching for another cigarette when the door behind him opened and Li-Sing announced softly: "A lady to see you."

"A lady?" Ivor swung round.

"I tell her," said the houseboy calmly, "that maybe you plenty busy and no can do, but she not go away till I come find out. It is Missis Danvers," he informed.

Ivor frowned. "Say I am sorry, but I *am* very busy and no can do!"

The boy went out, and was back almost as quickly. "Missis Danvers say velly important. Must see you one time quick."

Confound Iris and her importunity! The last thing Ivor felt like was seeing her just now. His frown deepened. "All right, Sing—I'll see her on my way out." He hastily picked up a leather case from a table as he passed it. If he said he was on his way over to the hospital he would be able to get rid of her! But when he reached the threshold of the room he came face to face with his most unwelcome visitor.

"Hello, Ivor," she said. "Sorry to butt in if you're working. But I've something rather important to talk to you about."

He was really annoyed, and showed it in the curtness of his manner. "Sorry, Iris—I'm just going across to the hospital." Sing had withdrawn, and they were alone.

"I suppose it can wait," she said. "And—as you are so keen on the hospital, and what I have to say concerns it, I think you might be —wise to spare me a few minutes."

There was something in her tone, in the little triumphant smile she threw him, which arrested his attention.

He looked at her coldly, and, shrugging his shoulders, turned back into the room, shutting the door.

She passed him, and, going over to an armchair, sat down in it. "So you got back," she observed. "Apparently—only just in time."

"What do you mean?" he demanded.

She opened her eyes wide. "Isn't it true that if you hadn't arrived Chu L'iang's wife would have died because there wasn't anybody here to operate on her?"

"What nonsense are you talking?" he asked, but his eyes were alert.

She said: "Oh, if Doctor Blanchard isn't telling the truth, he ought to be stopped. He's been in the dickens of a stew, because apparently he entrusted a case of his to the private wing here, and there was no one of authority to give the right directions for treatment."

Ivor said furiously: "That's a lie! We saved the life of his patient —which is more than he was capable of doing."

"Yes, darling," she smiled. "That was because you turned up in the nick of time. The stories of your miracles will get out, you know. What is apparently annoying little Blanchard is that he rushed his patient off here, and when he arrived there was no one except Terry

O'Dare to consult with. He was told that both you and Doctor Grey were absent."

"Well," snapped Ivor, "what of it? He agreed that the operation must be performed——"

"He's a nasty little man," said Iris thoughtfully, "and we all know that he is an extremely bad doctor, and always relies on you people to pull him out of a jam. His story is that Terry insisted there must be an operation, and if you or Doctor Grey had been there you would have known better—or something like that. He's telling everybody that the hospital is inadequately run." She hesitated, and then, lowering her voice half pleadingly: "I'm telling you this because I think you ought to know why—the person you left in charge was not at her post, and—where she was."

There was the briefest pause. Ivor's gaze rested for a moment on the sleeping cat, and then moved to the slender, smiling girl whose eyes met his with a hard triumph she could not hide.

He thought: And they insult perfectly good cats by comparing some women to them! Aloud he said: "That's very—thoughtful of you. But I happen to know that Doctor Grey was with Lady Amanda, and afterwards with your brother, and also why she was there."

It was the last reply Iris had expected, and for the moment it left her nonplussed. Ivor regarded her, his eyes slightly narrowed. "It was unfortunate that her professional conscience made her feel it was necessary to remain with Devenham," he said quietly, "but extremely fortunate for him that she was there."

"I suppose she had a very good explanation for how she happened to be there?" sneered Iris, beginning to recover herself.

"Certainly." He did not think it necessary to go into the matter.

To do Iris the very little justice which she deserved, she had no real idea of how Jennet had come to be with Philip the night before last.

"Ivor," she laid a hand on his arm, "are you mad to let yourself be fooled like this? Can't you realize that Philip is crazy about Jennet Grey, and until she decided how good it would be for her professional career to marry you, she was quite ready to encourage him? Then, as soon as your back was turned she thought it would be rather amusing to——" She broke off, something in the steady gaze of the golden-brown eyes fixed on her making her stumble over the words.

"That will do, Iris; I don't think I should say any more if I were you," he advised quietly. "And now I am afraid I have not another minute to spare."

A wiser or more subtle mind than Iris's would have accepted the snub and perhaps left it at that, but wisdom was not Iris's long suite —especially when she was blinded by jealousy.

"If you don't see what a fool she is making of you, you must be mad!" she exclaimed. "Perhaps you will realize it when you know the whole place is aware that she spent Tuesday night alone with Philip, and that she was just leaving as the servants returned at dawn. If you think that is all right, it is up to you—I, for one, mean the trustees of the hospital to know exactly how well she does her work."

She moved towards the door, but Ivor barred her way. "Just a moment," he said.

She stood still, laughing, an unpleasant little tinkling laugh. "I thought you might not be in such a hurry when you heard that."

He said: "Please don't make any mistake. I am not in the least interested in your very unpleasant fiction sense. But I am interested in the reputation of the hospital, and in the reputation of my colleague, who also happens to be my future wife——"

"Of course if you marry her now you will simply ruin yourself," she flung at him.

He told her between his teeth: "If I hear one more word of this story which you have invented, there will be a scandal—but not the sort you want. Listen to me!" His fingers closed on her arm. "It is the easiest thing in the world to prove that Jennet remained with Devenham because he was too ill to be left, and you would be the one who would look very foolish if you found yourself answering a suit for slander. Your boy would have to tell the truth then—besides, Blanchard had Doctor Grey's note, unless your boy failed to deliver it."

"He said nothing about a note. Certainly if he had been told to deliver one he would have done so," she replied quickly. "I know Philip is ill—but he was quite well when Wang turned up. I tell you, Wang met Doctor Grey just as she was leaving. Even if Philip was a bit under the weather, he managed to get to bed—it was later in the day when they sent for the doctor. Wang said nothing about a note—how easily you are deceived!"

"How easily you think I could be! You had better go and jog your boy's memory," he advised. "Otherwise—there will really be some trouble."

"My dear Ivor," she retorted, "you can't bully me into protecting your lady-love. Don't! You're hurting me!"

His iron fingers had closed unconsciously on the arm he was holding. But he would have liked to hurt her very much more than that.

"Get out of my sight, for Heaven's sake! I'll deal with you later," he said.

She shrugged her shoulders. "You'll have to deal with quite a lot of other people, too. Don't be absurd, Ivor—you know how they talk in a place like this. You won't be able to keep them quiet." But he was holding the door open for her, and after a moment she thought it advisable to go through.

Her car was outside, and he did not attempt to wait for her to get into it before he shut the front door and turned back into his study.

For a space he stood quite still, his frowning gaze fixed on the chair where Iris had sat. But he did not see it—for a time he was far away from this charming room. He was seeing another sort of room altogether—plain cream walls and a long, shining oak table, the room where, every so often, the Board of Trustees who managed the affairs of the Eldred Chambers Trust met.

The more he thought of it, the more he was convinced that it was a complete wangle on Sir Bruce Ferguson's part. Of course, Sir Bruce had the casting vote over these appointments. He was the head trustee—but Jennet had never gone, as he himself had done before he came out here, before that Board. Even in the midst of the dismay which was gripping him now, Ivor's lips lifted a little at the corners at the memory of that half-dozen highly respectable and old-fashioned men and women.

But this was no time for humour, and Ivor's face was immediately grave and very troubled again.

Iris meant to make mischief—she had probably made a very good start already. And somehow—no matter how, she had to be stopped. Not only for Jennet's sake (that was important enough), but for the sake of the hospital and its honour of which they were both custodians, he must stop at nothing to prevent any real scandal.

He knew that, once started, the flame would spread like wildfire. The fact that there was far more invention than truth about the story Iris had so neatly constructed did not, alas! count.

He might even carry out *his* threat, and see that Iris was sued for slander—it might be easy to prove that Philip had been too ill to be left, to force the Chinese servants, who had probably already been primed and bribed by their mistress (I'd put nothing past her! thought Ivor furiously), to tell the truth; but the mud flinging would have started. And—mud sticks.

There was one way of scotching this snake before it could really strike, but desperate as he felt he shrank from taking that way.

He roused himself with a sigh, and as he picked up his case again his eyes were those of a man who is very deeply troubled.

That trouble was with him throughout the next two hours. He had promised to have a cup of tea in Jennet's room if he had time, and he managed to get there after she had waited ten minutes for him.

Although he was smiling and apparently serene she saw at once that something was wrong. "What's the matter?" she asked quickly. "Not another relapse?"

He shook his head, seating himself in the chair opposite her. "No. She's getting on very well."

There was a slight pause while she waited, knowing that he would explain in his own good time. Then as she poured out the tea which had followed quickly on his entrance, and handed him a cup:

"What made you think there was anything wrong?" he asked.

"You looked worried when you came in. Wrong diagnosis?"

He shook his head. "No; right as usual! But surely," he smiled across at her, "the woman isn't going to guess all my moods?"

"Looks like being my job, doesn't it?" she asked. "A good wife should always know her husband's moods—though if she's tactful she won't always let him know she does!"

"Pearls of wisdom!" He put down his cup, and, rising, went over to sit on the arm of her chair. But he attempted no more intimate caress than a hand on her shoulder.

Jennet put her own over it, and waited for him to speak.

"Darling," he said, "will you please tell me again exactly what happened after you got the good Philip home."

If she was startled by the request she did not show it. Instead, she repeated briefly all that she had told him before.

"And you are sure the boy understood about your note? That it was to be delivered to Blanchard?"

"Well, I impressed it on him clearly enough. Although," she frowned, "he didn't strike me as being terribly intelligent. It was after his night out perhaps."

"Perhaps——"

She turned her head, glancing up at him enquiringly. "What *is* the matter, Ivor?"

"He apparently didn't deliver it. Iris Danvers came to see me this afternoon. Devenham's laid up at present, but she says the servants found him quite well—well enough to put himself to bed."

"He couldn't have been!" she exclaimed sharply. "Unless he did it in delirium. Ivor, what did that woman say?"

He told her.

Her eyes widened. "Good Lord! I thought I'd met all sorts. I've had to deal with jealousy of the professional kind from men and women, and even some other sorts of it. But I didn't honestly think that anyone could stoop to the sort of things she does."

"Didn't you?" he retorted grimly. No one knew better than he

173

did the petty, mean deceits and lies Iris was capable of to gain her own ends.

"Of course," said Jennet, "it would be easy to prove why I was with Philip—if it is really necessary to prove it. It almost seems to me that it would be more dignified to ignore the whole thing."

He rose to his feet, looking down at her. "I wish we dared, old thing. You don't quite understand. If this story gets abroad it's apt to lead to no end of complications. I mean, unless the Chinese boy tells the truth you have absolutely no proof——"

"Do you mean that people would really believe I spent the night there deliberately?"

"You're sweetly innocent, Jennet mine——"

"I'm a fool!" She sprang from her chair. "How utterly loathsome! But I do see now—and with this other story (unfortunately true) of my not having been in the hospital when I was wanted—— Oh! why had this got to happen? I could kick myself. I wish I had left Philip where he was."

So did Ivor, with all his heart.

She continued unhappily: "If only I'd thought of it I would have brought him straight here, and let someone else take him home. It was that beastly thunderstorm coming on. And now if there is any real scandal I'll never forgive myself. I deserve what happens to me for my stupidity, but you—and the hospital——"

He slipped an arm about her shoulders. "Don't worry, dearest. It will be all right——"

CHAPTER XXV

LADY AMANDA did not take kindly to illness.

On the day following Jennet's visit she had wakened feeling very much better, and when Jennet telephoned her maid had informed the doctor of the fact.

Jennet had hardly been feeling like facing the older woman that day—so with the excuse that she was very, very busy she had got Terry O'Dare to go along.

The old lady liked Terry, and had been amused. He had found her temperature had already returned to normal, and congratulated her on her marvellous constitution. He had, rather naturally, said nothing about what had been happening at the hospital, but had advised her sternly to stay in bed for at least another day, and then to remain in her room until the end of the week. To all of which Lady Amanda took very badly.

She would like to have seen Jennet again, and was inclined to feel a little neglected when the next day passed into evening without her young friend having turned up.

The reasonable part of her mind knew that half a dozen things might have made a visit quite impossible, but she loathed inactivity and was not feeling very reasonable.

In the evening she refused to stay another minute in bed, and, getting up, sat wrapped in her Chinese robes by the fire which her maid had insisted on having kindled.

And she was trying to read a novel which had come in a recently arrived box from England, when, lifting her head, she saw the small, immobile figure of her maid standing opposite her.

Su-Li informed, "Doctor Sinclair has called, my lady. He like to know if you will let him come up?"

"Doctor Sinclair!" Lady Amanda sat upright abruptly. "Bring him up at once!"

The maid padded away, and returned a few moments later, ushering Ivor in.

"Good man!" Lady Amanda held out her hand to him. "The old woman isn't quite forgotten——"

"How are you?" He retained her hand, looking down at her. "What do you mean by crocking up when I'm away?"

"Crocking up indeed!" she retorted scornfully. "Nothing the matter with me, but a slight chill and a tummy ache. How are *you*? Working yourself to death as usual?"

"Plenty of life in me still." But as he took the chair she pointed to, those shrewd, bird-like eyes of hers noted that he looked tired.

"High time you got married and had someone to look after you," she announced. "I only hope Jennet is going to look after you, and not spend most of her time doctoring other people." And as he made no reply, but sat, his eyes fixed on the fire: "How is Jennet?"

"She's fairly all right." He hesitated. It was going to be far more difficult to say what he had come here to say than he had imagined.

"Hello!" exclaimed Lady Amanda sharply. "Nothing wrong, is there? You haven't had a row?"

"Lord, no!" The smile he gave her faded quickly. "There is something, though, and I want your advice." Then as briefly as he possibly could, he told her exactly what had happened.

She listened attentively, her eyes never leaving his face, interrupting now and then to ask a sharp, curt question. When he had finished there was a brief silence. Then:

"It's time that girl was dealt with drastically," she said. "She has been in Mangtong quite long enough—but unfortunately, apart from cutting her myself, *I* can't drum her out of the place. Unless I could find out something disgraceful about her I'm almost powerless. Of course we'll disprove this story, but——"

"Quite," he said quietly in answer to her look. "There can still be a lot of trouble stirred up. And it is unlikely to end there. Those people in London are not what you might call broad-minded—and if Iris carried out her threat of writing to them, even Sir Bruce would not be able to stop the demand for an enquiry."

"Why doesn't Jennet resign—chuck the whole thing before anything can be said?" asked Lady Amanda. "Lord knows I'm not for taking the line of least resistance ever. But——"

"I won't hear of her resigning—ruining her whole career by giving up her appointment with any sort of shadow over her."

Tut! thought Lady Amanda. She's got another career all ready-made. She kept the thought to herself, however, and said instead: "Well—didn't you know Iris before she came out here? Can't you drag up anything horrid from her past that I can advertise? Once she was cut socially she wouldn't stay here long. Who *was* her husband by the way?"

"I don't know. He had made his money in South Africa—or South America. I can't remember which. He was at the Cape when he died of T.B."

"A patient of yours?"

"No; I never saw him."

"Why on earth did he marry her?"

"I imagine quite a lot of men would have been glad to."

"Probably. Men are fools!" Lady Amanda frowned. "Did you hear who *she* was?"

"I think the father was a country parson," Ivor answered drily. "She—Iris—left home, and went on the stage. I fancy that is how she met her husband. He backed a show she was in, or something like that."

"Hum!" muttered Lady Amanda. "Always thought she was a bit theatrical—the cheap sort. Well, if she can't have you she means to make things as difficult as she can for you and the girl who is getting you. The woman's crazy about you. Look here," she continued, "something has got to be done. Of course, I'll stand by Jennet——"

He rose, and, walking to the other end of the room, came back to her. "There is one thing I can do," he said. "But I hate doing it. I came to you in the rather forlorn hope that you might find some other way. I see now that you can't—but you can still advise me."

He put a hand in his breast pocket and, taking out his wallet, selected an envelope from it and put it in her hands.

"Read those. I never meant to show them to a living soul. I don't know how I came not to destroy them. . . ."

* * *

A couple of afternoons later Jennet was made to realize for the first time in her life that the things people say about one can make life an uncomfortable and complicated business.

It was the afternoon on which, unless anything very untoward was happening, she was always employed on her own personal concerns, and she had gone to do some shopping in the principal store of the town, meaning to go and have tea with Lady Amanda. She was just leaving the stocking department when she came face to face with two women whom she had met several times at Lady Amanda's and elsewhere.

Jennet smiled and half stopped, but the ladies looked straight through her and passed on.

There is something particularly hateful about being cut dead; realizing that was exactly what had happened to her, Jennet walked on, her head high, a deepened colour in her cheeks. She didn't care a hang about either of those women, important as they both thought themselves from the social point of view, but she knew that she had to care for the reason that had made them hand her that gratuitous insult. It meant that the beast of gossip was let loose, worrying her reputation to bits. And because of her position, because she was not just an ordinary girl who could live it down, but a member of a profession in which scandal meant ruin, she must care. She would have to fight back with every possible weapon; but even if she won through, she knew that some of the mud would stick, and she felt sick with anger and misery.

She went through and finished her shopping. If there were any more direct cuts coming her way, she was ready to meet them. What she met instead was a cordial: "Well, well, young lady! I am in luck this afternoon!" And there was Sir John Selham, monocle in eye, looking as if he had just been lifted out of a bandbox in his white suit and sun-helmet. "I think a spot of tea is indicated," he added as they shook hands. "You can't be cruel enough to refuse the old gentleman!"

"Old gentleman indeed! And I never refuse a cup of tea," replied Jennet. She liked the dapper little baronet, and had learnt already that he was a much cleverer and shrewder man than he appeared to be. She could not help feeling amused and a little triumphant as she walked into the tea room with him, and the first people she caught sight of were the two ladies who had cut her a little while back. They bowed beamingly to her escort, and it was her turn to look as if she did not know them. She could not help wondering if Sir John had heard anything yet; she had the idea that as he made even more fuss of her than usual, he might have done.

If he had he gave no sign of it, and that tea cheered her up while she was having it. Afterwards he insisted on giving her a lift back to the hospital gates in his car; but when she had departed from him depression descended on her again. Her whole instinct was to go at once in search of Ivor, but she told herself: "He's worried enough. I can't go running to him with any more trouble—anyway, until this day's work is ended."

Then, the first thing she saw on entering her sitting-room was a note from him. She tore it open quickly. In his hardly legible doctor's scrawl he had written:

"Please come over for dinner this evening. Lady Amanda is coming. Love. I.S."

Then she smiled as she read the note through again. It was not exactly a burningly poetical love letter—and it was the first note she had ever received from him! But how like Ivor it was—scribbled on a piece of paper seized at random. "Love. I.S." With the memory of what a perfect lover he could be, she was sensible enough to realize that more lay behind those scribbled words than a ream of writing could express. But she could not help feeling that there was some serious implication behind Lady Amanda's visit that evening, and she was a little apprehensive when she dressed later.

She was ready very early, and, having time to spare, was glancing through some notes when someone tapped at the window behind her, and, turning her head, she saw Lotus outside. She had not seen the Chinese girl alone since that night at Lady Amanda's when Ivor had been wounded; and she could not help feeling that Lotus had been avoiding her.

She sprang up with an exclamation of pleasure, and threw the window wide. "Lotus! Come in——"

"You are not too busy?" asked the other.

"No; I'm going over to Ivor's for dinner with Lady Amanda. But I'm quite half an hour too early."

"I must not stay long in that case," said Lotus. "I felt that I wanted to see you, Jennet; to tell you that in a few days—next week—I shall be going away from Mangtong for perhaps a very long time."

"Going away. Giving up your work here?" asked Jennet in a mixture of dismay and amazement.

"Yes. It has been wonderful of Doctor Sinclair to let me continue with my studies here. I have learnt so much." She twisted a big, blood-red ruby on her finger, bending her head down over it. "One has only to be near him to learn. But—I am going to be married almost immediately. And my husband and myself will then be able to work together at a hospital nearer the war zone."

"Oh, Lotus, must you?" Jennet could have bitten her tongue the moment the words were spoken, but Lotus was regarding her smilingly now.

"Yes, my dear friend—I must. I shall be very happy, and it will add to my happiness to know also that you are happy."

"And—of course we shall meet again," said Jennet.

"I hope so. If not, I shall always remember you. But I feel that when you are married your husband will take you away from the East before very long. My grandmother feels that too—and she is very right. She wants to see you again one day. Please go and see her when I have gone away."

"Indeed I will—if I may," Jennet agreed, and then: "All this— your marriage is very unexpected, isn't it?"

Lotus nodded. "Yes; I did not think my future husband would return so soon. But there is this work which we shall both love doing. And—it was always arranged that we should marry as soon as possible after he came back."

She seemed very contented and even gay, and remained chatting for another ten minutes. Then she rose. "I must go. And so must you." She hesitated. "Will you—please tell the doctor my news. And—ask him to treat me as if it was something that had always been expected to happen any day. I do not like to discuss goodbye."

"Yes, dear," said Jennet gently. "I will tell him."

"And this too," said Lotus, "is our good-bye—though we shall see each other again. And we shall always be friends, Jennet?"

"Of course," Jennet promised warmly.

The soft, dark almond eyes met hers. "We shall love each other the better perhaps because of one memory." She hesitated, but the desire to speak was too strong for her. She put her hands on Jennet's shoulders, raising herself a little to look into her face. "Make him very happy——"

"I'll try." Jennet felt no trace of resentment as she kissed the smooth, ivory cheek. "Be happy yourself, little flower," she added in Chinese.

"Of course. I have my work, and a very good man—and I shall have kept faith," replied Lotus.

They parted a few moments later outside the door. And watching Lotus, who was truly like a bright flower herself, passing through the flower-filled courtyard, Jennet felt a lump in her throat. Lotus was brave and strong and splendid—she would do good work, and brave any danger. Strange, Jennet thought, that she should feel such sisterhood for one girl who had loved the man she loved, and such utter dislike and lack of understanding for the other who was of her own race—but then, what different types of love! . . .

* * *

When she was shown into his study, Ivor was alone.

"Hello, beautiful person!" He took her in his arms, and bent to kiss her. Then with a long, slender forefinger he smoothed between her brows. "Don't frown!"

"Was I frowning?" she asked, straightening his tie. And then: "Who let Lady Amanda come out?"

"I did. There's nothing the matter with her."

"If she gets another chill——"

"She won't, darling. She's tough, believe me!"

She sighed. "You usually know what you're talking about."

"Thank you, doctor!"

Her answering smile faded almost at once, and, releasing herself gently, she sat down on the arm of a nearby chair. "I had tea with Sir John——"

"You did, did you?" Ivor glanced round from examining the decanter of sherry which stood amid slender-stemmed glasses on the tray which had been set down on a small low table. "Do you wonder I'm a jealous man?"

"I adore Sir John!" said Jennet serenely. And then, forcing herself to the subject which she had been hedging away from behind this light conversation: "Ivor—I was cut this afternoon. People *are* talking. Your girl friend has been busy, I think."

He knew it. That was why Lady Amanda was dining here. "Did Sir John say anything to you?" he asked.

"No. I suppose he knows?"

"Yes," Ivor admitted. "He rang me up. He's one of the committee, you know. He's furious, breathing death and damnation to the mischief-makers. He and Lady Amanda can be pretty formidable together——" He broke off as the door opened and the Number One boy announced:

"Lady Amanda Trent."

"Who's taking my name in vain?" demanded Lady Amanda, shaking hands. "I heard it mentioned, I think?"

"You did. I was saying that you and Sir John——"

"We are. But we won't talk about unpleasant things until after dinner," said the visitor crisply. "Bad for the digestion. Is that the same sherry you gave me last time?"

"It is," he admitted.

"Good. How are you, my child?" she touched Jennet's cheek. "You look pale."

"What about you?" asked Jennet. "Ought you to be out?"

"Good Lord, yes! Germs don't live in me—they get smothered in the creases!" The old lady grinned impishly, accepting a glass of sherry from the silent-footed Li. "Well, here's confusion to our enemies!"

Dinner was announced almost immediately. Lady Amanda seemed to be in excellent spirits, and enjoyed her food with an appetite which her recent indisposition did not seem to have impaired.

It was afterwards when, a cup of coffee at her side and one of her favourite cigarettes between her fingers, she commanded: "And now, Jennet, tell me what has been happening? I know most of it—why on earth didn't I think to ask how on earth you were going to get back that night? I took it for granted you would have a rickshaw waiting."

"It wouldn't have made any difference," said Jennet.

"I'm not so sure of that. Even a rickshaw man can be a reliable witness. Experienced any unpleasantness from anyone?"

"Yes," replied Jennet. "I was cut by Mrs. Aldeney and her girl friend the Hon. whatever her name is!" She tried to speak lightly, but her voice trembled a little.

"Lands sake!" exclaimed her ladyship, the use of the idiom of her far-off youth showing that she was unusually moved. "I never heard such damned cheek! Considering the reputation that Aldeney woman had before she netted that poor fool of a husband of hers! As for the other female—she'd give her head for the chance she evidently imagines you had!" She glanced at Ivor. "It is time it was stopped, though. We don't want to have to go to law."

"No," he answered. "You're right. It's too complicated and too—uncertain. I——"

Once again the room door opened, and the small, blue-uniformed figure of Li appeared, bowing a visitor in.

"Mrs. Danvers."

Iris crossed the threshold, moving a little more quickly than usual. Her eyes were on Ivor. And then as she saw that he was not alone she stood still while the door closed softly behind her.

Lady Amanda removed the long jade holder in which she was smoking her cigarette, and nodded unsmilingly. "Good evening, Mrs. Danvers."

"Good evening." Iris ignored Jennet, her glance on Ivor again. "I got your note. I didn't know it was a party."

It was Lady Amanda who replied. "It isn't. It's a Council of War!"

"Really. How interesting!" In spite of her effort to appear so, Iris was never quite at her ease with Lady Amanda.

The latter said: "You know Doctor Grey?"

"Oh, yes; Doctor Grey and I know each other very well," drawled Iris, not attempting to hide her insolence now.

Jennet, having recovered from her surprise at this unexpected arrival, was not at all inclined to be affected by her rudeness. Her serene eyes meeting the other girl's said quite plainly: How cheap you are!

But Iris, though she coloured slightly, looked back at her with unveiled triumph, feeling that at least she had the whip hand of her rival. If other people meant to put her—Iris—on the carpet, they would soon find how little chance they had. She was not afraid of old Trent—for once the old woman would find that she had met her match, that even her influence would not count against an overwhelming public opinion. Ivor would have his beautiful Jennet, but both their careers would suffer. Let them find out how they liked that! Where the streak of cheap vulgarity in Iris had come from was an insoluble problem. Perhaps it was that the gentle, widowed bookworm of a father had left both his children too much to the care of over-trusted servants who had been either too strict or not strict enough—so that Iris, naturally self-willed and inclined to rely on her wits to get what she wanted, had developed her worst traits to the full.

For the first time she had found it impossible for all her wiles to get her what she wanted; and she was not going to be "done" without someone else suffering for it.

Ivor drew forward a chair for her, requesting her gravely: "Will you sit here?"

"Dear Ivor—don't make me feel as if I was going to have the state of my appendix enquired into," she requested.

Jennet had seated herself on the settee. Lady Amanda, her ridiculously small feet on a footstool, leaned back smoking her cigarette.

"I suggested that you should be asked to come here, Mrs. Danvers," she said, "because I thought you were the person who could help. As you know I am the chairman—or rather the chairwoman—of the hospital committee. And especially since so much of China is at war, the Board over here become more and more responsible for the hospital. So that naturally we are concerned when an unpleasant slander is spread abroad concerning one of our chief medical officers."

"Yes, I suppose so." If Iris had meant to pretend to misunderstand, she changed her mind when she met Lady Amanda's eyes. If the old So-and-so's hostile, she can jolly well have it in the neck! she told herself. "But then, of course," she added, "it's up to you, isn't it? Of course I know there's an awful lot of nonsense surrounding doctors. I mean, that things ordinary people could do without any fuss matter so much to them. They know that, and it seems to me it's up to them not to do silly things. And if I were on a hospital committee, I should take good care that unless the doctors behaved themselves they lost their jobs."

Lady Amanda gave Ivor, who had gone white with rage, a warning look. "Quite," she agreed. "But I am not asking what you would do. What I want you to understand is that one of the doctors in this hospital is being very grossly slandered, and that you—or your brother—can quite easily put the matter right."

"My brother is ill," said Iris.

"I know that. Otherwise I should have asked him to come here," replied Lady Amanda. "If he had not been ill, this story—this distortion of the truth could never have got about. You know, of course, to what I refer?"

"Oh yes, I know!" Iris admitted. "But since the story is true, I fail to see what I can do. It isn't my fault if people are talking." She looked straight at Jennet. "You shouldn't be so indiscreet. Or if you wanted to stay you should have got away before the servants saw you."

Lady Amanda looked at Ivor again. "I don't think we will waste time arguing," she said. "Mrs. Danvers evidently does not mean to help us. Doctor Grey can, of course, go to a solicitor——"

"But a slander action would not be very pleasant for your darling hospital, would it?" enquired Iris, her inward spite spilling over. "I mean—it would be rather silly to go into court and tell the world that your immaculate woman doctor——"

"That's enough, Iris!" Ivor interrupted. "I think we'll get to business."

"What do you mean?" she asked. "If you think you can bribe me——"

"Listen." He walked over, and stood in front of her, and there

183

was something so menacing in his quietness that in spite of herself she shrank back a little. "Scandal, especially about a woman, *even if she does not happen to be a doctor*—is not pleasant. Social ostracism, for instance, is not a nice thing."

"What do you mean?" she asked again. And then: "You can't get me ostracized, you know. Even if Lady Amanda decides to say I'm an impossible person, there are quite a lot of people who won't follow her blindly."

"That depends," he returned. "Do you remember Simon Barton, Iris?"

"Don't be absurd! Of course I remember him," she retorted.

"Simon was very popular, wasn't he? Not only popular, but he had some very influential relatives. His father was a great friend of Sir John Selham's."

"Well," she asked defiantly, "what has Simon to do with this?"

"Nothing. But it might not be very nice if the story of why he died so suddenly and tragically got out," Ivor told her.

"Don't be silly! Simon died because his car skidded," she countered. "You can't blame anyone for that."

"No?" Ivor reached out, and, drawing forward a chair, sat down in it, facing her. "Supposing there was proof that Simon crashed his car deliberately, because a useless, worthless woman had encouraged him to go mad about her, and having made him believe she cared, told him she was desperately in love with someone else; taunted him with having allowed himself to be used as a cat's-paw to rouse the other man's jealousy? God knows, it was inexcusably weak of him to think that a life which might have been of use to his fellow-creatures was no longer worth living because *you* of all people in the world had turned him down."

Suddenly there might have been only the two of them in the room; equally pale they faced each other, his eyes hard and cold and accusing—hers defiant, a little frightened.

"You're talking utter nonsense!" she exclaimed. "You've no right to accuse me of that. You have not an atom of proof."

"Have I not?" asked Ivor, and Jennet, listening, thought: Oh, he can be cruel! "What about the letter you wrote him the night before he—crashed? There are various ways of committing murder, but they all end in the same way. Unfortunately you can't be punished for what you did, as you should be. I have that letter, though, and the one he wrote me saying what he was going to do."

"I don't believe it!" she exclaimed. "You would have shown it to me before—you'd never have kept it to yourself."

"All I asked was to be able to forget it," he replied. "I didn't want anyone to know what he had done. There were his people to consider. The stigma of suicide smirching his memory. But now I have that other thing to consider; the honour of a living girl is more to me even than the honour of a dead friend. And unless you and your brother tell the truth and tell it damned quickly, those letters are going to be seen by more than one person."

Iris was so taken aback that she could not think at all clearly. She could only protest, almost weakly: "You don't mind blackening one woman to save another. You can't tell me that you would really be such a cad as to show my letter—and tell the world that your friend and colleague killed himself!"

"He doesn't need to, Mrs. Danvers," said Lady Amanda. "The letters are no longer in his possession."

"You've got them!" Iris sprang to her feet, swinging round on her. "Well, you can do what you like with them. I've no illusions. I know what you can do to me—along with a handful of other old cats who are your cronies. That won't help your two paragons!" She was working herself up, her hands clenched, her voice rising.

"Don't you have hysterics on me!" warned Lady Amanda sharply. "I know all about your tempers. Please remember I am not your Chinese maid. Any nonsense from you, young woman, and I will have a bucket of cold water thrown over you!"

"You old——" Iris choked, staring at her antagonist.

"Sit down, and don't be a little fool," ordered Lady Amanda. "You know very well that I can have every door in this place shut against you. Talk as much as you like about popularity—the women have always disliked and rather suspected you; and there was not a man who didn't like Simon Barton—poor young fool. If I had written that letter, I think I'd give a good deal not to have it seen by people."

It was not that Iris would not have tried to think of some way of wriggling out of this, so much as the fact that she was up against a will so much stronger and more ruthless than her own, which broke her up. She sank down into her chair again, covering her face. She was nothing more than a social butterfly, and no one knew better than she did what social ostracism could mean, especially in a community of this sort. Nevertheless, she did not give things up easily, and perhaps she would have still fought if that sudden pause had not been broken by the entrance of Li, turning up again like some bland Nemesis.

Ivor's Number One boy sidled up to him confidentially. "Mister Devenham would like see Doctor Gley—plenty quick and most particular," he announced.

"I want to see Doctor Sinclair, too!" Philip walked in through the open door. "Forgive my lack of ceremony, but——"

"Philip!" Iris looked up in horror. "I thought you were at home!"

"I told you I was all right," he answered impatiently. "I went to the club, and—Jennet!" He turned to her, something new in the careless ease of his manner. "I'm glad to be able to see you and—thank you for the brick you were last Wednesday night." His glance rested for a second on Lady Amanda and then went to Ivor: "Heaven knows what I should have done if she had not been such a Good Samaritan to me. I have only the vaguest remembrance of what happened, but I'd probably be dead if I'd been left on my own."

"You probably would," said Ivor briefly.

The two men regarded each other, and Philip said abruptly: "Can I speak to you for a few minutes, Sinclair?"

"Certainly. If the ladies will excuse us——"

Iris was on her feet; she moved in front of her brother, her eyes glittering angrily. With her usual lack of self-control she seized on the idea of someone to vent her temper on. "What do you want to come here for?" she demanded. "Are you in this blackmail racket? I suppose you've invented some wonderful story, and are going to say you really were ill, when you know perfectly well you were quite all right until the next morning."

For a moment he stared at her in amazement. "What the dickens are you talking about? I told you I was practically unconscious when Wang arrived back. He said Doctor Grey was sitting beside me, and only went away when he arrived. Then apparently the fool left me alone, and though I don't remember doing so, I put myself to bed. Wang didn't send for old Blanchard until much later in the day because he said he thought the other doctor would be coming back——"

Jennet said quickly: "I left a note and told him he was to deliver it to Doctor Blanchard at once."

For a moment Iris forgot her own danger. "A pretty story," she exclaimed, "if you can get anyone to believe it!"

Her brother stared at her with a sudden new intentness. Then he took her roughly by the shoulders. "Look here," he demanded angrily, "is it by any chance you who have been spreading this other 'pretty story' that was repeated to me at the club tonight? Since we're on the subject, Sinclair, perhaps there isn't any need for us to talk alone. Perhaps you have already heard this canard that someone has circulated. The man who repeated it at the club just now didn't happen to notice me until too late. I don't think he'll tell it again in a hurry." It was perhaps the first time anyone had ever heard Philip speak so firmly.

Iris threw him a poisonous look as she twisted herself free of his hands. "It's part of the education of a gentleman to lie for a woman, isn't it?" she asked. "And you must try to be a little gentleman, mustn't you?"

"So it *was* you! I thought as much——" It was clear in that moment that he had as much temper as she had when he was crossed. "Good heavens, Iris! You can carry your spite too far. I'm not being a party to this——"

"No? You're crazy about this woman too—she can't do any wrong in your eyes——"

He flushed darkly under the taunt. "Hold your tongue!"

"I won't! They thought they'd found a way to make me, and I nearly gave in to them, but——"

Lady Amanda said from the background: "Mr. Devenham, I do think you had better try and make your sister see reason. Otherwise she will find herself in a very unpleasant position. I would like you to look at something I have here." She opened her bag, and took out two letters. Holding them in her hands, she hesitated for a few seconds. "I have your word of honour that you will give these back to me?"

"Of course," he answered in surprise.

Iris stood, her eyes fixed on him. If only she could have got those letters, torn them in shreds! But Ivor was standing between them, and she knew he would never let her pass him.

There was dead silence in the room while Philip read. He was not an imaginative man, and he was shallow and at times quite unscrupulous; but he had one weak spot—his admiration for the beautiful creature who was his sister; a rather twisted admiration which had applauded her cleverness in having got where she was, married a rich husband, earned the fortune he had left her—and "got away with it" everywhere. They had quarrelled and rated each other during these last months, but he had been ready to play her game, hoping to win his own.

Until a few days ago—perhaps until this very night, there was little he would have stopped at if it would have brought him his heart's desire; and how amazed he had been to find how strong that desire was! Tonight, when Jennet's name had been flung at him in a coarse jest, something he had never suspected in himself had sprung to life. Perhaps the difference between him and Iris was, that though he had ignored it for the most part, he had a code of sorts. And now he had the burning humiliation of feeling shame for the person he loved and admired. Heaven knew, there were many occasions when he had been callous and cruel, but as he read the letter of dismissal Iris had sent to a man she had encouraged to love her the flippant cruelty of it sank into him; it was too much even for him. When he realized what the result of that callousness had been, he was horrified.

Without a word he folded the letters, and handed them back again. "I—didn't know," he almost stammered. "And—believe me—I had no idea—that Jennet's decency to me the other night——"

"I don't think you had." Lady Amanda spoke more gently. "Quite frankly, I've never had much opinion of you—but I don't think you would have encouraged this other thing either. I think we had better face the full implication of the story which could only have been put about in the first place by your sister. Mrs. Danvers, for her own reason, wishes Doctor Grey to be forced to give up her appointment and leave Mangtong. I am equally determined that she shall not succeed. I hate having to threaten, and because I was fond of Simon Barton I should equally hate having to publish abroad the contents of those letters——"

"I say, you can't do that!" He stared at her in horror.

"Mr. Devenham," she advised, "if I were you, I should persuade your sister to go. If she does not want to journey further, she might get quite a lot of amusement out of California. But before she leaves, I think it would be advisable to see that any libellous statements which may have emanated from your house in the first place are contradicted. I need not add that no one in the hospital believes them, and that Sir John Selham and myself are quite determined that they shall be killed."

"You needn't worry." Philip's tone was grimly determined. "Doctor Grey will, if necessary, receive a public apology. And—my sister will leave Mangtong immediately. Come along, Iris——"

"Philip!" she protested. "Are you going to turn on me now?—*you*!"

"For Heaven's sake don't be sentimental—after what I've found out," he told her shortly.

Her face set and sullen, she gathered her cloak about her as Philip turned to the others. "Good-night, Sinclair—good-night, Jennet. I don't know whether you'll believe me—either of you—when I say I'd have done a lot before I'd have had this happen."

Jennet held out her hand to him impulsively. "I do believe it, Philip. And—it certainly isn't your fault."

The gesture with which he bent over her hand and pressed it to his lips was still perhaps a little too graceful. Then he straightened, and, nodding to Ivor, who returned the nod unsmilingly, he took his sister's arm.

"Good-night, Lady Amanda."

"Good-night."

Iris had not spoken another word; when they reached the door she stopped and swung round. She was not at all beautiful in that moment, and she looked suddenly years older.

"Good-night, Doctor Grey," she said. "At least, you will always be able to remember what I told you before—you can have him for the rest of your life; but he belonged to me first!" . . .

* * *

Lady Amanda had taken her leave, and Ivor had gone out to put her in the car.

When he came back into the room he found Jennet standing just where he had left her, her eyes fixed on the roses in the blue glaze jar.

He went to her without a word, and took her in his arms. "Darling!"

"Darling——" She lifted her face, and then suddenly dropped it against his shoulder; her muffled voice came to him: "I do hate her—it's no use being superior and modern and sophisticated over it—I hate her!"

He touched her hair gently. "Not worth the trouble, Jennet mine." A pause, and then: "What was it that she told you before—and why didn't you tell me?"

She drew a little away from him. "I was so sure of myself at the time. I didn't believe it—or I wouldn't let myself. After all, I suppose it is stupid to let something that happened years ago——"

She did not finish, but he knew that she had been going to add: "spoil things."

It was inconceivable! And after a brief silence he sat down on the settee behind them, pulling her gently down beside him. "Sit in your own corner while I talk to you—and when I've finished, if you feel like it, come over to me. I hate telling you this story—not because there is any shame in it, except the shame of having been made a fool of—only it left a patch of bitterness in me that I've been trying to wear out; but it was you who succeeded in doing that.

"'*And sweare*
No where
Lives a woman true and faire——'"

He smiled slightly as she started. "I was a good deal younger, and very much less experienced when I marked those lines. I suppose you have got to hear it all. I met Iris when I was doing my house surgeon job at the St. Martin's. I had no intention at that time of giving any portion of my heart away. I had done pretty well up to then, and I had mapped out my life as young and ambitious fools do. But the Irises of this world—and I suppose much better and more real women—have a way of disposing of men's plans. Before I knew what was happening, I could think of hardly anything else—couldn't see life without her. Unfortunately I was an idealist, and I made the mistake of idealizing the girl I loved.

"She was playing a small part at one of the London theatres—though I gathered that she had no need to work. I knew her as Iris Devenham. And I wanted to marry her at once, but she insisted that she mustn't be rushed. We'll skip the weeks in which I lived in a fool's paradise. Then came the crash: she had talked at the beginning what I thought was a lot of hot air. Love ought to be free—she couldn't see herself tied up. She would love me for ever, of course, but she didn't see that it was necessary to get married. I believe I was rather horrified at first, but when she started impressing on me that I must not saddle myself with a wife too early in my career, I thought it was just her marvellous generosity! But I still had my own ideas—old-fashioned, and they included marriage to the woman I loved, nothing less. Men are only human, though, and I was mad about her; she was beginning to wear me down. She knew exactly how I felt, but she impressed on me how she felt too. Until at last I agreed to an unofficial honeymoon.

"On the night before we had arranged to go off for our week's holiday I was introduced to a doctor who had just arrived from South Africa, by one of my colleagues at the hospital. I couldn't get out that evening, and quite late I went to Evans's room for a yarn and a drink—where I met this man. In the course of conversation the inevitable subject of women cropped up. The South African was bitter against the sex. He told one story of a friend of his who had married a girl two years before, worshipped the ground she walked on, had given her everything—settled a private fortune on her. He was dying of T.B. at the Cape—waiting day after day for his wife to come to him, while she was here in England. The South African doctor had seen her, and gathered that she was too interested in another man to bother about her dying husband. He said: 'She's as lovely as an orchid, and as poisonous as the swamps they grow in, is the beautiful Iris.' I don't know why, but I heard myself saying, 'Iris what—not Iris Devenham?' He answered: 'Yes, that's the lady. Met her? Her married name is Danvers——'

"I won't tell the rest in detail. When I saw her the next morning she defended herself by saying that she knew if I'd known she was married I would have kept away from her, that all we had to do was to wait until her husband died—which wouldn't be long now. If you know what it feels to see something you've loved and thought perfect turn into a grinning skull and crossbones, you can understand something of what I felt. It was no use her swearing that she adored me—that she couldn't live if I turned her down. She just didn't exist any longer for me. Perhaps it was the shock of my discovery that left me so bitter—I suppose I was pretty ruthless to her——" he broke off. "Well, that's that! Looking back, I know how little like the real thing what I felt for her was; but I'll confess it was very real to me while it lasted. Only—if she told you I was her lover in actual fact, she was lying. It was just luck perhaps. I think if I had found that she had made me betray the honour of that poor, sick devil who was waiting for her, I'd have killed her. As it was—I simply broke with her."

Jennet was close beside him now. "Oh, I'm glad!" she exclaimed. "Glad! Of course I should have persuaded myself that it didn't matter, but I should have simply loathed to think—— Stupid of me, maybe; I shouldn't have minded anyone else. But *not* Iris. I could still kill her for hurting you like that."

He caught her close. "Sweetheart! What a very feminine creature you are!"

"Well," she challenged, "you don't want me to be anything else, do you?"

He kissed her closely and hard.

After a silence she said: "Ivor——"

"Jennet!"

"I hope you won't be disappointed," she flicked some peach-coloured powder from his coat. "I sent a long cable to Sir Bruce this afternoon——"

"Why should I be disappointed over that?" he enquired.

"I asked him to find someone reliable to take my place as soon as possible," she informed calmly. "I said I wanted to resign my position here."

"Why?" He turned her face up to his, studying it in amazed enquiry. "You didn't really let yourself get so rattled that——"

"No, no," she protested. "I'd made up my mind for quite another reason."

"What on earth——?"

"One has to face these things squarely." Her voice was steady. "I love my work—I hope I'll still be able to feel I'm doing it sometimes. But I'm taking on another job, and—for the next few years at any rate—I think it will need all my time."

For a moment he regarded her intently. And then: "Have you thought very seriously about this, Jennet?" he asked.

She smiled into his eyes. "*Very* seriously. I'm not saying that in a way it hasn't been rather a struggle to decide to do what I am doing. I love my work, as I said before, but," she coloured slightly, "for now I think my energies will be needed for other things. It's so important that a woman should make a success of—marriage and motherhood." Her smiling gaze was level and unfaltering.

"Darling!" His arm went about her, but she strained back a little.

"So you see, I'm not running any risks of a divided allegiance at first. I know that I can keep in touch through you. And one day, perhaps, I'll practise again."

"You must," he told her. "Dearest of all, I'm not going to pretend that the most selfish part of me isn't pleased—terribly bucked about this. Ought I to let you do it, though? You remember what I told you? You're not just a 'good' doctor, you've the makings of something exceptional——"

Pleasure deepened her colour. "You've been marvellously generous about my work, Ivor. And I don't think you'll ever feel about women in the profession the way you did before you met me. Perhaps it's selfish of me to give up, to want to be—just your wife for our first years. But don't let's argue any more. I've burnt my boats."

There might be times when she would look back, longingly to the promised land from which she had cut herself adrift, when her mind would soar after other heights than the ones she had chosen—they both knew that.

Perhaps it would have been heroic of him to insist that she should not make this sacrifice, but he was wise enough to know that she knew best.

His arms closed about her, and before he quite knew what he was saying the words were out. "To think that you're really going to belong to me!"

Strange how that simple and perhaps egotistical little speech made her finally certain that her decision really had been the only possible one. Other women might find happiness in running a career along with marriage, but for her and the not always easy man she loved with every fibre of her being the road to success lay along the route she had chosen.